Advance praise for

THE TRUTH IS

"In her luminous, raw, and open-hearted exploration of identity, grief and first love, NoNieqa Ramos has created an unforgettable character in Verdad. *The Truth Is* offers a complex look at a brilliant, queer, neurodifferent girl, the mother who loves but doesn't understand her, and a fabulously drawn group of street kids who can't save themselves but just might save her. A brilliantly written breathtaking book. I couldn't put it down!"

—Michelle Ruiz-Keil, author of *All of Us with Wings*

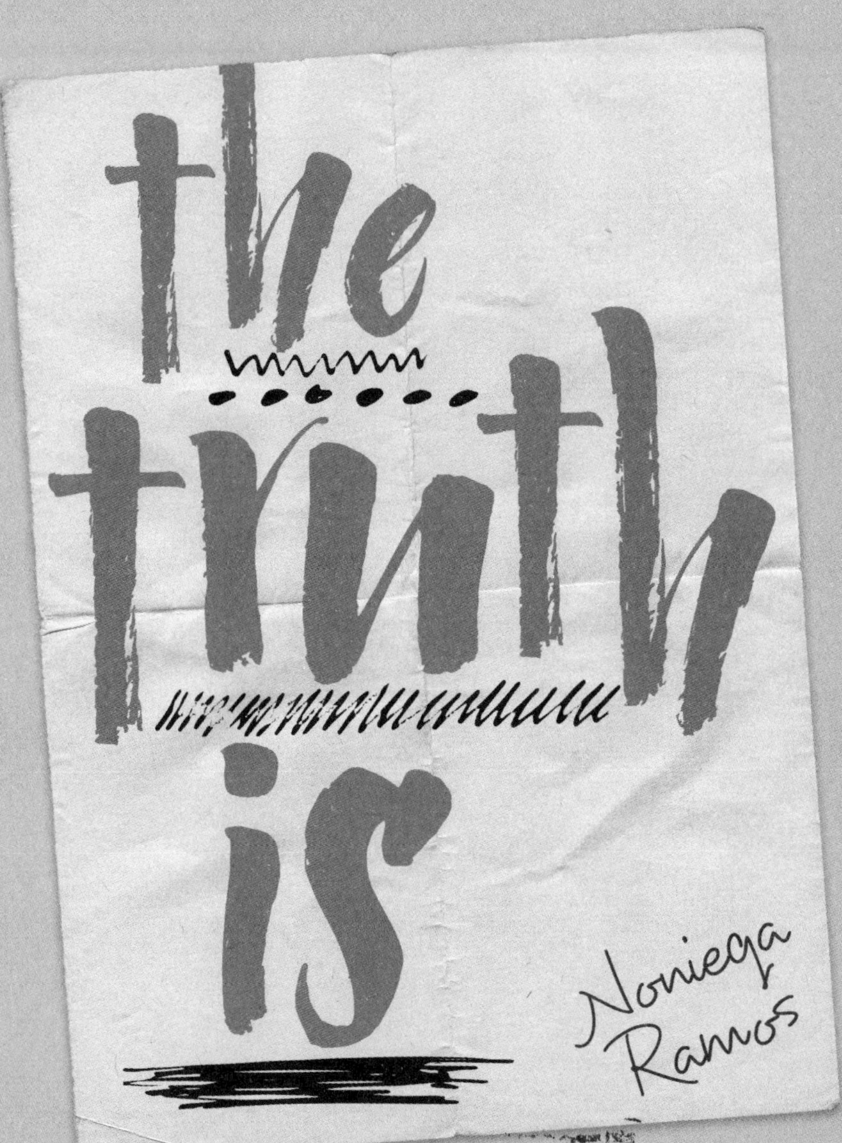

carolrhoda LAB
MINNEAPOLIS

Carolrhoda Lab™
An imprint of Lerner Publishing Group, Inc.
241 First Avenue North
Minneapolis, MN 55401 USA

For reading levels and more information, look up this title at www.lernerbooks.com.

Image credits: Milkos/Getty Images (hands); njavka/Shutterstock.com (bananas); Magnia/Shutterstock.com (herringbone); Stephen Rees/Shutterstock.com (paper); Creativika Graphics/Shutterstock.com (scribbles); mhatzapa/Shutterstock.com (speech bubbles); Ursa Major/Shutterstock.com (waves); Vera Holera/Shutterstock .com (title font).

Main body text set in Janson Text LT Std.
Typeface provided by Linotype AG.

Library of Congress Cataloging-in-Publication Data

Names: Ramos, NoNieqa, author.
Title: The truth is / by NoNieqa Ramos.
Description: Minneapolis, MN : Carolrhoda Lab, [2019] | Summary: Closed off and grieving her best friend, fifteen-year-old overachiever Verdad faces prejudices at school and from her traditional mother, her father's distance since his remarriage, and her attraction to a transgender classmate.
Identifiers: LCCN 2018042053 (print) | LCCN 2018049450 (ebook) | ISBN 9781541561038 (eb pdf) | ISBN 9781541528772 (th : alk. paper)
Subjects: | CYAC: Interpersonal relations—Fiction. | Grief—Fiction. | Transgender people—Fiction. | Racially mixed people—Fiction. | Family life—Fiction.
Classification: LCC PZ7.1.R3656 (ebook) | LCC PZ7.1.R3656 Tru 2020 (print) | DDC [Fic]—dc23

LC record available at https://lccn.loc.gov/2018042053

Manufactured in the United States of America
1-44717-35554-1/25/2019

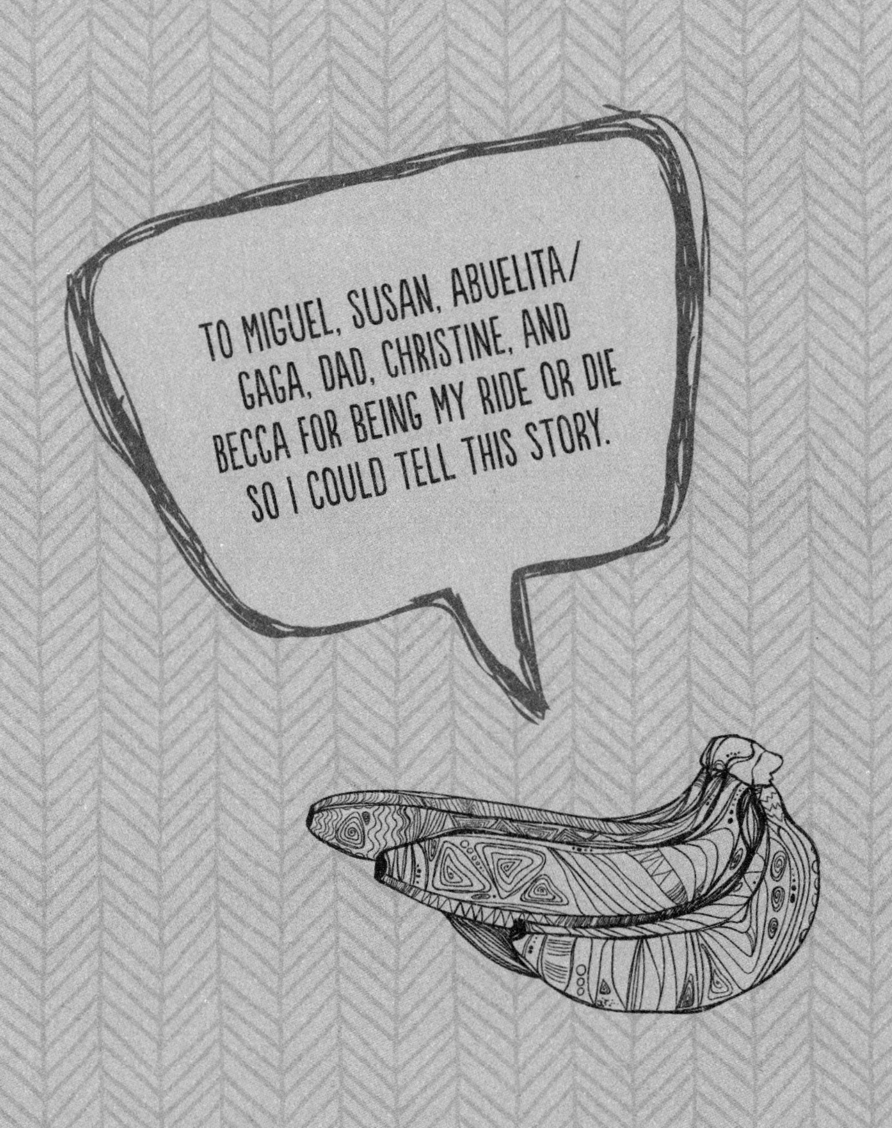
TO MIGUEL, SUSAN, ABUELITA/
GAGA, DAD, CHRISTINE, AND
BECCA FOR BEING MY RIDE OR DIE
SO I COULD TELL THIS STORY.

1

The Book of Love is blaring on my alarm radio app and I know to turn that shit off before my moms hears it. Once upon a time in a land ten years from divorce court, my parents danced to it at their wedding. They had met during study hall when they realized they were the only ones studying, and the rest is history. Now it's all math: who owes what to whom, an endless game of long division. I'm still playing the song though, because I don't get it.

Because seriously, who wrote the Book of Love? Who gets to decide whom, and why, and when? I'm fifteen and I'm supposed to fall in love like any minute now. It's biology. My moms is a nurse, so she knows this better than anyone.

I don't know what scares me more, falling in love with someone or my mother finding out.

The way I see it, love is just like your period. One day you're bleeding out of nowhere and it hurts, and that mess goes on for mostly the rest of your life.

My best friend, Blanca, didn't see it that way though. Blanca had been waiting to fall in love her whole life. If you can call fourteen years of living "whole."

She always thought we'd get married at the same time in Central Park. Honeymoon together in San Juan.

My moms flicks the lights that are already on. "¡Despierta, levántate y brilla! Thank God for a new day. Wakey-wakey," she sings, opening and shutting my bedroom door fast.

I hurl my chancla at the door. Mornings to me are like holy water to the devil.

Standing up, I trip over the baseball bat that my mother has always insisted I keep by my bed. What can a bat do against a bullet?

A holographic Jesus screensaver watches over me from across the room. I gasp. "Ma! What the hell?"

"You toss and turn so much," my moms shouts from the kitchen, where the rich aroma of coffee calls my name. "He's protecting you from bad dreams."

I scowl. Hurl my sheet over the computer, making Jesus a ghost. Fling open the door. "So let me get this straight. Like the white dude in the dress with the giant thorny bleeding heart glowing out of his skin is going to get rid of my bad dreams?"

I know Mami is signing the cross: "Forgive her smart-ass mouth, Lord. She gets it from her father."

Anything that's right with me comes from my mother's side, anything wrong from my dad's.

I lock myself in my bathroom and shed my favorite vintage *West Side Story* T-shirt that I will wear until it disintegrates. Ah—cough, gag—she's been burning incense again. Patchouli. To protect me from bad spirits. With all this protection, I'll be lucky if I don't die of asphyxiation before I leave the house.

Modern Christian music blares on the kitchen radio. Dudes are full of uber emotion singing about Jesus. I wish I could feel all pumped up like that about religion. But like how long has it been since Jesus has been here? Two thousand years. I remember waiting for my dad on the porch for hours when he didn't show up for a visit. Two thousand years is a long time to wait on a porch. Yeah, I'm bitter a little bit.

When the water is steaming hot, I step into the shower stall full of lotions and creams Mami stocks in here so I will smell like the botanical gardens. Because all girls are supposed to want to smell like flowers. *Be a flower.* It's true I got stems. Like my moms, I got the mile-long legs. She had to wear flats around my dad so she didn't tower over him. But just like stems, I'm hairy. I don't like sharp, stabby, prickly legs. Blanca's legs always felt like a cheese grater if it got cold. Mami keeps threatening to wax me, por que we girls can take natural too far, she says.

I lather up with my loofah, covering up the scar above my knee with bubbles. I rub and rub, imagining the scar—the hole torn in my leg and my life—has disappeared.

I step out of the shower into the mist. I love looking in the mirror and seeing me in the clouds, immaterial. They don't got homework in the clouds, do they?

I picture my moms and me sitting on clouds after we both die. "Pero, like, if you take one more class, you could be an archangel."

Once my hair—which Blanca used to call The Entity, like she was one to talk—is braided to my satisfaction, I head to the kitchen, where my moms is waiting for me with cafe con leche. She likes to have a convo with me before she's off to work. She always sits straight, rigid, like a beautiful statue that survived the volcano but got left alone in the ruins.

"Morning."

"*Good* morning, Verdad."

I pull out my chair—across from Mami's and next to the place that's been set for Abuelo for the past three years—and collapse in it. "Couldn't God put morning later in the day?" I prop my head on my right hand and stir my coffee with my left.

"Did you get any sleep, mija?"

"Couple of hours. Did *you* get any sleep?"

"Verdad! This isn't healthy for a young girl. You're not going to grow properly. You're going to get acne."

This from the woman who hasn't slept since 2000, who works at three different hospitals and builds Habitat for Humanity houses in her so-called spare time. "Mom, this isn't healthy for a grown-ass woman. You're going to start shrinking. You're going to get wrinkles."

My moms stirs her coffee into a whirlpool that would suck in the *Titanic*. "Verdad! Listen." She grabs my hand and holds me prisoner with her eyes. "A lot has happened. That we can't control. But what we can control is ourselves."

That's bullshit. I break free from her gaze and look away.

There are certain things you want to be true. My moms wants it to be true that if you work your ass off, you're gonna have this great life. You'll have the house, the car, the vacations. I mean, I know I have it good. Mami is a nurse, but everyone in the family calls her doc and hits her up for advice when they so much as have a sniffle. She bought us a house and made sure I had my own room and bathroom. We're the ones the family descends on for barbecues because we're the only ones with a yard. We got a car that runs most of the time. We got a YMCA membership. But like what's the point of a house if you're never in it? A bed if you never freakin sleep in it? My moms works 24/7 to keep us in the house we're in. The only place the damn car takes her is to work.

Mami sighs. She squeezes my hand and releases me. "You know you need to play a sport . . ." I lift my eyebrows. This is like telling an ostrich he should dance the tango.

"No no no!" she clarifies, images of me attempting volleyball flashing across her eyes. "I mean you should . . . run. With those long legs. You know, your dad used to run—"

"Used to?" He left us for another life. Got himself a new house, a new wife, a stepdaughter. But most of the time it feels like he's still fleeing the scene of his earlier crimes. My dad's present does not have room for his past. I haven't seen him in weeks.

"Verdad! I'm just saying. You run after school. Do your homework. That'll get you tired. Get you to sleep."

What my mother fails to comprehend is that I'm tired all the time. Of everything. Tired isn't the problem.

I nod. So she'll stop talking and also because I'm falling asleep.

"Okay!" She slams her hands on the table.

My eyes pop open. I droop from one side to the other like a rag doll.

"So I got to get to work. Give me the highlights from last night."

She got no time for details. I don't have any details anyway. I don't have no problems. I have no friends. Anymore. I don't want any. I have nothing to do except school and nowhere to be except home. That's fine with me. The real problem is my moms will lecture me for the above lack of problems.

I shrug. "Violin practice was fine." I have a school recital tomorrow—my first without Blanca. "And yes, I aced my history test."

"Music to my ears!" My moms slaps the table again, making the coffee cups dance.

"But I almost wish I hadn't."

"Excuse me?"

"Well, this girl Nelly who's in my class calls it the history of propaganda. Yesterday she went off about how all we ever learn about is Rosa Parks and Martin Luther King. Rattled off a bunch of names of African Americans I never heard of."

My moms walks her coffee cup to the sink and rinses it. "What does this have to do with your grade?"

"Nothing? It's just. I mean think about it. What about us? All we ever learn about is Cesar Chavez. And no offense, but . . ."

"We ain't Mexican."

"Word. There's over a million Puerto Ricans in New York alone, but they ain't one single one who did anything worth writing about in any textbook?"

"What about that Sonia Sotomayor?"

"That's one, Ma. White people get a thousand. We get one?"

She turns, leans against the counter, and folds her arms. "Well, after you get your college education you could rewrite all the textbooks if you like. And if you took another class, you could get to college faster. Today could be the day you change everything. Make a decision to move in the right direction."

"Right." Rewrite history. If only.

I stand up and push my chair in, careful not to scrape against the wood. My moms is super proud of taking out the nasty linoleum and installing the wood herself.

"All I'm saying," my moms says, grabbing my hand, "is have a good day. Okay?"

"Okay." I wash our mugs and set them in the dishwasher, our industrial-sized drying rack. I tie up the bread and reach up onto the fridge. Hurling the bread into the microwave on top, I expertly catch the bag of chips that falls out and toss it into my backpack. Time to catch the bus. On my way out the door, my moms sticks a piece of buttered toast in my mouth. And I head to school wishing I could go back in time, to this day a year ago, before what happened—happened. Back to when everything made sense. I made sense.

2

It's dead silent in homeroom when I walk in. Everybody's heads are down like they're praying. But in reality they're texting. I mean, kids are sitting right next to each other, but texting each other anyway. Blanca and I were rebels. In middle school we used to pass notes. Paper notes. Those you can keep. I have them all. I'm a freak.

I have two seats saved in the back of every classroom. One for me. One for Blanca. From both, you can clearly see the door. From both, you could clearly duck behind the piles of textbooks if necessary. Because it can happen anywhere. In a school, in a church, in a mall, in—anywhere. White dudes are pissed and packin. I mean a POC may kill you for your wallet. But at least they are not killing you for your existence.

I sit down and read a book. Like one made of paper. Yeah, paper. You know that shit that comes from trees? I wish life were like these books. They have one central theme. There's a quota on how much could happen to you. My life's got too many freakin plotlines.

Ms. Moore: "Verdad? Wish you were here."

I look up from my book. I missed roll call.

Me, dog-earing my book: "I'll send you a postcard."

As much as my vocabulary is off the charts, using words

with actual people is my Achilles' heel. I never know what to say to anybody. My conversation starters are generally like this:

Day 1: Freshman Year

The kind of guy that a girl dreams would ask her out looks at me and smiles.

Him: "Hey, girl. What's poppin?"

Me: "What do you want?"

The guy who will never speak to me again holds up his hands and turns away.

The nice girl from homeroom, who could be the person I sit with at lunch, looking over my shoulder: "So who you got for math?"

Me: "Why?"

The girl flares her nostrils and whispers to someone beside her.

So it's week four of freshman year at my new school and I have the same three friends, me, myself, and I. And even they sometimes don't speak to each other. Funny how Blanca's a ghost and I'm the one who's invisible. But with books you're never alone. And the characters never have to die. Because when you reread you resurrect people. Or like you could read up till the part that breaks your heart and just stop. Books are time machines.

Someone knocks on the door. My body clenches like a fist. I've already mapped out the room. Every room I sit in. I know where to hide. What to use as a shield, what to use as a weapon.

Ms. Perez, the vice principal, sticks her face in the glass and my brain registers how a normal person should act. Which makes things worse. Because now I'm all amped up with nowhere to redirect my terror. No matter what my brain knows, my body can't dial it back. I dig my nails into my palms, redirecting myself from terror to pain.

Ms. Moore opens the door for Ms. Perez. There's somebody with her: a new student. White, wearing a baggy hoodie and tight jeans, half a head of light blond hair and the other half shaved bald.

"Welcome," Ms. Moore says to him—her?—huh—after Ms. Perez hands the kid off. "Why don't you bring your paperwork over and we'll get you settled."

He/she/they doesn't go directly to Ms. Moore's desk, though. They stop in front of me, search my eyes like they're looking for a set of keys dropped in the dark.

I feel like when you've been dragging your feet against a carpet. Shock.

"You good?"

I exhale. How long have I been holding my breath? "Enough. Yeah."

He/she/they nods and moves on. While Ms. Moore is having a quiet one-on-one with the new kid, my phone buzzes. The group message on my phone is lighting up. The only reason I'm on it is because Nelly from my history class insisted nobody got left out. I never reply to any texts, but I can't help watching them roll in.

@ShutupU2: Can I ask it out or not? #thestruggleisreal.

A collective silence falls over the classroom, but the harder everybody tries to eavesdrop on the conversation, the lower Ms. Moore speaks.

@macncheesedaddy: My dude. That's a dude! I seen him before at the park. No girl throws a ball like that.

@Kidsister: That's sexist.

@ShutupU2: Name one girl we know that can. It's bc you have those itty bitty hands.

@Kidsister smacks @ShutUpU2 with her itty bitty white hands.
@ShutUpU2 out loud: "But I can't hit you back right?"
Kidsister: "No. That's domestic violence."
@shutupU2: "That's not sexist?!"
@XoXo: "I'm so confused."
@frodown: Wait. Those lashes. She's definitely wearing eyeliner.
@macncheesedaddy: Guyliner.
@rican_havok: Good point
@ShutUpU2: Check for stubble.
@macncheesedaddy: That don't mean it's a guy. I mean Mrs. Perez.
@blerdsneedluvtoo: LOL
@ShutUpU2: Can't see any tetas.
@frodown: That doesn't mean it's a guy neither.
@ShutUpU2: Guess not. I mean, what are you, anyway? An A cup? You need to do them exercises.

At this point @ShutupU2 pumps his chest in and out.

@frodown's phone hits @ShutupU2's head. "Ow! Damn! I was just making an obser—ah! A sugg—ow!"

Ms. Moore: "Okay, class, let's return to our regularly scheduled program—me. Frida, retrieve your phone and put it away. By the way, what kind of case do you have?"

"I know!" @frodown aka Frida says all proud, grabbing her phone. "You could drop it down a flight of stairs and it doesn't crack."

"Wait," says @ShutUpU2 aka Rudy, rubbing the back of his neck. "That's bullying. Ain't nobody gonna defend me?"

"And does that make you a guy or a girl?" I interject, folding my arms.

From the class collective: "Oh!"

From @frodown aka Frida: "She always chimes in at the last minute. I kinda like that. Feel that burn!"

From @ShutUpU2 aka Rudy: "Hey Ex-Machina."

I turn. "Huh?"

"Shut up."

Ms. Moore is just about done talking to the new kid and giving them a desk assignment. To my relief she doesn't put them in Blanca's empty desk.

@ShutupU2: 2 more minutes to get your bets in!

Two more minutes because Ms. Moore will do her routine intro of the new student, where she will create a profile that always sounds like a dating ad. It's our class's private joke. Like, *This is Nelly, who comes from the west coast, give her some California love. The only time she wants to perspire is lying in the sand at the beach. She enjoys photography, anything written by Brandy Colbert, and music by Childish Gambino.* Pair him/her up with a mentor for the day, and mission accomplished.

For the first time, Ms. Moore doesn't have to shut everybody up before she makes an introduction of a new student. Backpacks stop zipping, sneakers stop shuffling. Thumbs hooked in his/her/their! pockets, they stand in front of the room with posture that's too good for a guy. For some reason guys think females find scoliosis of the spine hot.

"This is Danny La Spisa."

"Danny?" Rudy whines. "Are you kidding?"

Danny, aka Daniel or Danielle, hangs his/her/their head, and the hood and the shadow it casts fall forward.

"Verdad, you're up. You'll be Danny's peer mentor. Today

just drop—Danny off at the office before first period so—Danny can get some kinks in—Danny's schedule worked out. Everyone, no hacking into the school website. Have a good day."

Rudy: "Whaaaaat?! But you didn't—"

Just like that, though, Ms. Moore turns on the smart board with her electronic marker and starts bullet-pointing lesson objectives for her second-period world literature class. Nelly holds up her laptop with her own translation:

Objective 1: White people write literature about love, hate, war, peace, food, hunger, religion, magic, nature, humor. Objective 2: Native Americans write about buffalo and eagles. Objective 3: Brown people . . . migrant workers? Objective 4: Black people write about race.

She gets major dap from Frida, Rudy, and a bunch of other kids. I jot down notes, not from Ms. Moore, but from Nelly.

The bell rings. Everybody scrambles to scoop up tablets, coffee cups, and phones. Too late! Like a tidal wave, the juniors crash our party. If Blanca were here she'd play sports commentator. Freshmen swim bravely against the tide but get swallowed. Danny grabs my sleeve. Except for being cross-checked by backpacks, we make it out alive.

"Thanks." I rub the possible concussion I have from a laptop. "I'm supposed to be taking care of you!"

"It's a team effort, I've found." Danny points to a poster on the wall.

I look up and read: "*There's no I in team*?" Eye roll. Ugh. I start walking north to the office.

He follows my lead. "But there is *meat* in team."

I snort. What did my face just do? "And meta."

"Impressive. And tame!"

"And," I proclaim at the top of my dumb voice, "Mate!"

Backtrack. "Like shipmate. Checkmate."

We're at the office now. In an Australian accent, Danny answers, "See ya later, mate."

What just happened?

****

In Ms. Belle's room, I reserve my two desks and go about my business until the scent of buttered popcorn smears the air. Just inside it hovers a cloud of J. Lo's Live. Ice sloshes in cherry soda. Blanca never needs a refill.

At our old school, Blanca and I used to be in all the same honors classes. My moms had to campaign to get me into them. And she did it for Blanca too because her abuela only spoke Spanish.

A kid turns around, sees nothing, turns back. Rubs the back of his neck. Ms. Belle scans the room but can't find anybody eating anything. Her evil eye settles on me, but all she sees are my folded hands (with my middle finger ever so slightly raised), and my homework neatly organized on my desk. She frowns, eventually finds her markers in her cluttered drawer, and starts the class review.

Me: See that? She gave me the mal de ojo.

Blanca: I can see she's not a fan.

Me: That's okay. I know how to play the game.

Blanca: Is that what school is?

Me: That's what life is. And from the looks of Ms. Belle, it's a game of Clue. I'm gonna end up dead with a compass sticking straight out of my heart.

Blanca: Maybe life is Candy Land. Every once in a while you

get stuck in toffee. But it's still toffee, man. Life is life. So exactly why does Ms. Belle want to end yours?

Me: Okay . . . I failed a few tests.

Blanca: You?!

Me: Well, because. Because, my mom. She goes, you can handle another Honors class, easy peasy lemon squeezy.

Blanca: Oh. Throwing another game, are we?

Me: It's war. I'm getting 100 one day, a 50 the next. Ms. Belle starts singling me out. Trying to teach me math like Elmo trying to teach the number seven on Sesame Street. Going, it's all about focus, Verdad. Organizing your ideas. Taking it step by step." The woman can't even organize her purse, but she's going to tell me about organizing my ideas? The other day she says to me, "You know your mom said this class would be too easy for you, but I warned her of the challenges." I go, "Did you warn all the other kids who went into Honors that they shouldn't because it's too hard—or just me?"

Blanca: And what did she say to that?

Me: Something along the lines of, "Itthatwhat?" To which I said, "You do teach math, but some English is required."

Blanca (laughing): How is it you can say what other people can't, yet you can't hold a simple conversation?

Me: Simple conversation is the least simple thing in the world.

Ms. Belle, squinting at Blanca's desk and clearing her throat: "You've entitled yourself to two desks, Ms. Reyna, so maybe you want to take two tests?"

Me: "Absolutely."

I finish them both in five minutes.

Me walking up the row to turn them in: "I corrected your question on number three Test B." I go up to the board and demonstrate why her dumbass equation cannot have an answer as it stands.

Ms. Belle could cook huevos on her head, it's so hot.

Ms. Belle (each letter starched and ironed): "Thank you." To the class: "Everyone, you make skip question three if you have Test version B."

Those with Test B: "Yaas!"

Blanca: Yup. It's gonna be the compass. Don't turn your back.

I pack up my one-hundred-pound backpack. I'm a freakin Marine.

Guy who I could peer tutor in math and who could give me tips about how not to end up unconscious in gym class: "Verdad's too school for cool."

Pink-haired girl I could be joking with in bio lab: "She's been like that since middle school. She's a walking calculator."

Boy with blue lipstick: "A robot."

Some dickhead: "Ex Machina."

The next bright and colorful circle of hell is Spanish. Orange, red, pink, and yellow picado banners surround tasseled star-shaped pinatas. Vases of terecitas, bouquets of puffy blue, purple, and pink flowers stand on either side of the serape runner covering the teacher's desk. The wall is lined with sombreros with enough silver sequins to make a solar panel for the eastern United States. Just like in church, I have a hard time understanding how any of what I'm seeing relates to me. Somewhere El Diablo is making another tally mark and my mother is signing the cross.

Ms. Hewitt writes the objectives on the board. "Please review present, past, and future tenses with irregular verbs." Her handwriting is as perfect as her neat blond French braid, pencil skirt, and crisp ruffled blouse. Her shoes do not match her outfit perfectly. She lets us chew chicle in class. She brings us guayaba. I hate her aerobicized ass.

Ms. Hewitt: "Verdad, please review your conjugations from last night's homework." Her accent is perfect like her teeth. My moms keeps threatening to stick braces on mine. I got gap teeth. I keep reminding her I know how to use pliers as well as she does.

Me: "Presente. Yo tengo. Tu tienes. El/ella tiene. Nosotros tenemos. Ellos tienen. Past. Yo tuve . . ."

Ms. Hewitt: "Verdad. Let's work on your accent. Repeat after me. Yo tengo."

Male half of "the couple" (his ear always has her red lipstick on it; she always smells like his cologne) detaching momentarily: "Yeah, girl. You sound whiter than the teacher. No offense."

Even Ms. Hewitt laughs. She's one of those teachers that likes to be all buddy-buddy with the kids.

I huff and start future tense: "Tendre. Tendras. Tendra."

Three Boricuas in the back crack up laughing, repeating the tenses as if the Queen of England is saying them.

Texts light up my phone.

@ShutupU2: Deja lo. It's not Ex Machina's fault. Spanish don't compute in her program.

Me looking at @ShutupU2 aka Rudy: "Chíngate!"

Some dickhead: "Uh-oh. Ex-Machina is mad."

Rudy: "She's at twenty-five percent!"

Me: "Mira, perras—"

Rudy: "Oh, fifty percent!"

If Blanca was here, she'd put everybody in their place. In

Spanish. Blanca never questioned who I was. When I was with her, I never did either. She would understand how I feel about Ms. Hewitt.

Me: It's just that I can't speak Spanish, but Blondie up there can? What the fuck?

Blanca: I get it. But Rubia speaking it isn't stopping you from learning how to speak it.

Me: I just wish I didn't have to work at it. At–being Puerto Rican. I mean white people don't work on being white. They just born like that. Nobody says to them, you're just not white enough.

Blanca (laughing): I guess not. Okay, Let's solve this problem. Pop quiz. What are the three things we put in our comida?

Me: Adobe. Sazon. Cilantro!

Blanca: And at every meal?

Me: Rice, beans, carne.

Blanca: Goya–

Me: Oh Boya!

Blanca: And if you didn't act right when you were a kid?

Me: El Cuco would get you.

Blanca: Fill-in-the-blank. Sana Sana–

Me: Colita de rana.

Blanca: You're a Boricua. Pass!

Me: Just pass?

Blanca: There's no 100 percent nothing no more, Verdad.

Me: Tell that to my mother.

Without Blanca, I'm lost. We might as well both be ghosts.

Off to history. I plant myself in my customary spot, with my customary reserved desk. The last row in the back of the room where I can see and access the door, as far away from the windows as possible.

We do lockdown drills here. Teachers cover the window with black paper. Kids hide in the back of the room away from the windows. Lockdowns do save lives. But the truth is somebody's already dead by the time a lockdown starts. The truth is, if it isn't you it's the person you were planning on sitting with at lunch. That person you once knew is now frozen in time, on a stage in your mind and they've forgotten all their lines.

Miss Kim excavates herself from her desk of ancient textbooks and stands beside her giant globe, which everybody learned fast not to spin without her say-so: "Good morning! Let me remind you to place your phones on my desk."

Rudy: "Can't you get your own? They got payment plans."

Miss Kim: "Now."

Rudy: "That's harsh. You're the only one who takes our sh—stuff."

Miss Kim: "That's a good point. I'll talk to the other teachers about that. We need to be on the same page about your sh-stuff."

Rudy ducking pencil missiles: "Ouch. Ouch. Ouch."

Me: "Most people get smarter at school. You're gonna have brain damage before lunch."

Miss Kim: "Today we are starting a new unit on current events. I want each of you to come to the board silently and write a current event that you feel passionate about."

Damn it, I don't want to share. I should be happy that Miss Kim is keeping it real, but I feel panicked. My raw unfiltered thoughts are safest inside my head.

A knock comes on the door. I crouch down a bit. It's Ms. Perez again, apologizing and signaling Miss Kim to step outside. Everybody's hair gel, colognes, body lotions overpower my nostrils. My sense of smell amps up every time I'm on the verge of freaking out.

Miss Kim, heading into the hall: "Xavier, you get this party started right. One by one. Row by row starting by the window."

The classroom door closes behind her. Xavier picks up his jeans to waist level, stands sentry at the board, and snaps for everybody to begin.

I always sit on the opposite side of any window. Of course, since I'm sitting in the back by the door, I have to deal with the crushing suspense of being last. I feel transparent. Aware of every part of my body. No matter how hard I try to relax, it's like the beat of my heart is audible to everyone. Can everyone hear my eyeballs moving in their sockets like I can?

From Row 1, Boricua 1 sprints to the board like an Olympic medalist. She chooses a red marker and sticks it: *catcalling*

Boricua 2, aka Penelope with the pink hair: *rape culture*

I can't help but stare, because something clicks in my memory, but the key is broken. She looks at me, but I look away.

Boricano 1: *paranoia #wejustwannatalk*

Boricua 3, with a Tierra Santa band T-shirt, chipped black nails, skipping a Chicana's turn: *#everydaysexism*

White Guy 1, who clearly has the Axe gift set: *#feminazi*

(He fist-bumps a bunch of guys as he makes his way to his seat.)

Boricuas 1, 2, and 3, eyeballing White Guy 1's groin: "Shake those maracas, baby!"

White Guy 1 blushes and hurls himself into the safety of his desk like it's a bomb shelter.

Las Boricuas: "C'mon. Don't be shy. Let me see you smile. Open that mouth. Show us that pink tongue."

White Guy 1 shrinks and pulls his cap way down over his eyes, shaking his head.

Miss Kim raps on the glass window of the door and points to Xavier.

Xavier: "If y'all don't stop she gonna give you a research paper."

Miss Kim gives a thumbs-up through the window.

Mexican Girl 1: immigration & DACA

Mexican—er, wait—AfroLatinx Guy 1: *dreamers.* (He also writes a *#lesbians* by White Guy 1's *#feminazi.*)

Boricua 4, with dope cat eyes: *colorism*

White Girl 1, aka @kidsister: *#EnoughisEnough*

Nelly, writing in bubble letters: *Enough Is Enough When Your Asses Are Getting Shot At, Huh?*

Me. I just want to walk up and erase the board. Erase everyone's memories. Unplug every TV and computer. I want it to be like the 1980s when my moms was a kid and you could actually shut everything off. Out. Every one of my nerves is charged to full capacity.

White Boy 2: *Religious Freedom*

White Girl 2, aka @XoXo: *#loveisloveislove*

White Girl 3, in a crop-top hoodie: *Right to Bear Arms*

White Girl 1 out loud: "A bear arm?"

Some dickhead: *I like pizza*

Everybody laughs hard.

Xavier, pointing to the door: "Shhhhh."

Nelly, back up at the board: *RIP #TamirRice #EricGarner #MichaelBrownJr. #AltonSterling. . .*

Black Guy 1 with waves and a low fade: *No Justice No Peace*

My scar radiates heat. I want to limp, but I autopilot it to the board. I am my mother's daughter. I am strong. Like her when she went back to work a week after her C-section because how else were the bills getting paid? Strong like when she made me go back to school two weeks after the funeral.

From Row 3, Black Guy 2 with some GQ glasses, working the sweater vest and khakis: *#BlackLivesMatter*

White Girl 4: *#AllLivesMatter*

White Girl 5, with henna on her hands: *The second amendment.*

Me. My body moves me forward like I'm a prisoner held inside it. I take my turn. I don't speak my mind. My mind speaks me. Whether I like it or not. My hand writes what I don't even know has been incubating in my brain: *#brownlivesmattertoo*

White Girl 4, standing up: "Right. Like I said. All Lives Matter."

Me, still standing up, towering over all the girls—and a lot of the guys—in my class: "That's not what I meant."

Nelly, sizing me up: "That's some bullshit, Maquina!"

White Girl 1 aka @kidsister: "What's she's trying to say is black doesn't matter more than white. Or brown."

Me: "Don't tell me what I'm trying to say." I may not know Spanish as well as my gringa teacher, but I don't need nobody speaking for me. "I'm saying our history is messed up too. Our people were killed, enslaved. Our people have suffered too." To Nelly: "Shit, at least you're in the history books."

Nelly: "And what is in those history books? Just a 101 on how to keep us enslaved. Talking about slavery as if it's past tense. Making our identity all about being slaves or being saved—by everybody but ourselves."

Black Guy 1: "Word, Nelly. Put Maquina back in her box."

Nelly, on a roll: "Those history books never talk about

African revolts, black concentration camps, Black Wall Street, Blacks inventing shit like half the music every white person listens to. I mean Mozart is great but you don't hear people blasting that from their cars, do you?"

Me: "All I'm saying is I don't want to be lumped together."

Nelly: "Lumped? No, Maquina, it's called *united.* Dónde está tu abuela, girl?"

Me: "Uh, what about my grandma?"

I charge up the row toward Nelly. She climbs out of her desk, stumbles on a backpack, and crashes onto White Girl 1. White Girl 1 shoves her off and Nelly smashes into a desk, sending the Mexican girl in it running for cover. Nelly regains her balance and charges, but White Girl 3 trips her.

I freeze. The beef she's got with those girls has superseded whatever was about to go down with her and me.

White Girl 4 headlocks Nelly, but she isn't having it. Nelly bucks and they both crash onto White Girl 1's desk. Boricua 1 pins White Girl 1's arms and drags her out of the desk. She and her girls hold back White Girl 1 from joining the fight. Meanwhile White Girl 4 yanks Nelly's hair. Nelly backs into her and head butts. White Girl 4's nose explodes with blood. Nelly spins on her knees and adds a complimentary shiner. White Girl 3 pounces on her back.

The door flings open and a security guard magically marches in, drags Nelly to the front of the class, and hurls her into the air like a crash test dummy. She slams against the wall, all the beads in her braids rattling.

Black Guy 1, standing up: "Don't touch her like that!"

Security Guard: "You better sit down, son. All of you. Right now."

We sit. We've been told. When you see blue, do what they

tell you to.

Black Guy 2 in the sweater vest: "Nelly didn't do nothing. It was them," he says, pointing to the White Girls 1, 3, and 4. "And her," he says, pointing to me.

A posse of black kids stands up and forms a circle around Black Guy 2.

White Girl 3: "Oh! So you're all gonna gang up on us now?"

Black Guy 1: "What, so we a *gang* now just because we're standing together? Just because we're black?"

Ms. Perez, charging in from the hallway: "Be quiet!"

Nelly, still pressed against the wall: "Get off of me!"

Miss Kim, standing beside Nelly: "Take a deep breath, Nelly. How about Officer Smith lets you go and Ms. Perez walks with you to the office?"

Ms. Perez backs everybody up to the side of the room by the windows and gets on her radio. A minute later the nurse comes in and sits with White Girl 4 aka Brooke. Helps her up and escorts out.

"Everybody to their seats now! Take out your textbooks!"

Five minutes after Miss Kim situates us in the Revolutionary War, I hear my name over the loudspeaker. "Will Verdad De La Reyna please come to the office?"

3

I go to Ms. Perez's office thinking of how I can keep my mother and the Lord Jesus Christ, who will inevitably be invoked, from being involved in all this.

"You got suspended?" Mami will shriek, making water rise out of the sink of dirty dishes like Poseidon raising a storm. "I hope you know this goes down on your permanent record . . ." (Wait. That's a line from a Violent Femmes song.)

Because a suspension is equal to a prison sentence in my house. Brings me one step closer to mediocrity, which leads to community college, which leads to me getting a low-paying job, which leads me to the ghetto aka hell.

The VP's office is plastered with awards and photos of smiling teachers. I imagine what the corkboards would be like if all the kids who sat in my chair were photographed. More like mug shots. "Have a seat, Ms. Reyna. Verdad. That's a beautiful name. What's the story behind it?"

My mother named me truth. Apparently, I'm the farthest thing from it. My answer: "I don't know."

"I need your account of events, Verdad."

"It all happened so fast. It's hard to remember."

"You too? I could call Sheriff Donahue in here to jog your memory, if you'd like." A Cheshire Cat smile spreads ear to ear.

"He seemed to be successful jogging everyone else's."

"No. No. I mean, Miss Kim was out of the room. I remember that. Maybe if she were in the room, you know, things would have turned out differently. But she was with you, right?"

"Thank you for that observation." Lots of shiny teeth under her plastic Invisalign, but no more Cheshire Cat smile. "How would you say this all started?"

If I say it started with me, it would end me, right here. I'm not going to ruin everything I worked for, for the sake of some kids who don't even know my name. "I would say I got up to write on the board like everyone else. And maybe that was misinterpreted. But I wasn't involved in the actual fight."

"What if I told you that's not what everybody else is saying?"

"I'd ask you, do I look like I even broke a sweat? I had nothing to do with that fight." I mean, I was *about* to get in Nelly's face. But all the other shit? Really, it was the backpack's fault. And ultimately society's fault. "Other than hearsay, there is no evidence to the contrary."

"All right, Ms. Reyna. You can go back to class. But I want you to know that we've met. That I know you." She taps a file on her desk. "I suspect we'll meet again."

I have too much in my head to handle. For the rest of the day my invisibility cloak malfunctions. Everybody's mal de ojo is on me, and everybody has an opinion. To keep sane, I go numb, to power-saver mode. If God made sense, He would have given every teenager the ability to camouflage.

Going to lunch woulda been like voluntarily going to the guillotine. I spend it at the library hiding in the reference section. I mean, adults can't even handle this #blacklivesmatter #alllivesmatter shit, but we have to make sense of it? We are all little snow globes that are getting shaken too hard. We're getting unglued. Cracked. The water is spilling out and none of us know if we can breathe actual air.

****

After school, I go to coding. Nobody cares if I don't talk in there. Most of the kids are working on this architecture program where you can simulate your dream house. I'm working on building apps. On Stanford college applications, one of the questions they ask is have you invented anything. So by the time I'm eighteen, I have to invent shit, take every advanced placement course there is so that by the time I'm in college I'm finished with college, stay on the Dean's List, win scholarships for being "Hispanic," play the violin like Paganini, and somewhere in all that shit eat and sleep (and shit).

I want an app that fast-forwards my whole life to getting my college degree. Because the in-between—as in, my life—is all about getting to that point. Delete today and every other day of destruction that seems to be the default in my life. Don't even keep that shit on the C Drive. I'm okay with amnesia.

I need to free up space. I need Blanca.

I head to the graveyard before I catch the bus home. Pretty crazy, all this neighborhood has is fast food, liquor stores, Lotto shops, and a graveyard—and yet, most of the people around me work fifteen hours a day and can still barely afford their rent.

Like cogs, they head to White Castle, McDonald's. They are the people in your neighborhood we learned about in kindergarten—service workers, transportation, construction. We dressed up as them on Halloween. The same people we are taught never to be by middle school.

Just a year and a half ago I ran these streets with Blanca. We tried on all the clothes at Rainbows and posted pictures on Instagram. We probably brought in tons of customers, but the owner didn't show us any appreciation. "I mean, you should be giving us a discount or something," Blanca shouted from the sidewalk. We ran before the cops were called. Death at Rainbows was not how we were going out.

The train above my head carries the weight of people and their dreams. People walk by with the force field of their phones. Me, I have my armor too. My book. That stupid trope where nerds crash into things because they're reading is bullshit.

I stop at our favorite food truck, Lechonera. "A bag of maduros and another of tostones, please. And one of those." I point to the Malta in the bucket of frosty beverages. I take the steaming paper bag of sweet bananas and my senses absorb all of it, the homemade warmth, like holding your mother's hand. The island smell in my nose takes me to where I have never been. If my brain don't get being Boricua, my stomach does. Bananas are like nectar to the PR gods and me.

My humanity is temporarily restored. And my throne beckons.

I down half the Malta and head toward the Hello Kitty store. The giant pink chair sitting on the sidewalk has a "Please don't sit here" sign. The closer I get to it, the closer the owner gets to the window. Ever play Marco Polo in a Hello Kitty store? Blanca and I did once.

Owner of the Hello Kitty store (a chinito with purple reading glasses, hanging over us like a bee over a can of coke): "Can I help you?" Five seconds later: "Can I help you?" Five seconds later: "Can I . . ."

Blanca (running her hand all over the trinkets, pencils, and erasers):

"Hey, let's split up. You go this way. I'll go that way. She'll have to chase us both."

Me: "You've been watching Scooby Doo again with your little cousins."

Blanca: "Shut up. Thanks. Now I have an earworm."

Me: "Scooby Dooby Doo!"

Blanca (covering her ears, her hula-hoop-sized hoopies dangling): "Damn it." (Untangling her earrings from her huge-ass head of hair.)

Owner: "Can I help you?"

Me: "I'm in! How about a game of . . ."

Blanca (running): "Marco!"

Me (eyes closed, banging into a life-size Hello Kitty): "Polo!"

I walk up the path to Our Lady of Perpetual Help Cemetery. For all the ugliness on the outside—the spray-painted rock wall that leads to the highway, the uneven gravel mixed with crushed asphalt, glass shards, and trampled weeds, plastic lids and flattened straws, the torn parachutes of grocery bags—the inside is always beautiful. The entrance is an arbor intertwined with jasmine. The exhaust and the exhaustion of the city is overcome by these tiny flowers. Trees surround the cemetery guarding against the ugliness outside. Bright autumn wreaths of orange, yellow, and gold sit like crowns on some graves, on others bouquets, some buds of white roses with sprays of yellowing baby's breath, some blue forget-me-nots shaking off petals in the wind.

Blanca sits on her tombstone the way she always sat on tabletops. Her legs swing like a little kid's: #shawtyproblems. Her Homegirl Red nails are painted perfectly. I could only paint my nails on my right hand. The left always got smeared and screwed up unless Blanca did it. She's wearing a pretty black ribbon choker and white jumpsuit. Her hair, a thick bushy brown mane, floods over her shoulders.

I toss her the remaining half of the Malta and her tostones. She likes salty. I am a sugar addict. I pull some tiger lilies from my backpack.

Me: Mami picked these from her garden for you.
Blanca: I love Mami!
Me: She says hola.

Blanca and me always used to joke that we were separated at birth. Her abuela was like my abuela, even though it was all she could do not to break a hip keeping up with us. My mother was always Blanca's mother—at least until Blanca went boy crazy. Even then, Mami gave us the same lectures: *Remember, girls. These guys, the only deposit they make is when you sleep with them and after the kid comes, their checkbook is empty.*

I plop on the grass and chow down on the sweet bananas.

Blanca smiles. Her braces shine black and blue in the sunlight. She taps her cracked, taped-up cell and plops down beside me.

Blanca: You're late.
Me between bites: Coding.
Blanca (talking with food in her mouth): Invented the app for world peace yet?
Me (talking with food in my mouth, because if we stopped to close our mouths and chew, we would forget important shit): Try starting a race riot.

I run my hands through my hair so hard I pull some of it out.

Blanca: Say what? And gurl, stop that shit with your hair!
Me: Okay!

I shove more maduros in my mouth. I give her the synopsis.

Blanca (punching me in the arm): No, no, no! You're supposed to be telling me about how you're hanging out with such-and-such who's dope, but she could never replace me. You're supposed to be telling me about all the papi chulos. Tell me again about the brotha in the sweater vest.
Me: I don't know. He's in a bunch of my classes–homeroom and history and PE. He's–wait! What the hell does that have to do with–
Blanca: No, no, no. Don't stop. Stick with Guapo. You need to fall in love. That's the solution.
Me: Nobody needs to fall in love. We all need to fall in–like.
Blanca: Uh? C'mon. You and the Brooks Brother in PE. You could be chasing the ball in soccer and trip like you always do and he–
Me, licking the sticky stuff off my fingers: What? You know me. I don't chase balls of any kind.
Blanca (wiping her hands with a napkin, practically begging): Isn't there anybody you're crushing on?
Me: Blanca, think about the word *crush*. Does this word not alarm your ass? It is assumed that at least one of the two people involved in the relationship is being flattened.
Blanca: That's one way to look at it. Or, you know. Crushed. Flattened. Flat on your back.
Me: You are a prevert.
Blanca: Pervert, you dummy.

Me: Prevert. Because the only person you've kissed is me and you're already talking smack about losing your virginity.

Blanca couldn't stand the idea of not knowing what we were doing when we had our first kisses. And kissing our hands was out of the freakin question. She said she thought of Thor when she kissed me. (So maybe I cracked her head a little on the landing.) I thought about sex. Like how I wished I could just get sex over with a friend so it wasn't this momentous deal I had to dread for the next five years. Guys get to wait with anticipation. They get lucky, they get street cred. What do we get? Bloody sheets and a rep. My moms says that hasn't changed and it never will.

Blanca (shaking crumbs from the paper bag into her mouth): It's not smack. It's reality. It's gonna happen one day. I mean you are in high school now.

Me: What is the point of sex in high school? If you're lucky enough not to be date-raped you're outed as a slut . . .

Blanca (leaning back against the tombstone): Damn, Verdad! You're such a romantic!

Me: Romance? Okay. So I become a couple with some dude, and maybe we go to the prom. Prom, one of the stupidest inventions of high school, BTW. Anyway, then inevitably we're planning for college and I want to take a year off and my dude wants to go to the military, so we just end up breaking up.

Blanca: Gurl! You think you're maybe skipping a few things? Like somebody waiting for you in the hall after class? Like you're drinking water at the fountain, and he bends down to drink too just as you come up for a breath . . .

Me: You got this all thought out, huh. But look, if I know a book has a stupid ending, I'm not going to waste my time reading all the shit before it.

Blanca (smacking her hand against her forehead, rubbing her temples, and taking a breath): Maybe life isn't a novel all the time. Where we're always trying to see what happens in the end. Maybe sometimes it's poetry. Every syllable of living counts.

Me: Shit. That was like profound. Like, wait. I gotta write that down.

I do. In pen on my arm. This annoys the living shit out of my moms. Why can't I just put my thoughts to paper? she asks. One, I have too many thoughts too fast and if I waited to get to paper, I'd forget it all. Two, the only reason my moms wants me putting thoughts to paper is because she wants me to enter them in an essay contest and win a grant or scholarship. And this is the reason I'm generally covered in ink head to toe.

Blanca (smiling high beams): You got all that down, girl. And write this too: Sometimes those syllables got to be like ooooh, Sweater Vest brotha, mmmmm–

I throw a maduro at her. She pinches my ass, hops up, and takes off. I chase after her weaving through tombstones. Running backwards, she makes crazy porn faces at me. I flip her the finger and trip. Whatever physical activity I do involves a possible trip to the emergency room.

Regaining my balance, I stand up. Damn! I've lost her.

This is the way it happened in real life.

In middle school. We were chasing each other through the halls. She slammed into an actual guy. Fernando with the lips you couldn't help but watch as he talked. That's the way Fate happens. She sees that the plotline is happy and she's like *Bam! Take this rising action! Smack! Take that turning point.*

I stand still and watch the clouds from Blanca's footsteps settle into minerals and dust. The sunlight interrupted by leaves breaks into shards on the grass. She was always two steps ahead of me. Blanca was never afraid of what comes next.

4

My mother's "Mercedes" is in the driveway. It's our private joke to call that broke-down piece of shit Toyota Camry a Mercedes. What isn't a joke is that how much Mami works should have got her an actual Mercedes but didn't.

The familiar base pumps through the walls. In my casa, we got music playing 24/7. Partly because then the assailants will think, *Hey, Bad Bunny is playing, better let them enjoy their jam*, and hit the next house. I prop open the screen door with my backpack, use three keys to unlock the door, and hear over the music, "That bastard!"

"Mami?"

I check the photographs on the entertainment center in the living room. My eyes scan past the framed photos of titis, tios, and primos, to the photos of Rita Moreno, Celia Cruz, Daddy Yankee. J Lo, Felipe Andres Coronel aka Immortal Technique, Benicio Del Toro. A couple years ago Lin Manuel-Miranda joined the family.

When I was little, I thought they were all my familia. Let me express how much it sucked to tell all the kids at school that Tio Daddy Yankee wasn't coming to my birthday at the roller rink.

Yup, Mami is pissed. There is a sticky note over my dad's

face, in the one pic of him that she keeps for my sake. My mother is even organized in her rage.

I head toward her bedroom—the bedroom I slept in for two months after Blanca died. My moms is sitting on the edge of her bed. Her head in her hands, she's massaging her temples.

I sit by her and rub her back. "What is it?" She sits up and I rest my head on her shoulder.

"Your dad. He didn't make the payments for your violin lessons. Says he needs the money to send his stepdaughter to private school. Can you believe that shit?"

I guess that means he isn't going to show up at tomorrow night's recital. In a way, I feel relieved. I can focus on the music and not keep scanning the seats to see when he's going to come. Last time he made it for the last fifteen minutes. *I had a meeting, but I did my best to stop by.* Stop by. What he means is drive-by. Drive-by parenting. At the end you have holes in your heart.

"Don't cry, Ma. I'll practice at home. I needed a break anyway."

That statement dries up her tears. "A break? You got a job? You kids always say you need a break. School ain't no job, it's a privilege. It's Club Med. You need a break from what?"

There is no satisfactory answer to this. My mother's family believes you've earned rest when you're dead. Back when Abuelo was alive, even though he was 180 years old, he still insisted on sweeping the house to earn his keep. Never mind that we had a vacuum. He had to suffer.

"Listen." My moms pulls a folded Kleenex from her bra and blows her nose. "You get a break after you finish your college education. Then you could have your break in France. Keep your eyes on the prize. Don't get distracted."

By "distracted" she means no crushes, no lust, no sex. She and Blanca butted heads a lot after Blanca went from *Aw, Hello*

Kitty! to *Whoa, hello titty* in like zero to twenty seconds. When we were little, Blanca was the one who went off the mile-high diving board first. (I was the one who watched her plummet and said hell no.) She dove into puberty the same way.

Of course, while Blanca was checking out guys, I was still checking out library books. The only characters I want to take to bed are the ones between the pages of my books.

I kiss her on the cheek. "Guess that's my cue to start on homework."

My moms starts changing into her pajamas. She puts on her sleep mask to block out the afternoon light.

I grab my backpack and swing by the kitchen. Yes! My moms left me jamón con queso and some dulce de coco. I could make the same damn sangwich and it would taste like cold cuts and bread. Mami makes it and it's magic. I gobble it down, smack my lips together, and head to my bedroom.

After two hours of homework, research for projects, and violin practice, I'm ready to collapse. The real reason Sleeping Beauty pricked her finger on the spinning wheel—she was all like, *I could just kick it and skip dance/archery/Chinese? Hella yaas.* I shower and towel off in my room. Until I notice Jesus watching me.

I turn my laptop around. "No offense, Jesus. I mean I know you made all these parts but . . ." I slip on my fave baggy jeans and unbraid my hair. Get up and find a tiny pair of scissors from the bathroom and play surgeon, operating on each split hair, the fork in an otherwise perfect strand that I didn't choose.

I think about tomorrow. The recital and the stranger who will sit beside me on the stage. Instead of Blanca, some girl, somebody whose name I still don't know. The chair in the audience that my dad won't fill. My life is full of empty chairs.

But no matter how my mind can fill in Blanca's place, when it comes to my dad, the file will not upload. We're completely incompatible. Thing is, even when your dad is a complete asshat, you're wired to love him forever. My heart feels cold, abandoned, obsolete. The trouble with tomorrow is, tomorrow is always today.

5

"Schtmrphx." My moms mumbles something as she crawls toward her bed and I crawl to the coffee maker. She's gonna catch a few hours of sleep so she can make it to my recital. I've learned how to be so quiet I could out-tiptoe Misty Copeland.

I'm on my own. I always fix myself coffee that is too weak or too strong. This time it's butane. I take two sips and leave the cup at Abuelo's place that's been reserved at the table since I was ten. The man ate pork chops down to the marrow. He'd like coffee that put hair on his chest.

On the bus, which I have mapped out too, I sit in the way back by the exit door. The problem is I got no plan mapped out for the dude walking down the aisle eyeballing me from the legs up. Almost every other seat is empty but of course the dude with the hat on backwards and the Kanye T-shirt has to park himself right next to me. Five more stops and I can get off.

I crack open my book and initiate force field mode. Four more stops. I flinch.

Ew, is it a cockroach? No. Worse. A hand brushes my hair from my shoulder, flicks the pages of my book. "Hey, girl, what you reading?"

My body stiffens like I'm all bone, no flesh. "Oh, what"—I brush off my shoulder and scooch onto the end of my seat—"because you want to discuss slipstream literature?" I reinitiate my force field, which is a hardcover and may come in handy.

"Oh, c'mon girl," says Kanye, snaking his arm over the back of my seat. I sit up. "I just want to talk to you."

"Touch me again and I will papercut you."

"You gonna what?"

I grab my backpack and stand up to change seats.

"What's your name?" Kanye runs his finger on my belt loop. "Oh my God, you got that back packed, don't ya?"

I turn around and wield my backpack of library books like a mace. Kanye falls out the chair.

"Bitch!"

The only advantage I have now is I'm standing and he's sitting.

But in a second, he hoists himself up and hurls me into the aisle ass first.

"Hey!" yells the bus driver, his face glaring in the mirror at us. "You two! Cut the shit and sit down!"

"Us two? *Us?* What the hell?" I lurch forward, grab my backpack and turn to make a run for it. Kanye grabs my backpack straps. He lifts me up and drops me on my culo. Thank God I been padding it with plates of Mami's pasteles.

I gain traction and scramble forward like a cartoon.

Kanye curses. "Where the fuck you think you going?"

But just like that he's pulled back. Like someone opened the exit door on a plane and he's sucked out.

"Damn it," Mr. Socially Conscious driver hollers, "Don't make me pull this bus over!"

Kanye is in a headlock by a dude almost my height. Blue flannel sleeves choke his neck.

My savior is wearing an unzipped hoodie jacket and Dickies

with hems cuffed above the ankles. A lock of his blond hair spills out his hood. I can hear him breathing hard, but he's not saying a word.

"Get off me, cunt!"

Cunt?

My savior is clearly Wonder Woman. In a blink the Rhodes scholar and his donkey kicking Timberlands are being hoisted up the aisle. I look at my savior's hands. They're beat up like the hammer missed the nail and hit every finger.

The hood falls all the way back and—oh shit! It's the kid from homeroom. Danny.

I can't even. I'm ded.

The bus stops. The bus driver puts it in park. He helps pin Asshat by holding one of his arms behind his back while my savior holds the other. He and Danny spin around and shove him to the front exit. Asshat tumbles down the stairs and into the gutter where he and his thoughts belong.

In conclusion and to be fair to men of all cultures and colors: YOU SUCK.

I stare at Danny as he/she/they climbs back onto the bus. The bus driver, meaty like a porkchop, stands at the top of the stairs and folds his arms waiting for asshat to try and get up.

"Your ass gonna be walking if you ever act like that on my bus again. You hear me?"

"Fuck you bitches!" Asshat apparently has a schedule and runs off somewhere to discuss the canon of western literature.

Bus driver to me from his seat: "You all right?"

I'm off the sticky floor and dusting the staphylococci off my jeans. "Yeah. I mean I'd be more all right if you had intervened earlier."

"Maybe you'd be more all right if you wasn't so hostile.

Have a seat. I've got a schedule," he says, turning his back on me. "Damn kids don't know what's it's like to earn a living."

The bus lurches forward. Shit! Half of my books are on the ground surfing under the seats. I bend down to collect them when, of course, people start pouring in at the next stop. By the time I have my books and shit together, Danny has situated themself in the front. A flood of people push their way through the front and back doors, taking seats. I hold onto a hook and stand swaying as the bus turns. I didn't even get a chance to thank him. Her? Ugh.

"No matter!" I shake my fist and shout toward the front. "We will meet again!"

A lady with no eyebrows sitting next to me mumbles, "Drugs," and clicks her tongue.

6

Outside homeroom, I look through the glass at the potential battlefield. Walk into homeroom and do my usual safety assessment. I know which windows I could jump out of and only break a bone or two before hitting the pavement. Nelly and White Girls 1, 3, and 4 are absent, I assume because they've been suspended. But all the other empty desks? None of Nelly's friends are here either.

Were they *all* suspended?

Blanca's not here, but I'm in the mood to pass notes. I lay open my sketchpad on my desk. I hold a pen by the cap and position my hand upright like I am holding a compass.

Boricua 2 aka Penelope, pulling her long pink hair out from under the nail in the desk: "What is Ex-Machina doing?"

Like what I'm doing is the weirdest thing in the room. A group of girls is watching a YouTube video on how to pierce their own arms. Another chick is filming the inside of her shirt. Her boyfriend is filming the inside of his pants.

"I tried to sit with her once. But she's so hostile," Boricua 3 says over the sound of music blaring in her ears.

"Yeah," Boricua 1 says over her own music. "We have lockers right next to each other, but she stares straight ahead. I guess her model's got no peripheral vision."

White Girl 2, aka @XOXO, with the glitter braids: "Maybe she's autistic!"

White Girl 5, with the faded henna: "Maybe she's just"—lowers voice—"a bitch."

White Girl 2: "Don't use the word *bitch*. It's sexist." Lowers voice. "But she is."

White Girl 5: "What is she anyway? Her hair is, you know . . . but she talks white."

Boricua 1: "What do you mean she talk white?"

White Girl 5: "I just mean—you said yourself she doesn't speak Spanish."

Boricua 1: "She don't. But that's not what you really mean. What, because she knows vocabulary and shit, she can't be Spanish?"

White Girl 2: "I'm so confused."

White Girl 5: "This is a private discussion."

Boricua 1: "There ain't nothing private about stereotyping."

The words tap against my consciousness like a fly hitting a windowpane. Albeit a big fat blue bottle fly.

Me: Did you send me a guardian angel today?

My pen inches over the paper. Makes a gentle 360 turn.

Blanca: :)

Me: Thank you. I'll come see you. Bring you some mofongo my moms cooked up. After I catch up with my savior. That girl. Guy. Person. Damn, this gender stuff is confuzzing. Anyway, I have to say thank you.

The pen slashes. Right over the happy face.

Me: Oh stop it.

The pen climbs up, down, up a jagged N. Slashes a sociopathic O.

Blanca: NO. NO. NO. NO.

Once Blanca brought me a slice of bizcocho mojadito from her abuela. Ay Dios Mio, my heart was in heaven, my stomach feeding a hunger only an abuela could satisfy, my brain in Culebrita where Blanca's family was from, my body swinging on a hammock between two flamboyan trees, my eyes gazing up at a canopy of fiery blooms. But no sooner had I finished my last bite, than my palms itched. My abuelo taught me that meant my conscience itched. I was in debt.

My moms always rolled her eyes when Abuelo talked like that, but she believed it more than anyone. She doesn't use credit cards. When we had to borrow money from the tías to put a down payment on our house, she worked triple shifts until she paid them back with interest they never charged. So being my mother's daughter, I baked Blanca and her abuela a whole cake to thank them for the slice.

Blanca, her giant brown bun bouncing on her head, her wiry baby hairs curling around her forehead: "My abuela says you got a problem. You can't receive."

"You mean, I'm not a moocher."

"No, I mean you aren't open to love. You always feel like you got to even things up."

"I guess I want to be debt-free."

"You can't be debt-free in a relationship, Verdad. Sometimes you're in the red. Maybe that's why people think red is the color of love. Sometimes you got to let someone else be the giver. If you love someone, you can't take that away from them."

"Shit, that was like profound. I'm gonna write—"

"That shit down." Blanca pointed to a pen and the empty skin on my arm. "Highlight it."

Me: Blanca, I have to say thank you to Danny.

I have to do something to show my appreciation. To make sure that he. She. They? Don't expect anything more from me.

My hand is going crazy now. Blanca's pissed.

Blanca: You want to even the score. But how can you even a score when somebody saves your life? That's a lot of freakin cake.

My hand drops and the pen shoots like an arrow across the floor. Someone stops the pen with their Vans, manages to flip it up like a hacky sack, and catch it midair. Danny.

I mouth "Gracias" in Danny's direction and stare like they're a pointillism picture and I'm dissecting every dot to see how it contributes to the whole painting. It isn't till their head drops and they blush that I realize I look like a dopey second-grader smiling for a school picture.

My savior hands me back my pen and I take it like I've been handed a wand from Hogwarts and it has chosen ME. At this point words should probably be exchanged. I'm thinking of how defined Danny's cheekbones are. Like a supermodel's. So of course, all I say is "Cheeks."

Danny's cheeks are now apple red. "Um, sorry?"

"Your cheeks. You have." One beat. Two. "Freckles!" I say triumphantly.

Boricua 1 to her girls: "I think there's a glitch in Maquina's program."

"Yes," says Danny. "I take after my nana."

Ha! I made conversation. Throw enough spaghetti at the wall and something will stick! And they called their abuela Nana. Que cute!

The bell rings.

"So, you're my fearless leader."

I blink. Slowly gather my belongings and remember. I get to lead Cheeks, and dang check out those other cheeks, to class.

"Okay. Let me see your schedule." The key to sanity is organization. Somehow for me, that freakin key is always the last one on the ring.

Danny hands me the schedule of regular and remedial classes. The tips of—their—fingernails are dirty, the skin cracked and bruised. Maybe they work in their dad's shop before school? Something like that? Maybe that's why Danny is three weeks late starting school. Family issues?

"Okay, your math class is gonna be this w—what the hell?"

We step into the sunlit hallway, and through the windows along the opposite wall I can see the campus grounds, the football field and stadium seats, the concession stands, the track.

And all the kids who should have been sitting in homeroom sitting in a field.

Some kind of protest?

I turn my back. Light pours in and spills onto the scuffed white tiles, and a vague sense of dread soaks through me. Light always makes me feel late, last, exposed. "Okay, let's go," I say to Danny, pulling on my own hood. Thinking. . .

Danny smiles. "Now you're in one cave. I'm in another."

I blink. Blanca and I used to do that all the time—think

the same weird thing at the same time. We were always in sync. "You know Plato?"

Our eyes meet just like in one of Blanca's stupid-ass novels (no offense, Blanca).

"No." But he nods his head yes.

A laugh escapes my lips. Meaning it drilled a hole in the prison wall when the guards were sleeping, slithered through tunnels of sewage, and escaped. "*All we see are shadows.*" I see the shadows under Danny's eyes. I wonder if they see mine. Another insomniac.

"*Because our backs are turned to the light.*" Squinting, Danny turns their(?) back to the window. "And we're chained. But what happens when we see the shadows of our chains?"

I can't help looking back outside to my classmates and the security guard now talking to them.

Me: "You're not much for small talk, huh?"

Danny: "Life's too short."

Tell me about it.

My heart feels like a car on a full tank getting pumped with gas. All it would take is one match. I'm panicked. Normally, I know what that means. My hypothalamus is trying to take over. The flight-or-fight response wants to kick in. But what do you call the opposite? Flying *toward* something in a panic? Shit, I feel like a bird about to hit a windowpane. I need to retreat. BREATHE.

"What are you two doing here?" Perez barks.

"That is the question, isn't it?" Danny answers, and we both laugh through our noses like only two dorks who read Plato in their spare time can.

"To class. Now."

I motion for Danny to follow me down the hall and I break

into a jog, leading my savior and philosopher king/queen to their remedial math class.

****

I'm sitting in AP bio. Time to compartmentalize. I tie up The Entity in a bun with a rubber band that I know will hurt if I touch it, so I won't waste time messing with my hair.

"Dónde está tu abuela?" Nelly says in my head, trying to shove me out of the cave. How long will she be suspended? What will it be like when she comes back? Was that posse in the grass protesting her suspension? Should I be walking outside into the sunlight to join them instead of sitting here?

I picture my brain like a car about to go on a road trip. In the trunk go the distractors. Nelly first. Then there's Danny, who's going to be waiting for me after class—every class, in fact.

I hear Blanca's words from the cemetery again: *How about you're skipping over a few things? Like somebody waiting for you in the hall after class? Like you're drinking water at the fountain, and he . . .*

Shut up, Blanca. He? She? Shut the hell up, me. Gotta adjust my mirrors.

Maybe Danny will even want to eat lunch together. Hopefully by lunch they'd already have somebody to sit with. Because our first conversation was maybe the best (I feel a pinch—JK, Blanca, *second* best) conversation I've ever had. I'll only ruin it if we talk again.

But what would sitting together mean? What would it look like? It's one thing to be assigned to Danny. It's another thing to choose.

And lately, I'm choosing to be an asshat.

I always saw myself as a "think outside the box" type of

person. But right now I'm feeling a weight, like my mother is sitting on the box and I'm poking holes for air. I don't know what to think . . . I know what to feel, though. I feel uncomfortable. I feel wrong for feeling uncomfortable.

The mystery of Danny has to be solved. *I* have to be solved? And this will be accomplished by . . . showing him the bathroom. That would verify he is a he, and I'm not . . . Damn! I feel like a bigot. First that shit with Nelly. Now this.

I close my eyes. It's like I've thrown a body in the trunk of my compartmentalized car analogy. But that body got its gag off and it's screaming, *You think you might be a lesbian? Are you a LES-BI-AN?* I slam the trunk down tight, but I know my analogy is burrowing through the car seat.

Time for cruise control. The best way to forget about one problem is to freak out over another. There's my violin recital tonight. And the teacher asking me to explain the quote, "Everything changes but change itself." Time to accelerate.

Vroom.

Made it through class, didn't get pulled over, no tickets. Afterward I've got some questions for Ms. Mercado about our investigation, so I'm kinda late getting out. Danny's not there, so I rush on to math to beat the bell. Just in time to catch a wave from Danny as they saunter into their class. How does someone who moves so slow keep getting ahead of me?

Blanca: Because you're just running in place.

After frowning at the ceiling aka Blanca, I motion for Danny to wait up as I apologize for my failure as an orientation buddy.

"It's all good," Danny calls out, their voice reaching me

through the talking, sneaker skidding, locker slamming. "For the greater good. I got my bearings! See you at lunch."

My heart flutters. Not like a butterfly, like a bird when it accidentally flies into your house and is freaking the hell out. Can he stop saying shit like that? Who says shit like that?

Blanca: Everybody. When they find the right person to say it to.
Me: Shut. Up. BLANCA!

Lunch. Everybody who has it fifth period heads for the bathrooms first. This is when the plot thickens. Because I see Rudy stationed at the bathroom, scrolling on his phone, and I know what his dumb ass is up to. The same thing my dumb ass is up to. I've got to know.

I go into the girls' restroom and wait in front of the mirror. I feel like I'm in Plato's cave again. Am I seeing myself or shadows? Who is myself? There is the same girl from yesterday. Long, muscular arms just like my mother's, made for carrying heavy things. Mami always jokes I'm the best daughter and son she could ever have. Blanca used to always be pissed. *You do one push-up and you've got a washboard stomach. I got to do seven hundred if I eat one potato chip.*

Blanca had major body dysphoria. I loved her body. Everything about her was soft, her heart-shaped lips that broke me when I thought about her kissing Nando, her hair you could actually run your fingers through, unlike my hair, like a tangle of wires on the brink of an electrical fire. Her skin. You couldn't see veins through it like mine, like I really have a circuit board under my skin. I wish I could be soft like her, not all angles and lines, muscles and bone.

I rethink my thoughts like I'm rereading a passage in a book I didn't get. Ay Dios Mio. I sound like a lesbian.

Some girls from homeroom and their cheap-ass perfume barge in, their reflections crowding me in the mirror.

"What's she doing?"

"Must be a short circuit. Anyway, my mom will pick us up from track . . ."

Anyway. Anyway makes me invisible. Anyway gives me license to be—myself? The girls talk without consonants reapplying their lipstick. Compare shin splints. Discuss IcyHot and bacne, exit.

Am I attracted to these girls? I didn't think I was. Time for answers. I google: *How do you know if you are a lesbian?*

Google's response: *The Ten Ways You Know You Are Going To Hell.*

It sucks when you believe in hell more than you believe in heaven.

Blanca: You want the answer to who you are to be multiple choice, fool? The answer is a three-part essay question. And remember, there is NO time limit.

By the time I step outside, everyone is in the cafeteria. Everyone except Danny and Rudy, who is leaning casually against the wall like the neighborhood drug dealer.

"You emerged from the cave," says Danny. "Your hair looks—"

"Crazy, girl," Rudy says, making a circular motion in the direction of my pelo negro with one finger, texting with another. "You ain't got no accessories like a brush and comb?"

Without realizing it, I've pulled every strand of hair out of my braid.

"Natural," Danny interrupts. "Extremely—natural. I like it."

I attempt to contain my hair with my hood. Like one of the grow capsules you submerge in water, it's grown to three times its size. "You should see it when it's humid." Tendrils crawl out of my hood like Jumanji vines.

"So, I already ate," Danny says, acknowledging my lengthy bathroom visit, but not blinking at its strangeness. "I brought you a banana. It was the only thing I could get out of the cafeteria."

"I know. The cafeteria ladies previously worked in the FBI, I think. No butter roll gets past them. You must be pretty talented."

"At stealing plantains? A total phenomenon. I'm auditioning for *America's Got Talent*."

"Ha!" I say, a grin escaping my face like a prisoner dodging a bullet of the tower guard. "I could audition my amazing expanding hair."

"Damn, I want to touch it, but I know better," Danny says, smacking their hand. "We could be a duo."

"What, like I could be a decoy and hide the plantains in my hair? What are you trying to say?" I ask, all mad, even though I'm just playing.

"I'm sorry. Is that—insulting? I only meant—you could be a distraction. Because your hair is—beautiful."

Cheeks is blushing.

Someone is stomping. We both turn toward Rudy, who's waving his phone in the air. "Ain't you gotta go to the bathroom already?"

"Uh," I say, shooting Danny a WTF look and throwing Rudy side-eye. "No, I'm good."

"Not you!"

"Dude," says Danny. "Do you normally monitor that sort of thing?"

"I mean," I say, "that's like sexual harassment, right?"

"Me? No. I—sexual what?" Rudy hitches up his backpack. "Why everything got to be sexual harassment?" He struts off muttering, "And what sex am I harassing anyway?!"

I turn back to Danny. "So, where are you headed?"

Danny hands me their schedule. "PE."

"PE!" The locker room cannot be avoided. I will have answers! "I have PE. I'll walk you to the locker rooms. The boys side is on the left . . ." I avoid their eyes.

Danny looks straight into mine. "Et tu, Brute?"

Now it's my turn to blush. "Oh, no. I—" Can't talk with my big-ass foot in my mouth. Somehow in the minute that I've known Danny, I've befriended and then betrayed them. "I'm so embarrassed."

Some random dude: "You should be. Hanging out with that." The dude shoulder bumps Danny and walks down the hall.

Danny regains his balance and grabs their schedule back. "I know where I'm heading, Verdad. Do you?"

The day finally crawls to its conclusion, flails, and dies. I can't decide if I left for school one person and returned another, or if the real person I am was just exposed.

Fast forward to the violin recital. Behind heavy burgundy curtains, I'm waiting backstage, finally in a space where I control my reality, where precision, practice, and planning matter. If only life were an instrument you could master with the right balance of control and improv.

The lights are being adjusted on the stage. Kids are talking smack around me and adjusting their outfits: white blouses and black skirts for the girls, white collared shirts and black slacks for the guys. I ignore the mal de ojo I get from the director when she scans my black slacks.

I don't do skirts.

I own my scar, and nobody is allowed to question or interpret it but me. I used to have this nightmare about cutting it out of my leg. But then of course I had a bigger nastier scar. At the end of the dream, all that was left of me was a scar. If I keep following this train of thought, I'm gonna wreck . . .

Blanca: You never liked skirts anyhow. Remember THE DRESS MANIFESTO?

I smile. Blanca used to get so embarrassed when I went off: If girls gotta wear skirts, why don't guys? Why I gotta wear a bra or I'm a slut? I've seen plenty of dudes who could use support bouncing around the track at PE. Why don't guys gotta worry about being raped 'cause they running around without a shirt? My moms always tells me to close my legs like a lady. But those pendejos on the subway sitting with their legs spread over two seats?

But back to reality. And thank you, Blanca.

We all get in our positions on the stage. I scan the props of the production in progress. Blanca and I were the backstage crew at all our middle-school productions. When we did *The Wiz*, she and her abuela created all the costumes by hand. My moms and I did the sets. Mami kept saying I should audition because, por supuesto, it would show college admissions I was well-rounded. I answered her by eating a big-ass bag of Takis and smacking my culo. Blanca knew my secret though.

I *had* auditioned. I tried for the part of the Tin Man. Why shouldn't the Tin Man be a girl? (Why did I choose the machine? *What would I do if I could feel . . .*) But my chickenshit self couldn't get a word out onstage.

"Take your places, ladies and gentlemen."

Ladies. Gentleman. And Danny, I think as the curtain opens and we see all the parents seated in the audience. While the music director does her spiel on the importance of music and where they could send their donations, I think about how Blanca's abuela used to sit in the audience taking pictures with this ancient camera, filling roll after roll of blur. Her abuela died a few months after Blanca, from a broken heart.

My violin instructor announces, "Verdad will be playing 'E Major Partita' by J. S. Bach—E Major first movement solo."

I step into the spotlight that isn't big enough for my greatness, according to my moms. She's sitting in the first row, scowling at the arrangement of violin players seated on the stage. Specifically, at who sits in the first and second chair. In middle school, Blanca used to be first chair, me second. Funny but you wouldn't know there was any white people in this school unless you looked at the violinists. They fill every seat but mine. I guess we POCs are just supposed to play the bongos or something. Not that I have anything against bongos—I love you, Tio Ray! #justsayin.

Back in middle school, Blanca and I were first and second chair. We were so proud to make the music director choose us. Yes, make. "It's unavoidable," he said, sighing. "God, the calls I'm going to get from parents."

What little clapping there is dies down. With my bow, I do what I can never do any other way: feel. Like skin is supposed to do. I can't even get a paper cut without overanalyzing it. Does this hurt? It would hurt most people, so I can determine that it is painful. Therefore, I should react. Freakin *ow*.

According to my mother, there is nothing I can't do. But I know better. I can do quadratic equations, but I can't figure out how to be a human. Except like this, holding my violin. The violin, like the coffin, is hollow, empty inside, but the emptiness is integral to its purpose.

Emptiness is space of such sacred design that only death and music can fill it.

Blanca: Not speech. Speech is just clutter, thoughts scribbled sloppily by the tongue.

Thank you, Blanca. Note to self: Write that shit down.

The audience is silent, surprised. I can never cry through my eyes, but I can do it through my fingers. Sadness is something I read like sheet music.

The auditorium is full, but as always, I play for the empty seat in the house. My father's. This fact, I know, breaks my mother's heart. I mean imagine that shit. You bust your ass as a single parent, and your kid treats the absentee parent like a rock star. But love is like water and it slides over the smooth places. Sinks into the cracks.

My father not showing up is probably better than the real thing. This way the father I imagine high-beams a smile and sheds a tear on cue. He apologizes for not being there for every show, for every moment my mother tried to fill, but only a father could. Emptiness is the fullest thing there is.

A best friend can't fill the emptiness, but she can carry it with you. And Blanca would go the distance, even uphill. Blanca shows up and plants herself in my dad's seat. She and her bow she's using as a conductor's wand, her big-ass cherry slushie that's splattering all over her leotard and white off-the-shoulder fuzzy sweater. Blanca.

She was the black swan, the swaggering ballerina. She could play the violin like an electric guitar. She danced hiplet. She pissed every teacher off because she refused to follow directions. She was a trial-and-error kind of person. She broke shit. But when she figured things out, she understood things better than the person trying to school her. She was intuitive. Everything I could never be. Now I play for her. For Blanca.

The air is a low tide and the notes of my violin stud the sand with whorls and wings of shells. The audience scoops up sea glass with their buckets. But Blanca dives in after the elusive conch. And disappears. Someone walks out of the waves and takes her place. I blink.

My posture, the position of my bow, fingertips, my elbow, tell you nothing. But if you measure my heart rate, my brain waves, you know something happened. That people got up out of their seats to make room for someone who showed up late. That someone is Danny, sitting in their cave listening to the music coming from mine. Really listening. Not the kind of listening most people do where they say, *Damn, I wish I could do that.* Or *Damn, I never knew that loser could do that.* Or *That girl is on the right track for college.* The real kind of listening. The kind of listening that makes you come out of your cave. Danny's hoodie slips down.

I blink. I bite my lip, but my fingers don't waver. They continue to play mathematically, solving note after note. Even when I do the unthinkable: I look through the force field of blinding purple lights straight into Danny's eyes. For a moment, I play for them.

By the time I play Bouree, autopilot ends, and I return to my body. I finish Gigue, flourish my bow, and take a bow, squinting in hopes that I can see a reaction from Danny. He is the only person not clapping, though. Not moving. The next violinist prepares her sheet music and Danny stands up. Like dominoes in reverse, people stand up one by one and let them through.

Why is Danny here? Doesn't Danny hate my homophobic guts? Could you be a homo *and* be homophobic? Wait, should I even be thinking the word *homo*? Queer, is that the right vocab?

The show ends. We bow. The audience starts clearing out through the clapping. I secure my violin back in her case and make my way to my biggest fan.

Hot dude I pissed off the first day of school: "Wow, Maquina, that solo was lit." He holds out his hand for some dap. I raise my hand in a lukewarm wave. Hot guy forms my hand into a fist and bumps it against his.

Random girl to random guy: "Can a violin solo be lit?"

"Verdad," my moms says, waving her phone in my face, "say hi to your tías! I had them FaceTime in."

By the time I am done FaceTiming with my tías, Sujei and Matilde and Clarissa, and mis primos, the auditorium is empty. My moms takes the cell back.

"Yeah, Sujei. I know. First chair." Blah blah blah blah. We're going to be here for at least ten minutes before Mami moves on to the cookies and lemonade in the cafeteria. I want me some nom noms, damn it.

Two lady custodians wheel a squeaky cart out of a closet. I smile at them and they smile back. I wonder how they're not scared to death working here at night.

A minute later I catch something in my peripheral vision. Did someone—Danny—slip into the custodian's closet?

I motion to my moms that I'll be right back and she waves me off. All sorts of racket is happening in the there. The screech of a shelf drags across the tiles. Brooms fall over. It suddenly occurs to me—what if it isn't Danny?

I glance at my moms. She's giving the play-by-play about my dad and tuition. I flag her, but she waves me off. Maybe in the past year I've taken the whole "see something say something" drill a bit too far? But this time could be different.

The custodians are long gone. I'm gonna have to handle this. I approach the closet door. I snap open my violin case and extract the bow.

"Aha!" I shout, I'm not sure why, as I whip the door open

and brandish my bow back and forth.

"Ow ow ow!" Danny shrieks, taking a step back.

I lower my bow. "I'm so sorry! I thought—"

"Just for clarification. You came in here armed with a violin bow?"

"Don't judge me."

"I won't as long as you don't judge me." Danny grabs a roll of toilet paper, checks if the coast is clear like in a cartoon and bolts out the door into the hall.

"By the way," Danny calls over his/her/their shoulder, "you were incredible center stage!"

****

My moms is headed into the shower before she heads to work, and I'm about to jump in bed. The hum of her toothbrush chills me out. All I need is my white noise app on my phone to block out the questions. Did Danny come to see me? Or to raid the janitor's closet? And for what?

Ugh, forget the white noise app. I'mma just turn on the vacuum and set it by my bed. Crossing the kitchen to my room, I catch the old-fashioned Presto ringtone of my mother's phone.

I plop down on a chair at the table and stretch my back muscles. Cradle the phone on my shoulder like a pillow. "Yeah." The buttons I accidentally press with my cheek beep.

"That's how you answer the phone?"

"Papi? I thought it was one of Ma's bosses." My spine straightens, dragging me with it.

"Did your mom tell you I been calling?"

A Mariana Trench-sized yawn rounds my mouth.

"I'll take that as a no."

I lean back, finger combing the tangles of my hair. All this hair that I spend hours and hours trying to make perfect, but it never freakin is. Blanca told me once I went cross-eyed, staring so long at my ends. "We been busy."

"Well, I'm glad I caught you then." He clears his throat. "I want to explain my absence today. Veronica, your sister—"

"My sister? Say what?"

"My daughter—"

"Your *daughter*?"

"Your stepsister. Stop interrupting and hear me out. Look. It's been tough—"

"Yeah." In theory, my dad is all about atonement and used to take me to church for confession even before I was old enough for communion. "*Forgive me Padre for I have sinned . . . I think a stole a cookie from a cookie jar?*" But when was the last time my dad asked for *my* forgiveness?

"Is your mom there?"

"She's getting ready for work."

"So you're gonna be alone."

"I'm gonna be asleep." Okay, I'm gonna be in bed.

"You're alone too much, mija."

"And you're trying to pin that on Ma?"

"She doesn't have to work that much. She could be there—"

"She is here. You're there."

"Listen. Maybe we could get together some time. Maybe next weekend? Wait, no. Wait. How about—"

"No. No more waiting. I'm not a middle schooler anymore, waiting on the stoop for a car that never comes."

Shit. I said it. When you lose someone, you learn to say what needs to be said before you don't get the chance again.

SIGH-lence on his end.

Mami's shower turns on, the running water my favorite lullaby. "I gotta go." Before I fall asleep in this chair, slide onto the floor, and get a contusion. Again, I can sleep anywhere but in a bed.

"Okay. I understand." Long pause. "I get it. I sowed nothing, so I can't complain nothing was reaped. I been served. No question. But, I'm still your father. For better or worse, you're still my daughter. I've made mistakes, but you were never one of them."

The biggest mistake here is me picking up the phone. "I'm tired, Papi."

"Verdad, we need to talk. How about I surprise you sometime? Just out of the blue. Show up."

"Surprise? That would be a cardiac arrest."

"Okay. Maybe you could surprise me."

My left eye pops open.

"You just call a cab and come over. Anytime. I'll pay for it when it arrives."

"Yeah, okay. And if you're not there when it arrives? How's that gonna work? Listen, thanks for calling. I gotta go." I hang up.

I'm so tired, I almost brush my teeth with my mother's tube of acne cream. I collapse into bed.

Of course, this is where I'm most awake. I seriously think I should put a school desk in my bedroom and a bed in my classroom. Now my mind has a mind of its own and pops the trunk. Nelly's words escape: *Dónde está tu abuela?* Why didn't I ask Blanca what this meant? Because I was embarrassed. Embarrassed at not knowing? Embarrassed at looking like a racist?

I wiggle out of my cocoon and head to my desk. Pray to the

Google god. Get my answer from Puerto Rican poet (there are PR poets?) Fernando Fortunato Vizcarrondo:

Yesterday you called me Negro, And today I will respond to thee: My mom sits in the living room, And your grandma, where is she?

My hair is kinky, Yours is like silk, Your father's hair is straight, And your grandma, where is she?

Your color came out white, And your cheeks are pink; Your lips are thin, And your grandma, where is she? . . .

Yesterday you called me Negro, Wanting to embarrass me. My grandma steps out to the living room, And yours hidden from everybody . . . And I know her very well! Her name is Mrs. Tata You hide her in the kitchen, Because Negro is really . . . she.

Wait. Is Nelly Puerto Rican? Am I black? We black? My head hits the keyboard. I feel like a shapeshifter. Who am I?

I crawl into bed with a stranger. Me.

8

I walk into homeroom on three hours of sleep and short about three hundred hairs. My scalp is sore. My brain is the closet of the room you were told to clean, the closet you crammed everything into. I'm cranky. I lean on my palm and stretch out my legs across Blanca's chair. I'm about to catch a cat nap when the phone lights up with the homeroom group message:

@ShutupU2: No Danny this morning. The pool is over 200 dollahs!

@macncheesedaddy: Wow. I could buy a third of a smart-phone with that.

@blerdsneedsluv2: How many people are swimming in this pool?

@shutupU2: Well. About 200.

@frodown: But wait. This is a 50/50 bet. So let's use a random number and say 100 kids think Danny is a guy and 100 a girl. Then half of us win—

@blerdsneedluv2: 2 dollars LOLLOLOLOL

@XoXo: He can pee next to me. #loveislove

White Girl 3 out loud: "That's a T-shirt. A slogan. Not reality. Your dad would pitch a fit. Assuming he has a penis,

I don't want it in my bathroom, okay. Bathrooms should be based on biology, not on personal preference."

My eyes pop all the way open at the sound of her voice. What the hell is that puta doing here? I straighten up and scope out the situation. White Girls 1 and 4 are back too. Nelly still isn't here.

White Girl 2 aka @XoXo, chipping the pink polish of her nails: "I don't think gender is a preference. I'm sure everybody would prefer that they were born in the right body."

White Girl 3, who's now wearing cornrows(?): "The right body is the body you have, not the body you have to surgically alter."

@blerdsneedsluv2 aka Black Guy 2: "Why can't they just have their own damn bathroom?"

@frodown aka Frida: "Really, Alphonse? Their own water fountain too?"

@blerdsneedsluv2 aka Black Guy 2 aka Alphonse I guess: "That ain't the same thing."

White Girl 3: "I don't want to worry about getting raped in the bathroom. How am I supposed to know if a guy is in there because he thinks he's a girl or a guy is in there because he's a sicko?"

Frida: "So you're saying that rapists would dress up as a woman and attack you in the restroom stall?"

White Girl 3: "Tell me your father is okay with guys being in the bathroom."

Frida: "Why wouldn't rapists have dressed up as women to attack women in stalls before?"

White Girl 3: "I'm waiting."

Frida, fiddling with the flower in her hair: "Okay. No. My father would not be down with brothas in the restroom."

@Rican_Havok: "Forget my dad. My sister goes here. If that dude steps into the bathroom, I will kick his ass."

Boricua 2 aka Penelope: "Excuse me. Sorry I'm late to the convo. But what if he has she parts? Then can they use the girl's bathroom?"

@Rican_Havok: "No. A fictional penis is still a penis."
Frida: "So you're good with him using the boys' bathroom?"
@Rican_Havok: "I'll kick his ass."

****

Danny doesn't show all morning. I head to the bathroom before lunch. I've brought my nail clippers today because that is more civilized than using my teeth. To make up for the three hundred hairs I pulled out, I'll snip three hundred split ends. I sit on the toilet tank and find my rhythm.

Knock knock knock. "I could just slip it under the door."

"Danny?" I jump off the toilet tank so fast, I almost step into the bowl. "Slip what under the door?"

A banana clutched by a dry, cracked hand waves back and forth.

I drop my nail clipper, I'm laughing so hard. Grab the banana. Gather my things: hair, backpack, nail clipper. Danny glances at all this but doesn't question it, my sanity, etc.

"Okay. Office hours are over." I push open the door and grab Danny's hand. Thank God @Rican_Havok's sister isn't in here. "Come with me if you want to live."

By the time we find the most isolated stairwell, I have inhaled the banana and am trying to figure out what to do with the peel. So Danny and I think we're hilarious and set it on the stairs.

"So where were you this morning? Your ears are pierced." I estimate 120 dollars' worth of piercings from a homie who may have raided the janitors' closet. Blanca and I did the research.

"Yeah." He has wooden plates inserted into his ear holes. "Buddy of mine owed me a favor. Did it for free. But I had to do it this a.m."

"Free? Except for the cultural appropriation, I like them."

Danny blinks in surprise.

"So a buddy, huh? You and Blanca. She tried to DIY a tattoo once by reading a prison blog." Ms. Trial-and-Error was planning on piercing her nose by hand and I was like hell to the no.

"Blanca?"

I said her name. Out LOUD.

"Is she in homeroom?"

Yeah. No. Yeah. "She's not here." Not on the stairwell. At the moment. Mostly. "Anyway, tats and piercings were her thing." Gonna be her thing. "She was into fashion. Costumes, actually. Girl loved petticoats. Other girls walked around in shorties and tank tops. She walked around in the summer with a parasol. She always said she didn't belong—" to this time.

"What's your thing?"

"I love the suspenders. And the hats: bowler, Panama, fedoras. I could tie a Windsor knot like nobody's business. Britches are badass." Wait. The correct answer was *I build sets.*

"I can just see the two of you."

"Actually, you couldn't. Because Blanca had the cojones to walk through the barrio with a Victorian touring hat. She wore her personality on her sleeve. My personality . . . is kind of stitched into a secret pocket."

"I love secrets. And pockets. But especially secret pockets."

I snort again. It's on. "So do you have a secret pocket?" And are there janitor's supplies stuffed inside?

A bunch of gossip-girling sophomores jogging up the stairs fall dead quiet at the sight of Danny and me. One of them makes a big show of squinting at Danny like she's trying to identify a bacterial strain. They get all whispery and then back away like they verified leprosy. Frida comes up from behind and stares them down.

"Sorry for staring, ladies. My bad." Frida squints. "But only two layers of makeup? I couldn't tell who you was."

They suck their teeth and strut off.

"Yeah!" I shout to their backpacks. I get a middle finger.

I'm embarrassed and grateful all at once, thinking back to that guy shoulder-bumping Danny and me not saying a word in their defense. I SUCK. Frida didn't flinch. The right words came out of her mouth at the right time.

"PS, you two know there is a cafeteria, right?" Frida says.

Danny laughs. His/their front tooth is chipped. He/they stops smiling when he/they catches me looking.

"Speaking of the cafeteria, do you think tomorrow, I could offer you a seat? One that doesn't have a lid. At the table?"

Snort. "I'd—like that. But first"—deep breath—"Danny. I swear I'm not placing any bets with Rudy, but . . . pronouns, please for the love of God."

Danny nods. "Thank you for actually *asking*." Now I feel even worse. That was all I had to do? Maybe it's something I should do all the time. With everyone. "He/him will work. You?"

"Me?"

"That's a new one. Would me come a little closer?"

"No! I meant . . ."

"I'm just messing with me." He looks into my eyes and laughs.

I laugh too.

9

Normally, the day is like an abacus, stones sliding from one groove to the next and back again. But the rest of the day felt like skipping those stones across a sunlit lake. Especially with the picture of Rudy slipping on a banana peel, shared on the group message courtesy of Frida.

Is it tomorrow yet?

In accepting Danny's invitation, I didn't think about my hair. Most people wouldn't be aware of not thinking about their hair, but I'm not most people. I'm always aware of what I'm thinking, of when I'm not thinking about thinking, and where the ibuprofen is located. I wake up earlier to cut all the hairs that I wouldn't be able to cut in the restroom at lunch.

I'm about to slip on my jeans and T-shirt, when I consider what I'd actually like to wear for the first time. Okay, maybe I'm not ready to step out in public in britches, but how about a fedora for starters? Not just to school where everybody bumper-stickers themselves with personality. (No offense, Blanca.) But everywhere: the supermarket where the neighbors inventory each other's kids, to church where neighbors predict your fate, best exemplified in hats for women, dresses and patent leather shoes for the girls. I face off with my screen-saver Jesus.

"I mean, Jesus, you're wearing a dress. So I can wear a fedora. And suspenders?" Yes. And so what if I want to dress *GQ*, suave and powerful.

But in the end, despite my blasphemy with Jesus, I dress basic, because basic is my invisibility cloak.

I canvas homeroom as I stand in the doorway, the way I do every room I enter, and instantly register there is a change in logistics.

White Girls 1-5 are huddled up in the back of the room. Nelly's desk has been decorated like a shrine. Kinda like the way the outside of the Dollar Theater was decorated almost a year ago for Blanca and the others, with flowers and stuffed animals. A banner across the chair reads, *Nelly Should be Here.* Is Nelly . . .?

Nelly's friends are back and talking about how Nelly's mom unenrolled her from school. Apparently the administration wanted to expel her, even though the white girls only got suspensions. Nelly's gonna go to the local Catholic school. Her mom refused the scholarship and is gonna take a part-time job to afford the tuition.

Each hair on my head feels like a tentacle absorbing every minute vibration, telling me to retract, bleach, calcify, die.

I recoil to my desk the way I'd hide under my blankets as a kid. Check my phone and see an invitation for a rally at tonight's school board meeting. "Justice for Nelly" meets at seven tonight in front of the admin building. Crowds of people will stand two hundred feet away from the building raising signs and chanting.

Crowds of people are unpredictable. In a school we're regulated, monitored, herded from one class to another, from one life event to another. But outside everyone is an outlier, a variable, a powder keg. It would take only a second for someone to reach into their pocket and change the future.

I delete the invite. I barely know Nelly anyway. Check social media and see Frida is inviting kids to her house to organize. There would be conversations to initiate, which might lead to a rapport, which might lead to a friendship. Friendships require encounters at regular intervals. Where I can't predict the setting, the stage directions. On the other hand, if I'm not there, conversations will lead to bonding and relationships that will hinge on these defining moments, and I will written out of the script.

A gentle pressure weighs on my shoulder. "Uh, Verdad," Danny says, "the bell."

I lift my aching head. Homeroom is clearing out. I nod and meet Danny, who looks like he's been spun in a blender, outside the door.

He leans back on his heels. "Tough night?"

My haze lifts. "No. Yeah. I mean nothing more than the usual. More like a sucky morning. Which is also the youzhe. You?" I pluck what appears to be a leaf off his shoulder, pretend to throw it on the floor, and stick it in my back pocket. I don't know why, that's why.

Blanca (wrapping her arms around herself pretending she's making out with some dude): Mwahmphmmmmmm!!!

Danny looks in the direction I'm gazing. "I'm good. No worries. The nurse hooked me up." He shows me a giant Wonder Woman Band-Aid across the top of his left hand. A lefty like me. I find the Band-Aid sexy. I find him being a lefty sexy. I find thinking of his hands sexy. I want to kiss his booboo.

"You're blushing."

"I am?"

"I don't know why. But I like it."

Two chicks float by, one a vintage thrift-store hippie chick, the other in an airy blouse and poofy pants, all twittery and giggly, their long, silky black hair swinging in sync. Both bat volumized eyelashes in Danny's direction. Danny nods and looks away, hiding in his hoodie.

I will cut them.

I adjust my backpack. "We should go."

Danny fist-bumps me and I head to math. Math, the solution to all "our" problems according to my moms, but the biggest problem in my academic life.

"English—anybody could do that. That's not going to get you no scholarship."

"Really, Ma? Thoreau, Neruda? Anybody could do it?"

"Verdad, the truth is you won't get no respect without math. When you step in front of an employer, they'll look at that face and they'll make all kinds of assumptions about you. Assumptions that start with can't. Won't. Didn't. Thoreau's not gonna change that. Knowing how to do calculus will scare everyone shitless."

Here's another assumption about math: that it has to suck as much as it does with Ms. Belle. I wish she could teach me right before bed so I could actually sleep. I mean just because she can *do* some math, she can teach? How can anyone make Zeno's paradox freakin boring?

I am slipping into a vegetative state with these math packets. "Oh my God, can you give us some kind of application of this? Architecture? Engineering? Poetry?"

I mean the poetry of differential calculus. Calculating points in time and space. The infinite movement we make in time, moving forward, but never reaching zero. Integral calculus, where we don't head to zero—we head to fucking infinity, man. Get as close as we can. But again we never get there. Because in nature we never get an absolute. Absolutes are bullshit.

I think I am having an epiphany. I think tomorrow I will be wearing a fedora and suspenders.

The class falls dead silent. Ms. Belle whips open her book and tears a page, which I know, symbolically, is my asshole. "Oh," she mumbles, "I can give you a problem."

Me, a little quieter this time: "I mean Pythagoras—what did people do before textbooks and worksheets?"

"You know what?" She slams both palms on her desk, looking like she's going to pounce. "How about *you* present a brain teaser to open up the class for the next few weeks?"

"Me? I have enough homework already. I don't want your job."

"That's it, Verdad." She spins her chair with maximum centrifugal force. "Outside."

I step out in the hall. Without all the warm bodies generating heat, it's as cold as a tomb. Miss Belle is not in a rush to join me. Being an outsider peeking into the classroom window, I feel like I'm in a dream. Is this what it's like to be dead?

The door whips open and slams shut. "I have had it with you!"

"To be honest," I say, backing up from her egg-and-bacon-infused wrath, "I've had it with me too."

Miss Belle rolls her eyes. "Listen! I brought you out here to let you know, I believe you. You need instruction I cannot provide. So, you're going to cut the crap with the erratic grades. Next semester you're going into an Honors class."

"I am?"

"Yes, you are. Because if not, I've got your mother on speed-dial. And I'm recommending you for the math team." Miss Belle slaps a folder into my hands. "Here's the work you'll be doing to prepare. You can set up your office in the back. That is, when you are not peer tutoring."

Ms. Belle takes a breath and, I swear, skips back into the classroom, slamming the door on my fate. Damn it, my mother will be so proud!

The rest of the morning my schedule is as follows:

Period 2: Autopilot. (2,4,6,8, everything white people ever did was great!) Danny!

Period 3: Something, something, something. (Faulkner.) Danny!

Period 4: Biology. Here I am totally focused. Just not on the biology of the cell.

Lunch!!!!!!

I step into the doorway and stop short. Our cafeteria in middle school was a cold, concrete, fluorescent bat cave. This cafeteria is more like a café. We are surrounded by windows and sunlight.

"Hey, you okay?"

"Sorry!" I turn around too fast and Danny and I are almost nose-to-nose. "Whoops! It's just light. And loud. And—"

"Extremely close. I get it." He pulls down my hoodie. "We can do this."

Danny gently ushers me to the food line where I achieve a plate of tacos. We're babbling about whether you can have a side of French fries with a taco until we're drowned out by the scolding going on at the register. A basketball-tall chinito—boy?—girl?—PERSON is getting bawled out by the cafeteria lady. Out of the person's coat comes bananas. Lots and lots of them.

I can't help but stare as I fill my tray with the least offensive mass-produced items: strawberry milk, cheese quesadillas, fruit salad with almonds. "Dude must need his potassium."

Danny just looks down, his ears turning red.

"Now you're blushing. And I don't know why but—"

"You like it?"

I smirk. More than our lunch is getting put on the table.

Danny slides in across from me and takes a meat-eater's chunk out of a massive cheeseburger. I prepare myself to eat, sticking a straw in the milk I would normally chug.

"So," he says, chewing with his mouth partially open, then swallowing, "I decided we shouldn't talk."

I slice triangles of quesadillas into smaller triangles—that I would normally just shove into my face. I catch a triangle before it flies off the plate. "Okay."

Danny lifts an eyebrow as he watches me almost shove the straw from my drink up my nose. Because I'm cool like that.

"Yeah," he says, licking mayo off the side of his lip, "that way we don't have to think anything up."

"Mmm hmm," I say, watching Danny pause and examine my utensils. He picks up a knife and fork and starts chainsawing his burger.

I crack up laughing. "Dude, no offense but what are you doing? Who does that?" I say as I'm eating strawberries with a fork.

He laughs. I laugh.

"I'll lay down my weapons if you lay down yours. One, two, three!"

At the same time, we both lower our forks and knives. Both pick up our respective hamburger and quesadilla and take a bite. Both laugh and manage not to spit out most of our food.

Somehow our silence becomes a mixture of mirror-me and pantomime. We don't talk the whole rest of the meal, but we laugh the entire time. By the time the day ends and I go home, I'm laughing at things I couldn't explain to anyone but Blanca. At things she could only tell me, before Fernando came along. I laugh to myself the whole way home. As it turns out, this is a great way to get everyone on the bus to sit somewhere else.

I don't sleep that night, but for different reasons than the usual. The usual being, feeling cold, weightless. Irregular. On an indeterminate point in time and space. My mother is Zeno trying to solve my irregularity—with her insertion of box after box after box of prepackaged notions of success. Subtracting my irregularity to get me as close as she can to something determinate, quantifiable.

I still felt weightless. But this time I'm not hovering, lifeless. This time I feel like I'm flying.

10

I wake up before my alarm and even make my bed. I still dress basic but decide to add a bright blue bow tie. I chug OJ from the container and actually taste it going down. Ahhhh. Toss some bread into the toaster and sit at the table. Maybe I'll even read the news. My toast pops up.

"Don't even think I won't, muthafucka!!!"

I topple off my chair. "Ay Dios Mio!"

From my mother's door frame: "Verdad?"

Whimpering from the floor: "Mami?"

Unison: "Oh shit!"

Unison: "What are you doing up?"

Me: "Why do you have a chainsaw?"

My mother's hand lowers the chain saw with one hand, her other is across her palpitating heart.

"I mean the bat was one thing!" I lay my hands on the table, breathe in deep, and try to get my bearings. Look up. "Does that chainsaw even work?"

Chainsaw: *Vvvvvvvvvrah Vvvvrah Vvvvra Herrrrr!*

My whole body is shaking down to my molecules. "Cortar la mierda! Para!" I ease myself back into my chair. My throat is thin as a drinking straw. I don't need to duck, I don't need to run. "Where did you get that?"

She lays the chainsaw by the coffee pot. "Home Depot. They were fifty percent off."

"You want to tell me why a chainsaw?" My scar throbs like a rabbit heart.

"There's been homeless people seen in the neighborhood."

"Damn. And you were going to build them a home?"

"Verdad, Roberta Chavez said she saw them casing the neighborhood."

Because of my moms I know how to plaster a hole, drop a ceiling. But I guess there's a big difference between making someone a table and inviting them to sit at your own. "Jesus, I hope I'm never homeless."

"Verdad!"

"I meant it in prayer." I kneel. "Dear Jesus, I hope—"

Steaming coffee in hand, my moms retreats into her bedroom, aka the weapons arsenal, mumbling about El Diablo. I butter my toast. Retreat to my room. Spend more time than I care to say smoothing and securing my hair into braids. Untwining and unintentionally frizzing my hair. Thinking I probably split ends doing it. Cutting to undo the damage in my hair, in my brain, in my life.

•••••••

Can't remember the last time I felt happy like this. I know I shouldn't be. Feels like if I'm happy, I'm dissin Blanca.

Blanca: You dis me thinking like that. I want you to smile. Smile like when you got to try on the jacket of one of the Sharks in our production of West Side Story. You spun in front of the mirror singing, "Boy, boy, crazy boy—Get cool, boy!"

I smile despite myself.

Until I see that security is circling the campus.

Nobody is huddled up outside, warming their hands and talking and vaping before class. My eyes register the track team running toward the school gym but my brain processes kids running away from gunfire. I crouch in the middle of the sidewalk because if I don't, I'm going to hyperventilate and pass out.

The security guard circles again and pulls over.

"Young lady," he says, jogging over. "You okay?"

I nod because I hate that question. Admitting I'm not okay makes me feel sicker than not actually feeling okay. My mother goes to work if she hasn't slept, eaten, or recovered from the plague.

I will get up. Eventually.

The guard radios for the nurse. I'm escorted to a gurney in the nurse's office and hydrated with Gatorade.

"You feeling better, honey?" Nurse Xu asks. "You look green."

"Yup. Just. Must have a bug or something. Just need . . . some ibuprofen—" Like a robot, I reach in the backpack I'm still wearing, pull out a giant bottle, and watch my shaking hands drop the entire thing on the floor. The red circles spray like blood. I stare, trying to will them back to being pills.

My eye twitches. A nerve like a loose wire vibrates under my skin. Like curtains, I close my eyes to darken my mind and just breathe.

I feel a pressure on the gurney. The nurse is beside me.

With my eyes still closed: "I hate medical offices of every kind." I got the flu really bad about eight months after Blanca left me. My moms had to carry me kicking and screaming to the doctor.

I don't want my history interpreted. Don't want to be asked if I'm suicidal. Don't want some doctor judging me because I have a bullet wound like I was the one who shot the gun.

But the nurse just sits there. "I understand. Maybe you could just use a minute."

I turn toward the voice of Nurse Xu and I blink in surprise because I realize I have never seen a chinita(?) lady up this close. I mean there are plenty of chinitos in the barrio, but the only other one I've ever met was that shop owner chasing me and Blanca out of the Hello Kitty store.

Me and Blanca were always jerks to that lady in the Hello Kitty store and, really, all Asians. We used to pretend to work in a nail salon with heavy Korean/Chinese/Asian? accents.

If you only meet one person, and say that person is a Korean, and say that person is an asshat, than that's why you think all Koreans may be asshats. Pero like it is statistically ridiculous to think one asshat means everybody else who looks like them is an asshat. Your sample is flawed. You need like thousands of people to realize what was obvious to begin with. You are being the asshat. Or more to the point: I. AM. AN ASSHAT. I decide we need more math. Statistics will save us all from being racist asshats.

"I have to go." I slide off the table. I am covered in sweat. For the first time, I thank God for PE because I know I'm not the only one who's gonna smell ratchet.

"You think maybe we should call someone?"

Hell to the NO. If I was going to interrupt my mother at work something better be broken or vomit better be involved.

"You know what," Nurse Xu says. "Maybe you could talk to someone here?" She pats my hands again. Her skin is soft and cool. "We've got a new counselor now! Ms. Quinones . . ."

"Nooooooooooooo." That's all I need right now. Mami thinking I'm losing it. *When I was a kid we didn't have no mental health. Work hard. Go to college. Then you can have all the mental health you want.*

I chug the rest of the Gatorade bottle and head out past the office. Past the reason the security guard was circling the building.

The office gossip explains the security guard.

Annie and Brooke—White Girls 1 and 4—threw down. A beef over the rally for Nelly. Annie went to the rally.

I make a mad dash for my locker. I don't want another subplot now. An obstacle to my happiness. I am not asking for fairytale happiness either. I just want to sit in the cafeteria and have lunch with—a friend? a crush?—and not on a toilet.

Is happiness just bait to lure you through life? Can happiness have longevity? Or is it like bubble gum? You chew on it, suck all the sweetness out. Someone bursts your bubble, or you blow too big a bubble and end up with it stuck all over your face.

In homeroom, Nelly's chair has been removed. Everyone is bunched in groups and the gossip is flying. Ms. Moore is not jotting her agenda on the board, but instead leaning on the lip of the board, watching and waiting like a lifeguard after a shark sighting. Danny is, of course, not here and I'm feeling like the fish with the hook stuck through its lip. Blanca's desk is way in the back by the closet.

I make it a point to give everybody a searing mal de ojo as I drag the desk back to its spot, making a horrendous screech the whole way. Everybody looks away except Frida. Pink-haired girl taps on Frida's shoulder and they both get involved in a private convo. I know from their side-glances, it somehow involves me.

Once I sit down next to Blanca's desk, I expect the familiar vibration and hum of comfort, as if she's the driver, I am the passenger, and we're sitting in the fine leather of a two-seater—and anybody else can just take the bus. I remember Fernando and Bambi talking about getting their driver's licenses so they could pick us up at our front doors. Where has that memory been buried till now?

"Imagine me pulling up to Blanca's house in a Porsche! I'd honk the horn, and she'd come running."

"My dude, that's terrible. You don't make a girl come running. You got to be suave."

"Okay, Mr. Suave, lay it out."

"Aight. I'd put on like her favorite song, let the car idle. Knock on the door and walk her to her ride so she hears the lyrics as she comes down the steps."

"Okay, that's suave, breh."

Blanca and me overheard those dorks talking in stage crew. Blanca made me casually mention her favorite song so he'd be playing the right one in the fantasy, even though ain't none of us had cars in reality.

The memory threatens to run me over, but it's like the thought of Danny jumps out and pushes me out the way. Danny makes me step outside myself. Or outside my suffering? Do I have a self without suffering? The truth is, the memory and me are both me.

I feel eyes on my neck. I don't know if I'm hearing the words "crazy" and "freak" because someone is whispering it or my own consciousness is accusing itself. I know how people see me. I know I should be humiliated at how I act. How I lose control. I should be embarrassed. I once took a selfie of myself pulling out my hair so I could shame myself into stopping. But shame isn't a cure for anything.

The bell rings. The bells. My body stands up like I'm operating heavy machinery on Benadryl. Danny being absent has plummeted me to the pit of hopelessness even though I know how stupid that is to think a person I just met is responsible for my happiness. Especially a dude(?).

The thing is, what would life be like if, IDK, I just shaved my head? Maybe I'd cut phantom hairs. What would life be like if I sat in one chair?

I know the answer. No matter how much I blink and reset the channel, there Blanca will sit sipping her never-ending slushy, sprinkling cherry juice on herself like always.

You could do an exorcism for a bad spirit. But a good one that's not ready to leave or you're not ready to let go, can't be banished. If I banished her, I'd banish me. Blanca is my phantom heart.

Period 4: The Genius Hour! Once a week in biology we get to work on a project of our choosing that integrates science with another subject like philosophy (Moms: "You know why all them philosophers in those pictures is wearing sheets? Because they can't afford no clothes, mija!") and poetry ("Well, it's a good thing you know how to play the violin. Pero you can have a big case for people to toss quarters when you're living in the street.")

I am obsessed with the concept of change . . . #irony. In physics, the law of the conservation of energy states that the total energy of any closed system remains constant—"conserved," or unchanged over time. My love for Blanca was a constant. Science calls it a closed system, I call it paradise. But with middle school, the system was opened, with Fernando Zarrin, Bambi Lopez, and a night out that made it night forever.

Ms. Mercado is sitting on her desk. "Energy cannot be

created or destroyed. It transforms from one state to another."

Knowing that there is a science to love consoles me. What greater energy is there than love? Especially the love between friends? "But what about hate?"

Ms. Mercado: "What is hate?"

"I've seen hate." Hate, I learned afterward, was six-five, 180 pounds, blond hair, blue-eyed. "I've heard hate."

The sound of gunfire is coming from the movie playing in the adjacent theater. Right?

The screams sound so real.

"Can hate be transformed into love?" asks Ms. M.

"People always talk about hate being an inverse of love. You know, light is love and dark is hate. But that's colonial bullshit. Hate stands in its own category. Its own genus. Hate is not an inverse of love. It's an absence."

When did the shooter stop being a human being? When did his heart harden into stone, disintegrate into sand? What pressure, what heat made that sand turn into glass, sharp, cold, deadly?

"Can love overcome hate?"

"I don't know. Once, I liked to think I couldn't hate anybody. Once..."

Fuck prison where he would get street cred. Where he would be housed, fed, get dental and medical care, earn the high school diploma Blanca would never get.

"Ms. Mercado?" A kid working on the biology of tears walks over.

"I'm good, Ms. M." I give her permission to go, so I can have permission to STOP. Back up. DELETE.

Lunch—as usual in my office. I have every hair under control. Until I detect what might be a split end at the tip of a braid. Which means I have to pull the whole braid apart. And if I don't hold the split end tightly enough, I might lose it and have to spend hours digging for it. Which makes my eyes all crossed and my back hurt and my mother think I'm possessed by El Diablo. Thus, I rebraid. Only to start all over again. It's my third round when somebody bangs on the stall. An apple hovers just below the door and disappears.

Danny takes a bite and holds it out to me again. "I don't pretend to get what you do in there. But I'm here to nourish you."

I hesitate. I look like Medusa. And FYI, Medusa wasn't cursed with snakes. She was just a girl having a really freakin bad hair day. But I don't want Danny to go. I stick my hand underneath the door. Grab the apple, chomp it, and hand it back.

"Okay." Crunch. Danny takes a bite and passes it back underneath the door.

I can't help but reboot and laugh.

"Tomorrow I hope to add the Holy Grail—a buttered roll."

We take turns eating the apple. I know Danny knows when I bite where he last bit. When we get to the core I have no choice but to step out of the stall. I can't fix my hair because my hands are sticky.

"Wow!"

I lower my eyes so I don't see myself in the mirror. "Don't be a hater."

"You look like a lion. Roar!"

I snort-laugh. "I think all teenagers are shapeshifters. This is but one of mine."

Danny looks straight into my eyes. "I like all your shapes."

Me turning into girl gush: "I like yours too."

From outside the bathroom: "That motherfucker better

not be in here."

That motherfucker bolts into the third stall.

The door to the restroom flies open and @Rican_Havok scans the stalls. "Go ahead, Nita."

Apparently Nita, @Rican_Havok's sister, has to pee and needed an escort. Nita with the blond 'stache. She thinks bleaching it makes it invisible. I personally want a day of rebellion where girls can brandish their God-given 'staches. God didn't give me one though.

"Dude," I say to @Rican_Havok, "you step one foot in here and I will pull off a toilet seat and beat you with it." Or the lid of the trash can. I also know I can escape through a dirty window on the back wall. And use the rusty nails as a weapon.

Nita scopes under the doors checking for feet. "Don't you have somewhere to be?"

"You know I heard if you hold your pee too long," I throw a glance at her lady parts, "you could get a major infection down there."

She rolls her eyes and locks the door in stall one. I go into stall three and pretend to have to pee. Danny is sitting on the tank. Nita pees, flushes, and then it gets dead quiet. I know better than to move yet. The tattle-tale creak of Nita actually leaving the stall breaks the silence. After a minute I guess she gives up. The faucet turns on. Another second of silence.

I get hit. With? "Uh! What the hell?"

Nita laughs and runs out the door. She threw a whole soaking wet toilet paper roll over the stall door.

"Oh, please tell me this isn't wet with her pee!"

Danny and I bum-rush the sink and bathe in it. We dry each other off with paper towels. Danny manages to finger-comb a strand of my hair.

I swear Danny's hand is an outlet turning my whole self ON. We're a closed circuit, and I don't want anything to interrupt our flow.

"I guess we should . . ."

"Yup," I say, pulling back a step because as much as my body is purring, this ain't going down in the bathroom. "We should . . ."

"So yeah," Danny says, backing out the door, "math. Off to be remediated."

"I can help you with that." I shuffle my feet. "Math. Tutoring. Not that you asked."

"No thanks." Danny grins, nodding yes.

•••••••

My moms won't be home for dinner. Wouldn't you know it, Danny will. We take the bus together, Danny carrying his skateboard under his arm.

A paper grocery bag sits on the kitchen counter. Danny uses the restroom while I unpack the Goya cans of red kidney beans, green olives, the chicken bouillon cubes, the box of Sazon packets into the already overflowing cabinets.

"When the fit hits the shan, we'll be ready," my moms will say whenever yet another can of tomato sauce erupts from the cabinet onto my big toe. Tía Sujei says Mami shops for Armageddon because she spent her childhood with an empty refrigerator. She'll never go without Goya again!

I'm in the mood to cook the sofrito myself. Oh, the liquid-gold olive oil drizzling into the pan, the sizzle of onions out-gleaming any diamond, crisp green peppers that poetry-snap if you break 'em in half, fresh garlic from our porch garden!

Danny returns and munches on the banana chips I set out on the table.

"So is that your room?" Danny inhales the crumbs and licks sweetness off his thumb with a flick of a perfect tongue.

This is where I'm supposed to escort his ass to the living room. Not follow him into my room and close my laptop to shut down screensaver Jesus. #Don'tJudgeMe. I trip over Danny's Vans because he slipped them off without missing a beat.

"Wow. Your room. Is backstage. I'm backstage." Danny shakes his hoodie off.

Danny is backstage on so many levels.

His silky blond hair hangs down to a jutting chin on one side; it's shaved on the other. I need to braid those hairs! He grabs a fedora off an antique hat stand and smiles at the flaking gothic mirror that still reads *Who's the Fairest of Them All?*

Danny makes a beeline to my bed and knee-crawls across my covers. My covers. The place where I was just imagining him lying beside me last night. They reach to the baroque shelf above it. "Is this the instrument?" His long slim fingers, fingernails bitten to the nub, run over the length of the case.

"Yes," I say, leaning over him and gently locking the clasp.

Danny faces me and we're almost nose to nose. "Oh! It's like that. I understand."

"No offense." My violin, I decide, is the ONLY thing he can't touch.

"None taken. To be that good at something—that's sacred. I respect that."

Danny props up my pillow and leans back, eyes whirling around my room. It's like he's in the museum of me. I sit down cross-legged on the opposite side of the bed and watch his eyes trace the billows of scarves on my ceiling, mushroom lamps lit with LED lighting in the corners of my floors. The path of Danny's gaze reminds me of everything I ever loved enough to pin to my walls: a psychedelic poster of an *Alice in Wonderland* production we did with hula hoops and rollerblades, my favorite quote by T.S Eliot—*Do I Dare Disturb the Universe?*—on a mobile of coffee spoons, ruby slippers Blanca handmade dangling from a doorknob that we used for *The Lion, The Witch, and the Wardrobe*, black and white cast photographs.

All things bright and beautiful that have managed to become just background to me. Invisible before, now back in full Technicolor.

"Is that her?" Danny zeroes in on a pic pinned to a cork board behind my computer. Three of us are in black T-shirts and jeans, smiling because we don't know our fate.

I nod. "That is her. Blanca. And Fernando. He painted sets." I'm smiling at Blanca; he's smiling at her. He was always asking to paint her. Just like in one of her romance books.

Danny's brow furrows. He gropes under my pillow. He holds up a cover from which spills rubber-banded chapters. "Shit. Sorry!"

"No worries. Blanca did that."

She gave me that book for Christmas. I opened the gold wrapping paper to find a book cover and one chapter inside.

"Um. Thank you. And huh?"

"This is my gift to you. So you don't read ahead. So you read page by page. Chapter by chapter. No cheating. No rushing to the end."

"Thank you, Master Blanca." I stood and bowed—which was pretty racist now that I think back on it. But funny. But racist. #Mindfuck. "For that valuable lesson."

Danny carefully slides the book back under the pillowcase. He sits beside me and a whole bunch of good scents swirl together, like when I took Mami's magazine as a kid and wore every one of the samples inside at the same time.

"You just smelled me." Danny laughs.

I giggle and nod. "No." I look in Danny's eyes and see myself reflected in them. The only mirror I've enjoyed looking into in a long time. How am I going to tutor without a freakin brain?

Danny crawls over and sets his chin on my shoulder. The tickle of breath warms my neck and I'm tingling from my head to my toes. My body is a slave and my heart is a beggar.

"You smell good, too," Danny whispers. "Like cloves."

His lips move against my skin and I feel every part of my body, separate and whole, light and heavy, my thighs soft and my nipples hard, between my legs warm and wet.

He lifts me onto his lap and I wrap my legs around him.

Danny brushes my hair from my shoulders and I know I won't cut a single hair he touched. "Like cardamom."

Those lips, kiss by kiss, slide across my chin up to my lips. "And honey."

We're leaning into each other hard now, our mouths both open like we were drowning and just coming up for our first breath of air. We kiss harder and deeper like we're starved, so long marooned on the islands of ourselves. Our bodies and tongues intertwine and there's no way to know where his ends and mine begins. The more we take in each other, the more starved I get. We are pressed—breasts to breasts—heart to heart. There is no left or right. Black or white. He lays me back and starts to unbutton my jeans, but I grab his hand.

"Sorry," he says in my iron grip. "I should've asked. We can slow down."

"It's not that. It's just—" I rebutton my jeans. "I've got this—scar."

"Okay." He takes a deep breath. Sits cross-legged on the bed. "Can you tell me about it?"

Can I? "I've been wearing jeans year-round. That heat wave this past summer? I sweated out half my body weight."

Danny nods and says, "You know, I've got friends who've had surgery. I might one day. I can't speak for anyone else's scars, but I can't wait for mine."

I shake my head, choke out, "The scar is a bullet wound. It's the ugliest part of me."

His eyes widen. He clasps my hand in his. "Maybe it's a tattoo. Of survival."

"I hate it. Whenever it's visible I feel like it's forcing me to put my heart on my sleeve."

Quietly Danny says, "Every day I walk out into the world, my heart is on my sleeve. A target."

Shit. By that measure, no matter what burdens I'm carrying, he's always going to be carrying something heavier. I feel all guilty and irritated at the same time, and then guilty for being irritated.

We both lie on our sides and face each other.

"I really know how to sabotage a moment, don't I?" I say.

"I don't see it that way. I mean, I grew up with two parents, but it was my mom who raised me till—the split. I'll never forget what I heard through the wall. Her not wanting to. Him wanting what he wanted . . ."

"I'm sorry."

"Well, on the upside it taught me how *not* to be with a woman. We can leave the jeans on, you know." He kisses me.

Presses against me and slips his hand inside my panties . . .

It feels good, but I'm overthinking everything: my body and his. Is it my turn next? What do I do? But he squelches all that. Holds my wandering hand and kisses it.

The outside door unlocks and there's the unmistakable sound of my mother's keys.

We pull apart and the chair in front of my desk is still spinning across the room with me in it as my moms walks into the room. *Weeeeee!*

"Ay!" My moms holds her heart. "You scared the shit out of me."

"Sorry about that." Danny stands up.

"Ay!" She takes a breath. "Christ."

I stand up. Lesson 1: How to lie to your mother who can smell a lie like a fart in a car. "Mom, this is—my friend—"

"Danny," he says, reaching out a hand.

"Danny." She steps forward. Shakes his hand for a very long time and studies it like a palm reader. Looks into his eyes like an ophthalmologist with a penlight.

"Ma!" I swear she's about to frisk him.

She finally releases him and pats him on the shoulder.

I stand beside Danny. "I am tutoring Danny," I remember triumphantly. "In math."

"Math." She purses her lips and folds her arms. "Okay. You know what? I came home because I forgot my badge. But I'm feeling a little run down. I'll help you two set up in the living room where you could get some work done. I got a card table you could use. Danny, you help me carry it."

My mother calling in sick? My mother has gone in to work in a blizzard with the flu. The only time she's ever taken off is for a funeral and once she tried to Skype in (in her defense it was her third cousin).

After she retreats to her room, I tutor Danny for so long, it's possible he can now do advanced calculus. Every plus sign adds to our hope. Every minus sign subtracts consequences we don't want to face. But the knob of Mami's bedroom door twists and the time comes.

"Danny. It's late." She looks at him the way she looks at stray dogs. She'll throw them a bone. Make a donation. But ain't no dog going home with us. "You got anyone you want to call? Or I'll give you a ride home."

"No. No, thank you. I've got wheels." Danny motions to his skateboard by the door. Pins like *Vagenda of Manicide* and *Pussy Strikes Back* and *Girl Mans Up* clink as he organizes our notes and packs notebook and pencils into an otherwise empty backpack.

I am compelled to think about vajayjays. I mean, my moms calls her period her "friend." Like "my friend is visiting" when she's got her monthly. But the vagina? Like Voldemort, Mami and I don't speak Her name.

I can feel my mother flashing me the mal de ojo. I pretend I'm picking lint off my pants and not inner monologuing with my genitalia.

My moms clears her throat. She stands up to her full height and motions to the door. Her robe is no longer from Target. It is now the garb of a priestess mid-spell. "I'll walk you out." Translation: Flaca, don't let the door slam you in your skinny little culo.

My moms returns to her kitchen to finish the meal I completely forgot about. She grabs a knife as if to begin a ritual sacrifice to sanctify her spell. With each chop of her onion, she carves her will into the cutting board.

I dash out in front of Danny, shield him against her incantations. Outside, we stop and stand facing each other on the stoop.

"Danny, I'm so sorry."

Danny cracks up. "I've never done so much math in my entire life. My brain!"

I massage his temples. Danny grabs my wrist and kisses it. "Nice tats."

"Uh?"

"Tats, you perv. Your hands."

My hands. The ink on my thumb reads, *I Dare Me.*

Danny whispers, "I dare you."

I lean in and kiss Danny. I am thirsty. And among Danny's lips and tongue I find a saltwater swimming pool and I could hold my breath for hours. In my nose blooms the bouquet of Polo, Versace, whatever Danny musta jacked from his daddy. The smell of Mami's onions creeps through the door cracks, poisoning an otherwise perfect kiss. I pull away. Unlink my arms from his waist.

"I have to go. Face the music."

"I'm sorry you're facing it solo." He cradles my chin and leans in for another kiss. "Here are my digits." Danny writes his number on my wrist. "Later."

I close the door behind me, picturing Danny looking toward the window, his eyes lingering for a glimpse of my shadow.

Back in the kitchen with my mother's onions, I get stage fright. Chop, chop, chop. Mami's ambidextrous so she could cut 'em with her left and cut me with her right. An onion rolls across the counter like a head from a guillotine. Forget facing the music.

"I'mma go to bed." I stretch and yawn. And make a mad

dash for my room.

"Sit your ass down."

I sit.

Chop chop chop. "I can't even." The pan hisses as my mother uses the knife to slide the peppers and onions off the cutting board. My eyes water from the onions. Hers never do.

I take a deep breath. Turn the chair toward the stove. Sit with my arms wrapped around the chair's back. "Mami."

"What do I do?" she says to herself. She stirs the vegetables in the pan so hard some peppers fly out onto the floor. "Call Sujei? Call Padre Gomez?"

"Call a priest?"

My mother whips around with a wooden spoon in hand. My arm gets burned by tiny drops of oil. Behind her the pan steams and sizzles. "She is never to be in this house again!"

I stand up. "He."

"He? *He* is on the wrong path. And you're not gonna follow *him* down it too."

"Being who Danny is is not a path!"

"I don't care what you call it. Shaved head. A blanquito wearing earrings like un negrito? What is with that cultural appropriation shit?"

"How could you be so woke and so 'sleep at the same time? How can you not appreciate his struggle?"

"That so-called struggle is self-inflicted. That kid has decided that school, God, family are less important than playing dress-up. This face," she gestures to her cheek, the unmistakable Taino cheekbones, the unquestionable African roots of her hair, "is who we are. We can't take this off."

"What Danny looks like—who Danny is—ain't a costume!" I feel like I'm lecturing my mother as much as myself.

"Open your mind—"

"This isn't about Danny." She reaches behind her and turns off the stove. "This is about you and your future. No one else. I know who you can become. And it's not gonna be some dyke. It was bad enough with boy-crazy Blanca putting all kinds of ideas into your head about romance. But this?"

"First of all, Blanca did not put things in my head. My head isn't just a hole." No. Blanca expanded my mind. Mapped the unchartered terrain in my hemispheres. We were two girls on the moon. Fuck gravity. "Second, 'being some dyke' is not an idea." (I don't think.)

Mami grabs my hands, looks at the ink, leads me back to the kitchen table. Sits me down. "I'm sorry. Sorry for Blanca. Sorry for your father. I can't fix those things, but I can fix this. Mija," she says, dropping my hands and squatting in front of me. "You got enough shit on your plate. It's gonna be one year in a few days. You don't need any more complications."

"I need to be happy. Happiness is the best complication there is."

"That." She points to my room. "Whatever that was all about is not going to make you happy." My mother rises, goes back to the sink. She rinses a colander of beans in the sink. Whatever hope I have of changing her mind goes down the drain. She pours the rinsed beans into the pan. Turns her head and throws enough shade to goose-pimple my arms. "Never again, Verdad. Not in my house."

Her house. I head to my room. Which is really my mother's room. My heart feels homeless.

11

I think I actually slept last night. It felt good to submerge. I don't remember dreaming. It's like my thoughts are too hard for my subconscious mind to decode, my reality a symbol of a symbol making everything mean everything and everything mean nothing.

Morning comes and I waste way too much time staring into a clouded mirror. I rush to throw on deodorant and dress when I start hearing a beeping coming from the front of the house. Somebody's alarm's probably going off. Shit. I'm going to miss the bus. The beeping comes again, and out of curiosity and annoyance I look through the peephole of the front door.

My tía Sujei is standing on the stoop about to impale the doorbell with her long pointy claws. Shit. My moms called a family intervention.

A badge showing her position as a professor at the community college flutters on what can only be called a bosom. A red scarf she picked up in Spain trails from her neck like a flame.

I grab my backpack and open the door. We kiss, we hug, we say what the fuck. I roll my eyes and follow her to the sidewalk. Slide into the passenger seat of her car.

"This is overkill, no?" I shift my seat back to make room

for my sprawling legs and buckle up. Her seat is almost up to the steering wheel, her legs are so short.

"Escúchame!" She pulls the car off the curb and onto the street. *Bonk*. "I personally do not share the same position as my sister. You can be a lesbian. I don't give a shit. But date a girl in remedial everything? A girl who has no one wondering where they are at night?"

Shit. Titi Sujei is a spy.

"Danny is a guy."

"Danny has a vagina."

I blush three shades of red. "So what?"

Sujei adjusts her heavy black glasses so her eyes can bore into my soul. I assume her third eye is the one paying attention to the road. "Don't you want a family? Children?"

"Jesus. For real? Not right now! And hold up. I'm so confused. All my life my mother tells me 'Don't get pregnant.' Now suddenly it's 'Don't I want to have a family'?"

"Your mom wants the best for you. Your mom—" She interrupts herself and sings to Old time Jose Feliciano crooning his eternal love out her stereo. "Your mom worked two jobs to get you from Section 8 housing into the projects. From the projects into your little house. All so you could be safe. So you could have a chance. Despite her sacrifice, giving up pursuing her own career, her own dreams, September 15 happened. She almost lost you. Not just to bullets."

Sujei grabs my hand and holds it. It has been pulling out my hair. A clump of it falls onto the seat.

"And here we are a year almost to the day." She kisses my hand and releases it. Flips the finger to someone who honks at her. "Life throws enough punches. You don't need to punch your own self in the face. You've been through so much already.

It's hard to be a Boricua. A woman. Smart. And you want to add lesbian—or whatever—to that?"

That's nineteenth century cross-dressing lesbian Boricua to you, I want to say. Yes, my fedora is in my backpack. And maybe a cravat.

"You know, I hate to point this out to you, but what if you're *not* a lesbian? You're only fifteen. What do you know? But once you cross that line everybody is gonna think they know you. Before you even know yourself."

She does have a point. I'm *not* sure I'm ready to call myself a—dyke. Dyke is the closest word I can come up with to explain me to me. What does that word even mean? I google the origin of *dyke*.

Dyke: Unknown origin. Dike. Earthwork, trench.

Dyke is a dumb word. How is that even an insult? Why not just call someone an end table? *You fucking end table! Don't be an end table.*

"I mean what's with the cross-dressing?" says Sujei. "I get gay, but a gay girl can still look like a girl. A gay guy can look like a guy. Unless you're in a rock band, what's with the makeup? Why so fucking complicated?"

I don't have an answer. Is Danny experimenting with gender? Am I? He the control, me the variable, and vice-versa. Could he decide tomorrow that he's a she and she is—a lesbian? Which would make me a lesbian. Right now he's a guy, so he is like—heterosexual? In which case, even if he has a vagina, that still makes me heterosexual?

Though the truth is my heart fell for Danny, and for whatever body he's in, before my brain or anyone else's had a chance to mess with it. I start picturing Danny in different outfits—dresses, pants, a frock coat—and he's a snack in every single one. If he turned out to just be a girl who dresses (insert covert googling) "androgynous," or some other gender identity—the internet offers up *gender variant*, *gender fluid*, *nonbinary*, *bigender*, *pangender*—I'd still be into Danny. This convo with Titi Sujei is not about who Danny is, it's about who I am.

Sujei turns the volume on Jose way up. *Corazón corazón corazoooooooooooooon! How do you uncomplicate your corazoooooooon?* "What I'm saying is KISS."

"Huh?"

"Keep it simple, stupit. KISS. You know. K-I-S . . ."

"I get it."

We pull up across the street from the school. Sujei puts the car in park and lets the motor run.

"Bottom line is your mom loves you." Sujei puts the car in gear. "I'll light a candle."

I grab my things and climb out. Walk over to the driver's side and kiss my titi good-bye. She blinks and hands me a Tic Tac. I back up and cover my mouth. "I couldn't find the toothpaste this morning."

"Here," Sujei says, popping one into her mouth, "take the box."

Jose breaks into another ballad that I can still hear as she rolls up the window and bonks off the curb into the street.

I chug a few more Tic Tacs as I cross the street and step onto school property. Two black girls walk by and whisper "cunt" under their breath. Nelly's friends.

I throw my backpack down. I'm feeling righteous about cunts right now.

The girls turn around and stare me down. The one with the BLM tee says, "Oh. So you gonna fight us?"

"Traitor," the other one spits like a racist-seeking missile.

"I. am. not. a traitor! I didn't do nothing!"

"Exactly." They both walk off in the direction of righteousness while I pick up my backpack and my dignity. I feel the words I hurled at my mother last night boomerang back in my face: "How could you be so woke and 'sleep at the same time?"

What a spectacular way to start the day!

••••••••

You'd think that the obvious solution to this mess is to avoid Danny all day until he corners me just outside the bathroom. Then have an awkward convo about how we can just be friends. We'd go our separate ways, Danny to the world of remedial everything, me to the world of the normative-college bound track.

The problem is the freakin cave. Once you step out of the darkness and see the light, how do you step back in? How do I sit in class and focus on the words in front of me when words like *bisexual*, *pansexual*, *gender fluid*, *nonbinary*, *pangender*, *genderqueer* are filling up the new dictionary of who I might be? How can I focus on one voice when there are fifty in my head? My mom, Tía Sujei, Nelly's friends, Danny.

The one voice that I'm missing—Blanca's.

I head to the exit, texting Danny with the number he tattooed to my wrist.

His response: *Meet up at 11?* with an address—the bowling alley in my old neighborhood.

So the plan: Mami's cell doesn't work well at the hospital(s) so she generally ignores it until she gets home. While she showers, I can jack it, delete the message from the school alerting her to my absence, and forge a sick note.

Am I really cutting school? No, I tell myself. Today, I'm going to the School of Life. Subject: Identity.

I wait to catch a bus to the cemetery, thinking about what I would do if Kanye/asshat and I crossed paths again. I'd end up getting into a brawl, and me and my fedora and cravat would be driven back home in a squad car. The bus comes and I climb on, keeping my head down until I find a seat. I unzip my backpack and unleash my fedora. Attempt to stuff The Entity inside. I get looks.

"Ven aquí, mija," a viejita in a diva white pantsuit says. She beckons to me and I cross the aisle and sit next to her. "Pero, like this." She takes off the hat, shapes it with her slim, smooth hands. Cocks it to one side. "There. Maybe you get some cornrows. There's a place on . . ."

I hop off the bus at my stop. The sun shines underneath clouds like a Kool-Aid spill that someone left the paper towels spread over. The trees are like lightning planted in the ground. The stones welcome me, sinking under my feet, as I walk up the path to the headstones. Flown by invisible pilots, newspapers and flyers whizz around me.

Today I have no flowers. I have no offering. I realize I am, for the first time, empty-handed. I make my way past a grave laden with potted yellow mums, buttery candle wax bubbled down the sides of the tombstone. Blanca's grave is clean, well-kept, but empty. The smoke of burning brush wafts past me as I sit and hug my knees.

A squirrel scrambles across the neatly trimmed grass. I wish I were the squirrel. The squirrel can't be anything but a squirrel. It can't be a giraffe. It doesn't want to be a damn giraffe.

I laugh. "I need to be a squirrel!" I write on my left arm, *I'm just a squirrel in the world.* I draw a squirrel looking like it's ready to jump from one finger to the next. Okay. I cap my pen and stick it in my hair. Time to get down to business.

"You're probably wondering what I'm doing here in the middle of the day." I lean back on my elbows. "I don't even know. I just have questions. I need to know who I am. You're the best one to tell me."

Tktktk Tktktk, the squirrel chitters.

"Hello?"

The wind has shifted the clouds. Freed, the sun floods the stage of sky.

I sit up on my knees and visor my hands on my forehead. Way back in the distance the caretaker drives a golf cart filled with rakes and chugs across the field. I wonder how many times he's seen me and said nothing. How many people he sees in a day, how many words to the dead he's heard spoken. How many answers.

A couple rubs a cloth over an aging stone. A bearded man in a soft, kittenish gray and black suit carries a teddy bear through a maze of withered tulips.

"Blanca." I knock. Blanca's always home. "Blanca!" I stand up. "Blanca, where you at?"

Everywhere is where Blanca usually is. She's been everywhere I've ever been. Seen everything I've seen, tasted everything I've tasted. Cried every tear with me, laughed every laugh. There was never an echo; we were always a harmony, in sync. Until the end.

I wonder what high school would've really been like if— Would we have joined all the same clubs again? Had all the same classes? I turn in all directions, a broken compass. Where the fuck is my north star? "Blanca!" A berry bush of annoyed birds answers back. Another bush of pissed off birds answers them.

"Shut up, nature!"

Nature. All around me nature is in-betweening, transitioning out of fall into winter. Would Blanca be cool with me no matter how I changed? I have a science flashback: *Change is the only thing that stays the same*. But what is change? The trees are still trees no matter what the fuck goes on with their leaves. That caterpillar butterfly shit? No matter what, it's a bug.

"Blan—fucking—ca!!!!" Fuck. I'm screaming into the wind and expecting it to answer back. I grab air and except something to hold onto.

A car pulls up the gravel road. The golf cart is no longer in the distance. Somewhere that squirrel and its squirrel homies, twitter.

"Where are you?" I'm walking backwards toward the road. My best friend is missing. I am missing.

It's so bright now, all I can do is squint. Through the light I can see dust, shadow, then the familiar bobbing bun, strands of hair streaking behind her like comets, her chanclas thwacking down the gravel road, scattering stones. The birds sing for her as she heads toward the outside world, the street.

Blanca runs toward my bus stop; is she going back to school? No. She veers north and leads me uphill. My muscles feel tuned as I run up one block, then two, chasing a shadow.

Sticky caramelized clouds of grilled mango escape with the open and close of La Cocina Boricuas' doors; somewhere in the back garlicky arepas fry in oil, bitter coffee boils. It's a competition outside a hair salon where morning cigarettes, hibiscus shampoos, and chemical dyes battle for dominance, where Rihanna competes for attention over the voice of gossiping stylists. I pick up the pace like I ate an arepa, like Rihanna was singing for me. I ain't even out of breath. I'm still chasing Blanca; chasing myself.

Up ahead, the bus arrives and Blanca gets on. Shit. I sprint to the bus and climb in just before my culo gets slammed in the doors. Flash my bus pass and can barely elbow inside it's so jam-packed.

Damn. What bus am I even on? To where? How am I going to tell when Blanca gets off? And crap, what time is it, because Danny . . .

Only ten. Good. We're driving outside of familiar territory to some residential areas my moms threatens to move us to when she clones herself to make more money. Don't none of these freakin people own a coffee maker? It's house, Starbucks, house, house, Starbucks.

The coffee shops end and the block is taken over by another century. Giant spiky medieval buildings cluster together and windows are made of stained glass. Behind high iron gates, dozens of white girls in navy-blue polyester skirts and blazers stomp their black rubber-heeled shoes onto a courtyard. My mother has threatened to send me to Catholic School whenever she gets to talking to her ladies about the heathen kids of today and their cafeteria Catholicism—you know, I'll take a heaping plate of salvation, a side of answered prayers, but go light on the hellfire. A herd of red-ribboned ponytails follows a chapel bell. All except one girl. The girl without the ponytail. The girl I see look up because she feels me watching her as the bus pulls to its next stop. Nelly? Oh, shit. This must be the school she goes to now.

I'm lost for the next few stops, watching for Blanca to take the back exit, my mind getting off at Guilt Street.

We stop at a deli, and my stomach demands a tripleta—chicken, ham, and beef slathered with ketchup, mustard, mayo, topped with thin, crispy fried potato sticks. I squeeze my stomach in to shut it up and lean back. The windows are a filmstrip of my past.

My past with Blanca. There's the dentist where Blanca got her braces, the dress shop where Blanca and I already had her dress picked out for her quinceañera—she chose white like a bride, and I told her *Blanca, you'll have slushie stains on that in five minutes, white picks up everything* . . . That's my life. A white dress.

We round a semicircle to drop people at a transfer station, and I feel like Blanca has blindfolded me in a game of Pin-the-Tail on the Donkey. At least I'm not the donkey. Right?

The adrenaline of the chase is wearing off. I'm tired. I'm hungry. I'm guilty. I'm confused. I'm panicked. My moms is gonna get volcanic if she finds out I skipped school. Instead of solving my problems, I'm just adding more. I need Blanca to laugh everything off.

•••••••

But the problem is my moms, I text Blanca.

She's in the eighth-grade honors math with me, at our old school, and she's had way too many Skittles so she's giddy. Giddy because of sugar, her sensitivity to food dye, and our plans for tonight. Blanca's all the way across the room because we get in trouble for talking. The teacher jokes that she's gonna have to move Blanca's desk into the closet because for real, the girl can hold a conversation with a rock. Even the autistic kid with headphones who only talks by holding up a whiteboard will talk to her. Shit, if Blanca met Helen Keller, she'd manage to hold a convo.

The problem is you always got a problem, Blanca texts back. *We're just gonna have fun. Don't make graphs and charts out of the fun. Just have it.*

But what if she finds out?

She's going to do what? Ground you? You're not allowed to go anywhere and do anything now.

Blanca speaks the truth. Anything past seven o'clock is past my bedtime. (Anything not related to academics. Part of the reason we joined stage crew was to get permission to be out late.)

Blanca, the boys, and I are going out to whatever ancient movies are playing at the Dollar Theater. Everything's a dollar. The popcorn dunked in artificially flavored butter swimming with trans fat, the igneous Junior Mints malformed from melting and solidifying a few times, Blanca's Skittles which, with the Twinkie and the Ho Ho, could survive the apocalypse. The cherry slushies Blanca and I love because of the brain freezes and cherry lips.

You know, maybe this will work out perfectly. Your moms would have to punish you by ungrounding you.

Anyway, we're covered. Miss K's got our back! Miss K is having a hard time having a personal life and being a drama teacher. She forgot all about a bridal fitting so had to cancel our stage crew practice without alerting our parents ahead of time. She said we could work on the sets for an hour or two then lock up.

Let's do this. We have to do this. This is the chance we've been waiting for. This is the chance YOU'VE been waiting for.

Wait. Verdad, Bambi is fine!

His name is Bambi.

So what? How could you not think he's guapo?

No, I do. He is. There's no question that he's good-looking. Soft, thick, light caramel hair, skin like eternal summer, the biceps, and the booty. The problem is I don't care. I'm not feelin it. If he tried to hold hands with me in the popcorn, he'd be wearing the popcorn. I don't like even the idea of a date. Once you say the word *date*, you give a dude permission to put his moves on you.

Then, this is gonna happen? Blanca presses.

I sigh and type my confirmation. *This is gonna happen.* Whether I like it or not. We've been talking about a double-date like this our whole lives. Now that it's about to be a reality, I realize I'm more interested in the fantasy. The mysterious someone in the dark laughing when you laugh. Passing you the Junior Mints. Tasting Junior Mints in one peppermint kiss. In that fantasy I never know who the mysterious person is, but I know it's not Bambi. But Blanca wants this to happen with Fernando, and that isn't going to happen without me . . .

••••••

I stand up. The bus's back door opens and out pops Blanca. The exiting crowd is rowdy. I get mashed against a pole among shopping bags and some Middle Eastern dude carrying a box that I'm telling my racist ass not to think is a bomb. But if it is, I'll tackle his ass.

By the time the bus clears, I know where I am. I'm almost in front of the Dollar Theater. The theater I have not stepped into in 360 days.

Blanca is literally going to take me hostage down memory lane.

12

My brain is a game of 52 pickup. The theater. She's kidnapped me back in time. But my brain spars hard with the hands of the clock and forces them forward. 'Cause look at the time! Danny. I've got to get to Danny. Away from here.

I'm surrounded by a pregnant lady who must be having triplets, a guitarist and his breh with the trumpet. A college student who must be carrying the complete works of Shakespeare in her backpack. I can't reach the bus cord. I'll have to wait to the next stop. I unzip my hoodie because I'm super-hot all of sudden. Pull out the fabric of my T-shirt to blow air on my chest.

I have too much spit in my mouth. The Middle Eastern dude gives the pregnant lady his seat and I have room to find my own. I crack a window to get some air but all I taste is exhaust. I want to spit, but I can't bring myself to do it. The bus doors finally open but I'm afraid if I move, I'm going to hurl. All the people talking seem to be sucking away all the oxygen. Somewhere on TV I heard you put your head between your legs to get over a panic attack. Shit, is that what I'm having?

Putting my head between my legs, I can clearly see everything that people stick under seats or falls out their pockets:

chewed-on lollipop sticks, cough drop wrappers, a condom, a cockroach that is making its home in a Snickers because it satisfies him.

My hat falls off and thankfully some heat escapes from my head. I grab it and fan myself. I might hurl in it if I don't get off the bus now. Up on my feet, I'm like Michael Jackson in "Thriller" dragging myself to the doors. In the gutter, I throw up the little breakfast I ate. Right next to someone sitting in the gutter.

"Sorry, man."

"Been there," the scroungy dude says, holding up Jack Daniels. "Want some?"

"Um," I say, feeling clearer in my head and lighter in my feet, "I really like to wait until," I check my celly, "eleven o'clock before I hit that. But thanks, man."

"No problem." He holds up the bottle in a toast.

I step onto the curb. The neighborhood hasn't changed. I swear that was the same dude in the gutter the last time I was here. In the year 3000, will we still have alcoholics in gutters? Can't we give them, like, some kind of BYOB bar where they could drink and pass out on a cot, free of charge?

And across the street, there are all the junkies in the park. I mean, really? Can we not just give them a place to shoot up that doesn't involve monkey bars and sandboxes? Would this not be a public service to everyone involved?

I squash my fedora way down low on my head and stick in my headphones. Just as Kendrick's about to drop the beat, loud laughter rounds the corner, followed by footsteps. Loud laughter that gets quiet all of a sudden. I leave the headphones in so I can pretend I don't notice the bunch, maybe three or four guys, so close they're stepping on my shadow. I hear their accents.

I'm catching words like "puchica!" and "cabal" and I mentally identify El Salvador. My neocortex drops the words gang and MS-13 and I remind myself to DIY pepper spray tonight. If I live that long. Hopefully these dudes are just out to rob me.

What am I doing here?

One dude: "Ta' chivo, ¿vá?"

Giggle. Giggle. Another dude: "Chera!"

Un otro: "Yo! The girl in the dope hat!"

I don't turn around and speed the hell up. "Fuck off!"

"No seas puta, damn!"

I jaywalk into traffic to avoid them and almost get sideswiped.

Laughter: "¡Te pelaste!" the El Salvadoran dude calls over the honk of a horn blaring at me, "We'll just keep it!"

I whirl around. Across the street of gypsy cabs and busted cars, are the would-be assailants in Yankees caps tossing something back and forth like they're warming up on a baseball diamond. Takes me a minute before I realize. I dropped my bus pass. OH SNAP.

I cross the street at the light this time. The dudes turn their backs on me and play it off like I'm not there.

"Give me my Metro card."

"Damn," the dude who likes my hats says, "She got no manners. Ghetto!"

"Ghetto? Like y'all hanging out here in the middle of the day?"

They all turn around and face me. Dude with the Puerto Rican flag tattooed on his bicep clears his throat. "We're on break. Been up since we opened at five a.m. this morning." He points to a White Castle. "About to head back. You?" He tosses me my Metro Card.

I don't catch it of course. Got to bend down like a fool to pick it up.

I'm a traitor to black women and a now racist against El Salvadorans and Puerto Ricans. "I'm"—I shove my bus pass into my backpack—"sorry," I mumble, scanning the landscape. I might scale that White Castle. It would make the perfect place for a primal scream.

I give up chasing Blanca and head toward the bowling alley. Right now I need Danny to say the right things, do the right things, and make me rewind to our kiss and delete every single thing that's happened since.

Right on time, Danny shows up on his skateboard with a bunch of kids in toe. We—as in me, myself, and I—are not pleased.

Here's the lineup: There's an Indian girl in a man-sized T-shirt and zebra-stripe pajama bottoms next to a white girl in booty shorts (her booty cheeks have goosebumps) and a crop-top (her belly button looks cold), each of them holding a skateboard. I'd say they're a little older than us, maybe juniors? I'm déjà vu-ing hard watching the Indian girl's ridiculously long black hair swing like a pendulum. There's a Paul Bunyan tall blonde. . . person in a man's flannel and jeans, and a tall skinny chinito/black dude(?) wearing these teeny-tiny reading glasses hanging onto the end of their nose for dear life. Chinito sports an AfroPunk T-shirt and purple shorts—that I know I've seen . . . in the cafeteria. That's right. Chinito is the one I saw stealing bananas!

But what stands out is Danny—and his shiner. "Are you okay?"

Danny looked like if he fell off a cliff and narrowly managed to climb back up. Greasy and uncombed hair lies wilted on one side of his head. His jeans look like a crumpled dollar bill that got forgotten in a pocket. And those hands.

"Just had to save my skateboard from a dastardly thief earlier," Danny says. "Everyone, this is Verdad." He points to the others and rattles off names: Prisha, Sarah, Jane, Baldwin.

"Later," says Chinito aka Baldwin, jumping on his(?) skateboard.

The black-haired Indian girl hugs Danny and says, "Under Graffiti Bridge."

I mathematically analyze the distance between her boobs and Danny's when they hug in relation to the time each hug took multiplied by commensurate eye contact.

The squad disappears from whence their wacky asses came, aka from the life that Danny leads that I know nothing about. Because I am mature, I instantly hate their asses. My ass is cuter.

Awkward silence.

"Graffiti Bridge. Speaking in code, huh?" I finally manage to say. "A secret hideout? From the looks of you, a secret identity?"

"Totally undercover." Danny slides his hands on the rim of my crazy-angled hat. Danny is wearing—nail polish?

"And you?"

"I don't know," I say, noting the cover-up pancaked over Danny's bruised eye. The lipstick? "Maybe I'm not in disguise for the first time." I can't say I like the way that feels. I want to go back to school. Home. Whatever page of my story where life made sense. "Let's get out of the hood."

"Hold up. This may be the hood, but where else could you get your shoes shined while you eat a chorizo and egg with a side of hash?" Danny smiles. His teeth shine unexpectedly white for someone who may possibly have climbed out from a dumpster. "We could explore the old theater. It's kinda fun walking around in there. There's a dope chandelier. Prisha says it's actually worth a ton."

Danny keeps talking, but I don't hear the rest.

"You don't look healthy. You good?"

"Yeah. No. I don't know. I just have to move."

Speed walking, I break into a jog. Danny's by my side cruising on their skateboard. HIS skateboard. She's a he. Right? I'm tryin to ignore the lipstick. Not 'cause Danny doesn't look cute. Because it's confusing as hell. Because that makes Danny a bio girl who's a bona fide boy wearing lipstick, damn it. That's my understanding. Is that Danny's understanding? Can you just decide that shit? Is that what Danny is doing? Can he just *snap!* undecide all of this?

Danny effortlessly cruises over cracks. I never decided how I felt about Danny. It just became a reality. Part of my story. Like one of those chapters Blanca ripped out and handed me one by one, I couldn't cheat and read ahead. I'm breathing in and out now, more like in meditation than a run.

It's a good thing I'm hitting Walk signs because I'm not paying any attention to the traffic rushing past. Just the traffic in my brain. Am I expanding my brain, or going insane? Both.

Danny holds out his phone and videos our path. I side glance at that jut of chin, the glint in his eye like the shard of mineral trapped in sidewalk concrete, the cocky smile. The hands bruised and beautifully cut like church stained glass. Even over a gaping pothole, Danny has perfect balance. We fly past a posse of guys checking me out like my boobs are jogging past without the rest of me attached. Danny does some kind of 360 jump and makes them flinch.

They shout, "Dykes!"

Me: "End tables!"

That's when Danny almost falls. He is dying laughing. "Out of all the things you could have said . . . I love your brain."

I blush. Danny loves my brain!

Should I say I love his brain back?

I should be out of breath by now, but I'm not. I feel like a cheetah that's been unchained. I'm stretching my legs. I'm seeing the possibilities. I'm hungry.

Danny and I should be able to be—whatever we are! With or without each other. Why do we want every damn thing to be the same? I think about the Holy Trinity, the statues of saints back at the cemetery. God is a hundred billion things but humans are expected to be one.

Blanca: Write that down.

I let Danny give me a peck, then pull away. "Sorry!" I gulp down the last of the Tic Tacs. "My toothpaste was missing this morning. Resume."

"Sorry." He looks genuinely sheepish.

"You'd be sorry if not for Tía Sujei's Tic Tacs." We kiss like a run-on sentence and finally after like seventeen semicolons, we take a breath. "Let's go."

"No." He backs up. "Not today."

"Not today? You do realize school is a five-day thing, right?"

Danny licks his lips, tasting mine. I get a mad tingle in my lady parts.

"Maybe I'll catch you after school?"

"Actually, I have coding. Then homework."

"Okay. How 'bout that theater sometime? Or just an old-fashioned movie."

"Movie? Uh." I back up a few more steps. I just realized I haven't watched a single movie in a theater, on a TV, or otherwise in almost a year. "That's something people do. Maybe . . ." I turn my back.

Danny hasn't moved.

I turn back around. "How about we do lunch? Only this time, we exchange lines of dialogue. You are still technically enrolled, right?"

"Lunch? That's something people do." He jumps on his board. "Maybe . . ." But he nods.

We part ways. I ring the bell and get buzzed in. The office is a madhouse. It seems like everyone from homeroom, everyone from the Nelly Incident is here.

I look behind me as I walk to the front desk. Some major evil ojos are lasering my back. "Verdad De La Reyna. Freshman. I'm late."

"No kidding," the secretary says looking at the clock and scribbling me a tardy slip. "Literally five more minutes and I would have marked you absent."

"Well," says the VP from her high horse, "you can mark yourself absent from whatever you have planned after school, young lady." She scribbles on THE PAD. "Report to detention promptly at three. You can join these bozos."

Those bozos. The girls who called me a cunt, plus White Girl 3 from homeroom and history class. For some reason, it surprises me one of them's got ballet shoes tied to her backpack. Then my mind blinks, and I think *Hello, Lauren Anderson. Misty Copeland.* Then I think, *Fuck, I'm so fucked up. How did I get this way?*

The other girl, the one with the BLM shirt, is mentally cataloguing White Girl 3's ensemble of boho shit from her feather earrings and dreamcatcher necklace down to her suede boots.

"The Native Americans sent a smoke signal," she says. "They want that whole outfit back."

"If Native Americans can even wear clothes, I can wear a dreamweaver."

"*What*?" says BLM Girl, getting in White Girl 3's culture-appropriating face.

"Do I need to call security?" The VP threatens BLM Girl as I plot my escape route out the office.

"Sure, that's how we handle problems, don't we? With security."

"That's how we handle violations of school policy, Tanya."

"It wasn't a violation. It was art."

"Art stays on the canvas. Once it leaves the canvas, it's vandalism—"

Tanya, neck-rolling and side-eyeing, "Said no artist ever."

A procession of blue-, purple-, and silver-handed kids from homeroom pour out the principal's office with expressions all along the spectrum from *My ass is grass* to *And I'd do it again, bitch.* The flower in Frida's hair glitters with spray paint specks and her jaw is set. She looks like she just climbed a hill that she thought was a mountain, and now she can see a mountain in the distance—but her ass is going on. Right behind her is Rudy, tripping on jeans so wide he could jump from the Empire State building and land safely.

Rudy: "Hey, Ex-Machina, you missed the party." He turns to Tanya and takes a five.

Tanya points to my detention slip: "She'll be there for the after-party."

I open the office door to see two custodians, white dudes,

one sporting what looks like a Robitussin-red beard and the other with enough hair in his ears to make a beard. One is carrying the desk in question toward the principal's office and I guess the other one inhaling a hot dog is providing emotional support. Both acting like the two gravediggers at Scrooge's funeral.

Custodian 1: "They behave like this and what do they expect?"

Custodian 2: "Get a free education. Free food. But they're never satisfied."

By "they" do they mean kids in general or do they mean us—people of color? Are food and education not bare minimums for all humans?

Gravedigger 1 sets the desk in front of the office. The top of it is spray-painted with the words, *You always got a place here, Nelly.*

Every kid that files out rubs their hand against it. I wonder what would happen if I touched it.

Zap!

13

It's the end of a very long-ass day. I'm back in homeroom, standing in a line to get my detention room assignment. From what I hear, different teachers have different methods of doing detention. The PE teacher has kids do push-ups. The math teacher makes kids do statistics correlating detention and college dropout rates. The science teacher collects cell phones, covers the clock, and then discusses the theory of relativity.

Rudy's taking bets again.

"Do you bet on everything?" I ask.

"You bet your ass your ass ain't safe from Tanya if she got to do push-ups. PS, the Danny Pool is up to four hundred dollars. I added in the category hermaphrodite."

"Hermaphrowhat?" Like I need any more categories. "He's a guy, okay? End of story."

Rudy situates his headphones so he can use them in detention without detection. "Whatever you need to tell yourself, Ex-Machina." I have a feeling he's not just talking about Danny's gender.

"Yo, Rudy. Why am I to blame for all of this? I had nothing to do with the spray-painted desk. I wasn't even here."

"You're never here."

"Technically I've never missed a day."

"Dang, you so literal. I mean, you are not present. You're the only one who hasn't asked once how Nelly is. You're the only one who hasn't gotten in touch. You know, even Annie went to the rally? Even when she knew Brooke was going to go after her ass."

"Look," I say. "This has gotten way bigger than me. I may have started something with Nelly, but I'm not responsible for all this. I just want to be left alone. Damn, I barely knew Nelly."

"Nelly's one of us. Ain't that enough? I mean damn, don't you care what happened to her? Do people normally just disappear from your life?"

"Fuck, Rudy. You have no idea."

Rudy blinks all surprised.

"Yeah, the robot has flesh."

After a beat, Rudy nods. Points behind him again. "By the way, the other desk. They took it too."

"What other desk?"

"The one you're always—using."

My eyes dart to the back of the room. My throat tightens. I can't believe I didn't notice the minute I walked in. I nod and walk out the room to the water fountain. I'm feeling too warm, and if I could take off my shirt I would. I'm trying to reset my brain, downgrade my temp before I pass out.

I douse my whole face in the fountain. I need to get control.

•••••••

Detention is in a classroom and not the gym, thank God. The lady presiding over our next hour-and-a-freakin-half is not anyone I know. Behind the front desk, she faces a laptop and messes with stations on Pandora that blast through the speakers on the ceiling. From the front door, two seniors lug in a pile of what looks like yoga mats. The teacher hasn't decided what she wants and switches from the sound of rain to chimes to Gregorian chants. Everybody around me is trying to guess why Ms. Esquivel has settled on brown noise, which I didn't even know was a thing.

"First, everybody's gonna push the chairs to the wall. Next, starting with the back of the room," and Ms. E points to me when she says this, "everybody is gonna take turns and come up to get a mat."

"Can she do this?" Rudy asks.

Boricua 2 aka Penelope, whose hair is now violet, nods. "She can do this and so much worse."

I trip up the row to grab my mat as every ally of Nelly all of sudden has to stretch and fall on the seniors handing out mats. Trip as one of them sticks their legs out when I make my way back.

By the time everybody has their own mat and is situated on the floor, every kid is joking about nap time in kindergarten and how they used to pretend the mats were really rafts and if they touched the "water" a shark would get them. A bunch of kids launch into a loud-ass rendition of "Baby Shark." Ms. Esquivel "accidentally" blasts the music and lowers it.

"Sorry, not sorry. But since I have your attention. No mantras to recite this week."

"Thank Goddess," mouths Penelope. "Got enough from AA."

Ms. E sits on her own mat in the front of the room. "There is a lot of tension going on in this room. A lot of talking smack. For just a bit, we're going to give it a rest. Give ourselves a rest. Speaking of childhood games, let's take ourselves back to kindergarten. Criss-cross applesauce. Hands on lap."

I watch everybody comply. They roll back their shoulders and straighten their spines, listening to the baritone heartbeat of cellos, but all I can hear is the telltale heart of my own panic. I'm desperate for push-ups or whatever other old-school draconian bullshit any of these teachers can throw at me.

"Your body is feeling exactly what it wants to feel. Let it. Your mind is going where it wants to go. Let it."

Just like Ms. E says, I feel like a tree planted at my mat, my roots extending into the ground. Only I'm not feeling centered and at one with anything. I feel directly connected to magma, and I'm full of fire. My roots are underground snakes. They slither to the same sacred haunts. The graveyard. The movie theater where Blanca tried to take me.

"Feel your arms, your branches extend upward. Outward. Feel the sun. Reach for it."

I reach for the light.

•••••••

The chandelier. In the Dollar Theater. It's ridiculous. It's like a top hat in the ghetto.

First off, the marquee of this theater is missing the first *T*. So it actually says *HEATER*. Which is funny because we all know it doesn't have one.

Blanca, Fernando, Bambi, and I are standing outside the 'heater waiting for somebody to reappear in the booth. The booth is spread-eagled with porn. It's awkward until Blanca launches into "Do Your Ears Hang Low/ Do they wobble to and fro?/Can you tie em in a knot/Can you tie em in a bow?" and we're all dying.

"That brotha"—Blanca points—"could make balloon animals with that thing."

"You could put an eye out like that," I say.

Just as the ticket dude returns to his post, a stampede of high schoolers cuts the line, daring us to say something.

Nando's and Bambi's muscles seem to inflate. Nando's jaw twitches. Blanca grabs her dude by the jacket sleeve and stands almost nose to nose with him. "It's all good. Gives us more time to decide."

The high schoolers are talking a lot of smack about who's already inside the theater and who's begging to get a beat down. To hear them talk you'd think their brehs were staking out every screening in the place, just waiting to start some shit.

We got our neutral faces on for the public, but Blanca catches my side-eye.

Nando puts an arm around Blanca. "What do you want to do, bae?"

Bambi takes a step closer to me and stops like a mosquito hitting a zapper.

Blanca looks from me to Nando. "I want to go to the movies."

I roll my eyes. Double-check the movies listed on the marquee. "Gimme your money, y'all." I fingersnap. "I got a plan."

Blanca knows I will carry her kicking and screaming with me if she don't comply. Fernando knows it too. He coughs up money for him and her, Bambi coughs up money for us and I hand him back my half, and I pay for my damn self.

I gather the change and dispense the tickets.

"Qué es eso?" Fernando says, scrunching up his eyes as he reads the title on the movie tickets. We elbow into the mosh pit of kids clogging the front door and beeline for the snack stand.

Blanca laughs reading her ticket. "Really, Verdad. What the hell?"

"You think any of those fools would want to see *this*?" I'm all proud of myself. Nobody tries to start shit in the middle of a freakin independent foreign film.

Fernando hooks up Blanca with prime movie snacks, one of her reasons for existence, which also include after-school snacks, PMS snacks, and sleepover snacks. Prior to tonight, Fernando pumped me for information about Blanca's faves so he was all suave, knowing exactly what to get her, enough jalapeno cheddar popcorn to feed a third world country and her fave cherry slushie. I let him have it. I'm happy for her. Ish.

Bambi steps up and knows better than to order for me, then joins the lovers. I step up to the counter. "And let me get a small popcorn and a box of Junior Mints."

"Sorry," the teenager says, looking stressed as he eyeballs a bunch of kids dry humping a Cardi B cardboard cutout. "We're out."

"Out? How you gonna be out? I just saw like a stack!"

I get yelly, snatch my popcorn, and stomp back to my crew until I see them. Ten of them. Boxes of Junior Mints in Bambi's arms. Blanca and Nando are dyin.

"For real?"

Bambi laughs so hard he drops a box. I throw him the kind of shade that killed all the freakin dinosaurs.

"How 'bout a deal?" he says. "You could share the popcorn. I could share the Junior Mints."

I nod. A movie without Junior Mints is like rice without beans!

"But don't try to put no moves on me," Bambi says. "Let your hand touch mine by accident."

"Oh! You're suave, my dude. I may be hungry, but not thirsty." I think that made sense.

We leave a trail of popcorn as we head to our movie. Choose the back row and plunge into ratty chairs, sticking and unsticking our feet stick to the floor. The previews are for movies we never heard of from places we never heard of. A mom in front of us is explaining to her daughter that this movie is in the dialect of their people.

"My abuelo used to take my moms to movies in Spanish too, hoping she would speak the language," I tell Blanca.

"Shit, Verdad." Blanca shoots popcorn at me. "This has subtitles? We go to the movies and have to read?"

I laugh. Eventually after many a popcorn has been fired and retaliated against, we leave the world of the movie theater and enter the world of the hotel. I'm not drinking a watery Coke and eating fossilized Junior Mints, glad it's dark because all the nail polish on my left hand is chipping off. I'm with my mom and dad at a fancy hotel leaving dirty dishes for the maids waiting outside my door.

My name is Amodini and I'm ignoring half my parents' instructions about what I'm supposed to do and not do while they're off at a business meeting and I'm at the pool. I'm Amodini leaving a trail of water behind me as I run back into the hotel room to get my favorite lip gloss and catch the maid's daughter eating my crusts.

Nando and Blanca agree they will kick Amodini's ass if she snitches and hold hands.

Then room service comes up with comida for the maid's daughter. Her name is Daysia.

Nando and Blanca are officially snuggling and feeding each other.

"It would be less gross," I whisper, "if y'all just made out."

"Damn," Nando whispers. "You hard."

"No"—I launch a fusillade of Junior Mints—"these are hard."

Many mints get launched, but in the end, with him having nine boxes of Junior Mints, I have to cry uncle.

Bambi and I are dyin laughing. So are Amodini and Daysia. They're running in and out of rooms, the kitchen, now a ballroom. They're pretending to dance when a crystal falls from the chandelier. Both girls pretend to get married. The diamond is the ring.

"Run, girls, run!"

The manager is after the girls. Of course, they get caught. Daysia gets her ears boxed by her moms because she could be fired. Amodini smuggles the crystal to Daysia as they're both being hauled away in separate directions.

Bang bang!

We all look at each other. Ask and answer with our eyes.

Bang! Bang! Crash.

We search inside the movie screen to see where the *Bang! Bang!* is coming from. The explosion of breaking glass. The screaming that must be coming from another movie in an adjacent theater. We sit up on our knees and scan the theater. Other people are looking behind them.

Light steals dark. Words that need no translation.

"Go back to your country!"

"Oh my God, oh my God!"

The spray of gunfire stifling screams. Heartbeats.

••••••••

I gasp. Open my eyes. My hands are slippery fish. A black hole is where my heart should be. I'm soaked with sweat. I feel panicked like when you think maybe your period leaked through the back of your pants. The nerves around my eyes are loose electric wires. Everyone else's eyes are closed. Like I'm the only one who survived. The clock tells me it's only been five minutes.

My chest. I need three hearts to hold this much pain. I walk out with the counselor hissing behind me, "Verdad? Verdad!"

She's propping the door open and dialing her cell.

I dig in my pocket for my bus pass. If they suspend me, so be it. I'm not going back to detention. Don't need to go to something that my mind attends every day of my life.

Damn it! My bus pass. Did I lose it again even after those guys gave it back? My moms is going to hit the roof. She does not lose anything: neither umbrellas, bus passes, keys, nor her fucking sanity.

I text Danny and tell him I'm walking northeast from the cafeteria, and he texts back that he'll catch up with me.

What was once a car but is now a rusting hunk of duct-taped metal on wheels pulls up. The passenger seat window is plastic wrapped. The cracked driver's window rolls open halfway, probably as far as it goes. If I look down on the ground, I'm fairly certain I'll see feet instead of wheels.

"Need a ride?"

It's Danny's broad-shouldered, flannel-wearing friend Jane, passenger side. I can't place her accent. Mississippi? Georgia?

Baldwin, wearing those teeny-tiny rectangular reading glasses, is in the driver's seat. Danny is squashed in the back with the Indian girl and the white girl, and Mental Note: their shoulders are touching. Mental Note 2: They are beautiful.

I will cut them.

"You got room in the trunk?" I say to LumberJane. "Because at this point, I'm willing to ride in it, I'm so tired."

Danny sticks his head out his windowless window. "This no-tell motel always got a vacancy. Hop in."

The whole scene is ridiculous. LumberJane, a Goliath, is impressively pretzeled against the dashboard. To fit, I have to sit on Danny's lap and stretch out my legs across the two girls in the back with us. *I have claimed my territory*, I think, eyeballing the girls, *and I bite*.

Danny seat belts me with his arms. I lean in fitting into the puzzle piece of his body. "Can you do that forever?"

He kisses my forehead. "That kind of day, huh?" Rubs his thumb against my cheek.

"That kind of year."

"Join the club."

One member of the club is eyeballing my sneakers. I side-eye the Indian girl. "No matter what size I am—trust me, you couldn't walk in my shoes." *I also kick.*

"Prisha, baby, I got you," says the white girl. "You'll swap spit but not shoes? C'mon!"

Prisha shrugs and rubs her *bare* feet against—her girlfriend?—YAS—in apology. "Sarah, it's not because I don't want to wear your shoes! What if you cut your foot again?"

"What if *you* do? I could not deal."

To Danny I whisper, "It's the middle of September and girlfriend isn't even wearing any shoes?" Now that I'm feeling less territorial with Danny, I can sympathize.

Danny whispers back, "They got jacked. Then, last time she wore Sarah's shoes, Sarah cut her foot on sheet metal. We got it cleaned up at the ER, but then her crutches got jacked."

I've been so comfortable for so long. My moms is the one who reminds me what it was like when we were living in Section 8 housing. When she tried to grow tomatoes on the balcony and somebody jacked the plant out by the roots. Half joking, I say, "Why don't you each wear one shoe?"

LumberJane beams at me in the mirror. "Oh, I like h— pronouns, please, Danny's new friend. In fact, let's all go around."

Pronouns are exchanged. I take notes. Jane, Sarah, and Prisha use she; Baldwin uses they. "I wish we could just all throw our own gender reveal parties like quinceañeras," I say.

Baldwin, our chauffeur, nods. "Word. Jane and I want to do like a naming ceremony or something. Why do the cis straight people get all the rites of passage?"

"Why do they?" They. If cisgender (thank you, covert googling) straight people are theys, am I part of the we that is something else?

Danny squeezes my hands, which have gotten restless again. "Jesus, now I get the bathroom stall transformation." He gently runs his hands through my hair, which proceeds to get trapped.

Baldwin: "Her hair is trying to eat you!" Blanca didn't call it The Entity for nothing.

"You know," I direct at Prisha, "the Salvation Army. They got shoes. That's where my moms got mine back in the day before she finished school and we moved out of Section 8 housing."

Sarah lifts Prisha's chin and kisses her. "It's time, baby." To me: "It's just hard. She had money. She didn't even do hand-me-downs."

Prisha: "I sound like a snob."

Sarah: "Don't ever say that. What you gave up for me . . ."

They make out. Before I can try to piece together what the hell is going on with these people, Danny is kissing my ear and my parts are turning to pudding.

Baldwin: "You *all* need to get a motel. Not that it matters to me, but where am I going?"

"Where are we going?" Danny says to me, his lips brushing against my neck.

"Nowhere fast," I answer.

"Well, fuck. It's official," says LumberJane.

"Got it," Baldwin says, adjusting the mirror. "Destination, Nowhere." Scrolls through their playlist.

Me: "Hey, Logic. That's my jam!"

Sarah: "Really? Rap? That crap is misogynistic. How about some Tim McGraw?"

Prisha's Indian accent transforms into an alarming drawl: "*Live like you were dyin*!'"

In the mirror Baldwin flashes a smile at Prisha and changes the station to Country FM.

I throw my hands up. "Buzzkill! First of all, country is racist." I return Sarah's nostril flair with a neck roll. "Well, it is. How many black country singers do you know? Latinx?"

Prisha actually smiles. "How many white rappers do you know? Excluding Slim Shady?"

Sarah smiles all crazy, trying to hide her messed up teeth: "She was on debate team, FYI."

"None, buuuut, to begin with, hip hop was about blackness and brownness but overall about repression. Country was blues that became white *because of* oppression."

Baldwin changes the station to Taylor Swift.

Everybody: "Turn that shit off."

Baldwin: "Oh my God, I'm so stressed out!"

Me: "Who's up for rock-paper-scissors!"

We all rock, paper, scissors. After two rounds, I am defeated by LumberJane. She claps and blasts tunes that apparently she and Baldwin know all the lyrics to—in Chinese? "BTS, baby!"

Baldwin: "Aw, for me, Baby Bear! I love you so hard!"

Me to Danny: "What high-pitched hell are we listening to?" Is it chinito? Anyway, at least it's not Tim McGraw. And it occurs to me how much I hate it when people think Latin music is only to be played on Spanish stations but white music is for everyone everywhere. So I chill.

LumberJane and Baldwin sing-screeching the English part: "*All the underdogs in the world. A day may come when we lose.*"

Everybody but me: "*But it's not today! Today we fight!*"

Danny holds my chin. Kisses my nose: "Today we will survive. Together we don't die."

Together we drive around going nowhere, doing nothing,

talking shit, and I feel better than I have in weeks. There's nothing like a full tank of gas and a car full of—friends? I maybe accidentally slip off my shoes because I'm going to maybe accidentally forget them in the car. It's all good. Till I wonder, looking at the sky, how long have we actually been throwing away our opportunities for college scholarships (shut up, Ma!), exactly? I check my phone. OH. SHIT.

LumberJane lowers the volume. "So tonight, Underdogs?"

Baldwin: "Tonight."

Sarah and Prisha: "Tonight."

Danny raises an eyebrow at me. Starts petting the hand that's yanking out hair.

Danny to the crew: "At the farm?"

Baldwin: "No. Meet at the soul garden. It needs watering."

Me: "What's the soul garden?"

"Our Lady of Perpetual Help Cemetery," Baldwin explains, and I wonder if Blanca somehow masterminded this whole thing. "You're welcome to come."

"Uh, thanks. I'll have to see. . . Can you just drop me off for now?"

I tell Baldwin where I live, and turns out we're not far away. (Have we been driving in circles?) Danny and I are now not speaking. I broke the spell.

14

"Oh God, pray for me," I say, glancing out the window as we pull up to my house. My mother is standing on the porch.

Danny: "Please tell me she's chopping wood?"

It's the chainsaw. I sign the cross and crawl out.

"Hi, Mrs. Reyna," Danny says, trying to be all polite to a woman aiming a chainsaw at him.

Prisha and Sarah have somehow morphed into the back seat.

"Ma . . ."

Once I'm by her side, she lowers her weapon. Walks up to the window where Danny is sitting. She takes a survey of everyone. One by one. Finally, she steps back to aim her finger and her curse. "You people," she says pointing at each one of them, "you don't come here to my house. To my street again. If I see you around here . . ." She handcuffs my wrist with her ninja grip.

". . . I'll call the police! Do you hear me? All of you!"

Baldwin clicks his—uh, *their* tongue and adjusts their glasses. "It's not really your street, Mrs. Reyna," they correct her. "This is public—Oh my God!"

My mother's chainsaw is making her cheeks vibrate. "My daughter is not for ANY of you!"

Baldwin peels onto the street. Back inside, she releases my wrist, launching me into the kitchen. It's going down.

I look at her. It's not my mother. It's the ghost of the woman who hasn't slept in weeks. Who she was haunts who she is. The hands that once built, soldered, drilled, nailed are now the machine. Her eyes are funhouse mirrors.

My pocket vibrates with a text. I know better than to check it right now.

She pulls out a chair and steadies herself with it. "I don't want to have this conversation. I don't want to say things you're not strong enough to hear." She lifts and slams the chair against the floor. "I don't want to make this a conversation you'll never forget."

From the time I left for school to the time I jumped in Baldwin's car, I've shrunk and grown, aged and regressed. I am square in the eye with the woman I used to look up to. I'm naked with the woman who taught me to dress. I'm all messed up feeling like I've outgrown this house, but I still want so freakin bad to fit inside.

"But you," slam, "put," slam, "me in this position. You make me the monster."

From me, silence. All the words in my head are coming out in a language I can't even understand. No hablo myself.

"Where," slam, "are," slam, "your fucking," slam, "shoes and socks?"

I'm barefoot with the woman who taught me to tie my shoes. A stray grain of rice sticks to the sole of my foot.

"They're—on Prisha. I think—"

"Who is Prisha? Where did you meet these people? I don't know them. But apparently I don't know a lot of things. Maybe anything. Why weren't you at school this morning?"

"Blanca," I mutter. "I thought she was missing, but she was hiding. Playing hide and seek. She hid and wanted me to see—"

"Blanca wanted you to what? Verdad. It's time to come to terms with reality, let go of the delusions. This past year I feel like I've been holding onto your ankles. You're so light, you could blow away. You just won't carry the weight of it."

"The weight? The weight of what?"

"The weight of sadness. Blanca is gone, Verdad."

I see myself holding Blanca by the ankles like holding a string of a balloon. I think I have the balloon. But then *bang bang!* it pops.

"Say it, Verdad." My mother's eyes are watering. "Let her go!"

"This from the woman who still sets a chair for Abuelo?!"

"Abuelo comes and goes as he pleases. Blanca is trapped. So are—"

"By me? What?"

The chair slams again. Again and again till the table rocks. "I'm not going to do this. You're standing at the edge. I'm not going to push you over. The issue with school. We'll say you were sick. That school. It isn't right for you. Where we live. It's better but not good enough. I'm going to figure some things out."

"Figure things out? I am not an equation. You can't solve me."

"Chica, you better watch your tone. This situation is a problem and we will solve it." She looks away and talks to herself. "Yeah. I could pick up another shift. I'm already halfway there with a down payment."

"Are you effin kidding me? You're solving me with suburbia?"

"You're not making the same mistakes I did—"

"Danny is not a mistake. And if it's not Danny," I say, realizing this argument is way beyond him, "it's gonna be somebody else. Somebody I want. I choose. You can't tell me how to feel."

How do you go from being a stranger one day to being a lover the next? How do you go from being a mother and daughter one minute to combatants the next?

"I can't tell you? You who got a roof over her head, warm food on the table, and somebody to provide for your every need. Those clothes, I buy. Those white teeth. I pay. And where is all the fucking damn toothpaste?"

"What are you saying, Ma? Really? Since we're not having delusions no more."

"I'm saying not under this roof. You gotta learn to earn. You gotta follow my rules. One day, when you have your home, you'll have rules too."

"There's no rules for love!"

"Yes, there are. Boy loves girl. All the rest is against my rules. God's rules. I ain't raise you to be—to be no dyke."

"A dyke? Definition, disgusting. Do I disgust you, Ma?"

"No. You're my daughter. The daughter I raised, the daughter I love doesn't disgust me."

"Because that daughter isn't a dyke."

"You are not a fucking dyke."

"Yeah, I guess not, because Danny's a boy."

"That ain't no boy. There's Adam. There's Eve. That. Is. It."

"No," I say, feeling strong. "There's God, Jesus, the Holy Spirit—*and* Mary who got demoted by the patriarchy." I mean I don't know who wrote the Book of Love, but I do know who wrote the Bible. Dudes.

Moms signs the cross. "What kind of crap are they feeding you at that school? That shit is against evolution *and* God's plan."

"God didn't plan for a lot of shit then."

I can tell she's not even hearing me anymore. "This shit is

a phase. A phase, a fad, a way of coping. In two days, this will all pass. We'll go on with our lives."

"I don't want to go on with my life. I want to *have* a life."

Moms sits down heavily in the chair she just did her best to break. "I'm tired, Verdad. You're fifteen, what do you know about life? As long as you're living it under this roof you will go to school, and you will come straight home until I know I can trust you again."

"Trust me?" For the first time I don't trust my mother. Add that to God, and that pretty much means in nobody does my ass trust. Is that when adulting starts? When you realize you can't trust anyone?

"I need to get some sleep so I don't end up in a car crash. Go to bed, Verdad. Pray."

•••••••

For the first time in months, I do pray. I grab my fedora, add a clip-on cravat to my outfit and another pair of sneaks my moms bought my undeserving ass, and all the cash I still have left from my fourteenth birthday that my tías wouldn't let me spend on books—gracias mis tías! Heading to the living room, I pray hard.

That I won't get caught.

Danny texted me to be ready for pickup at ten. I dump my backpack out and repack it book by book. Me without a book is like, is like—I have my books and my poetry to protect me. I am shielded in my armor! I don't know why but I pack up my violin. I want to feel grounded with the weight. Centered. Also, attention asshats: I have a baseball bat.

The baseball bat doesn't fit in my bag. But I have a grand

realization that I own a pirate costume for our middle-school play *The Jolly Roger*. So I dismantle and engineer the scabbard to fit my baseball bat like only a stagehand could, so I could look like a complete lunatic.

Nothing is stopping me from leaving except me. I close the door behind me. The distance between the porch and the sidewalk is the distance between starlight and a star. Night is everywhere. Light has its limits but dark reaches everybody and everything.

I haven't been out this late at night since . . . that night at the theater. The chill in the fall air snaps at me, goose-pimpling my arms. But I'm hot. I'm fire and ice. The backpack carries a history too heavy to hold. My shoes are prisons. My hat is a coffin for every thought I wish would die.

I squint and look up the block. Headlights flash in the distance. On. Off. On. Off. Then I hear the music. The Underdogs.

The lights turn off. The music silences. The car rolls toward me. Idles.

Fate is walking me like a dog, dragging me by the leash. I take a step off the porch.

"Jump in, baby." Baldwin adjusts the mirror and a shard of glass falls off. "The water's fine."

I climb into the passenger seat. Baldwin's hair is wet as if they really did just come out of a pool. "Where's everybody else?" Specifically, where's Danny?

"Watering the soul garden. Danny sent me to get you. He didn't want to leave the girls alone. He's real protective."

This hurts my brain a little. LumberJane is six-two. Could she not protect the girls? Does this mean Danny is taking on the traditional machismo role and Jane the submissive? Or am I being the dick assuming that because Jane is large she can fight? Or wants to?

On goes another chinito song I can't identify. I can't understand the words, but the music is beautiful. The perfect soundtrack for a journey to the soul garden.

"You look ready for battle, Verdad. And, I might add, a performance of the Pirates of Penzance."

"You look like you just came from battle. And, I might add, a swim through the Hudson." Their hair is dripping wet. A crack jeers from Baldwin's glasses. I reflect on Danny's bruised eye, Prisha's jacked shoes.

Completely ignoring my comment: "How long till your mom knows you're missing?"

"Under these circumstances, she'll probably call the school tomorrow morning to make sure I get there on time. She'll have me paged on the intercom so everyone knows I'm missing. She'll request campus police and dyke-sniffing dogs, but all to no avail. My tías will be called, including the ones in San Juan. Titi Sujei knows the barrio like the back of her hand, and when she finds me, she will slap me with it."

Baldwin laughs in Morse-Code *ha ha ha haha ha ha haha*. "So midnight's at about nine tomorrow morning?"

"I guess you could say that."

"Then I better get you to the ball, Cinder-ella." Baldwin says it as Cinder-*eya*. Even though I am prepared to use the baseball bat against Baldwin in case they pull a Jekyll-Hyde, I like their style.

Baldwin parks the clunker in a grocery parking lot. "Just gotta grab some snacks."

"Is this place chinito?" I ask.

Baldwin wrinkles their nose. "Chinese? No."

"I mean . . ." What did I mean? Chinito doesn't just mean Chinese. It means—pretty much—all Asians. My cheeks burn up. I flash to complaining to my moms about everybody assuming all Latinx was Mexican. And here I am assuming all Asian people are the same.

"Sorry. That was rude."

"AF."

I want to ask what their background is, but I know that would be rude AF too. Nobody does that shit to white people, do they? Like hey, you eat spaghetti and meatballs? Are you Italian?

"Totally," I say. "Forgive me? Snacks are on me."

"Then I absolve you in the name of the Baldwin."

"I like that name," I say. "For James Baldwin?"

"Yeah. I'm still test-driving it. Might land on something else. I knew who I was this morning—"

"But I've changed so many times since then." I smile, finishing the quote from *Alice in Wonderland.* Books can do that. Make friends out of people who, two seconds ago, were peripheral. Strangers. "Great British accent by the way."

"Thank you."

We wave to ourselves on the video camera as we scope out the store for sustenance. I am digging these strawberry-flavored biscuit sticks covered in chocolate. Baldwin grabs two banana milks.

"You have to try this."

"That sounds so so good."

We bring our goods up to the counter. Baldwin veers off to a case of steaming buns stuffed with juicy slices of meat.

Mmmmm. "I can smell the pork!"

"Oh lawd, and they have smashed cucumber salad!"

At Baldwin's direction, I buy a box of matches and two pork buns. We step out of the store and into the parking lot and agree to trek the rest of the way on foot. For the past year, my whole existence has been in the dark. Now I'm a bat flying in it. Free at last.

The soul garden needs watering. "I could walk to Our Lady of Perpetual Help with my eyes closed."

"Prove it."

Baldwin pulls a bandana out of their pocket like a magician. We cross the street and they blindfold my eyes. I step forward and stretch out my arms to make sure they're still there and not messing with me.

"That was my left nipple." They slurp their Coke. "I mean we just met so let's take it slow."

My turn to snort. Thank God a beverage isn't involved. "Sorry."

My brain reboots. I am the bat, nocturnal, knowing my place by sound.

"Here comes my favorite Lady of the Night at ten o'clock." I can tell Baldwin says this while walking backward as I walk forward. "Avoid the lawn chair to her left."

"Kinky," the Lady of the Night says of our game.

I walk two paces and stop, my toes just popping over the curb.

"Not bad. All clear. Walk."

Baldwin Mother-May-I's me across the street.

Beside me, the strip holds echoes of my past that speak of the hearse and the horsepower it took to carry the weight of a rhinestone tiara, petticoats from Perla's Party Palace, private jokes, unmade plans. Nobody wanted an invitation to that party. We all stood around strangers, not knowing ourselves. We ate food we couldn't swallow, drank from never-ending Styrofoam cups of tears. Blanca, she's a genie locked in the bottle of my brain. On this very sidewalk, Blanca and I talked about when we would get our driver's licenses. How we would cruise by the bus stop, roll down the windows, flip the bird to all the boys, blast out those bus-taking fools with "Sorry: Sorry, I ain't sorry! Sorry, I ain't sorry. I ain't sorry. No no hell nah!"

"Ew. Overturned trash can, ten o'clock." Baldwin coughs at the stench. "Pothole, twelve o'clock!"

"Not pothole. Crater of the moon."

Baldwin claps. "Yes. We are astronauts." They walk all trippy like the gravity is gone.

"Yup. AstroNOT. As in, I'm *not* ready."

Silence.

"I get it." Baldwin slurps up the bottom of their drink. "As in, I'm *not* cisgender. Not binary. Not a figment or a fraction. Whole."

The atmosphere is toxic with cigarettes. "Not a robot."

"Not a sin. Not going to your hell."

From a bunch of white boys crushing beer cans, "Hey, can we play?"

I pull out my bat. "Depends on the game."

Baldwin airlifts me and my bat off my feet. "Not now not ever, boys. Not toys."

I'm back on my feet.

"Doodoo, twelve o'clock, one o'clock, two o'clock!"

"Shit!"

"Out of luck. Inevitable."

"Foul! Which foot?"

"Left."

I drag my foot against the sidewalk. Mother May a few paces then stop at the smell of incense. "Church." All the candles of my memory are lit at once, but I blow them out one by one, camouflage in the smoke.

Baldwin holds my pinky and leads me through a crowd of churchgoers, choir members; some humming under their breath, some singing. One lays her ringed hand on my head before she passes. I can feel her hands sign the cross.

After a couple more uneventful blocks: "We're here."

Baldwin takes off the bandana. We're at the foot of the gravel road. Aquila the eagle, Cygnus the swan, Hercules, twinkle; their stories hover over us.

"How often do you guys come here?"

"All the time. Second only to the movie theater."

My stomach curls. I trip over nothing—without the bandana on. "Funny, I've never seen you. Any of you."

"Most people don't."

15

I've never walked so far back in the cemetery before. I'm in unfamiliar terrain. We walk to where the daffodils have died and been replanted for next year, where leaves once lay but now sit in giant plastic bags under the trees. Past mausoleums, which I only thought existed in gothic novels. "Wouldn't it be cool if we all got to be entombed in pyramids?"

"Yeah, it would." Baldwin straightens their reading glasses. Their hair is slick but not dripping anymore. "What would you take with you? If you could only take three things." Their stomach growls. One pork bun obviously didn't cut it.

"You had to make it hard. But actually the answer is always books. Books first. And a photo—of my friends." The one we took outside the movie theater, freezing smiles, icing time. "And—is there Wi-Fi in the afterlife?"

"Of course. I said heaven, not hell."

"Kay. But it is cheating, isn't it? Like making a wish for more wishes." Rose bushes surround us now, shedding the last of their petals.

"All right. No Wi-Fi."

"Then I'd take my props. *A* prop. The Sharks jacket Blanca and I made for a production of *West Side Story*."

"And leave your scabbard behind?" They smile and their

glasses shed another piece of lens.

"Ha!"

"Danny told me about you and stage crew. That's dope. Why the jacket?"

"I never felt more at home than in the theater. I was stage crew most of the time. Creating worlds."

"Being in control."

"Yup. But it was more than that. Sometimes I had to jump in, take over a role for an actor. I played a Shark in *West Side Story*. I loved it."

"The thrill of being someone else."

"Actually, no. The thrill of being me. I didn't want to be the girl in the window. I wanted to be out on the streets, dancing."

"Oh!" Baldwin grins. "You're pan!"

I think they mean pansexual. Or pangender? Both?

"It was fate we all met. The fate of star-crossed-dressed lovers!"

Baldwin twirls me, dips me, and drops me on my culo, but I add some stylized moves that look like a combination of break-dancing and going into epileptic shock.

"Ha-ha-ha-ha-ha!"

We laugh too hard and too long. "Okay already!" Baldwin helps me to my feet.

I dust myself off. Grab my backpack. "Your turn," I say as we start walking again.

"Well, first of all, I'd take my glasses. Ever seen Velma without them? That's been me for the past year. My librarian buys me these reading glasses from CVS, but as you can see," Baldwin says holding them up in the moonlight, "they are suited for grandmas by the fire. Not Underdogs in the cemetery."

Needing glasses for a year. I imagine not being able to

read for that long. I think back to when my mother offered me braces and I turned her down. I mean, I was turning down shit I needed. That's how well off I was. This poor kid—who's driving, no less—is squinting to read road signs. I wouldn't even dare ask if they have a driver's license.

Shhhhh. Tsssssss.

I jump.

"What is that?" I'm scoping the darkness for sickos and snakes of mythological proportion, hand on my bat.

"No worries, She-rah. It's just the fountain."

A fountain full of angels blowing trumpets is a few feet away, turned off for the winter.

"How 'bout you all?" Baldwin says to the shadows under the fountain's edge. "What three things would you take when you die?"

"I've already taken names, so I'd take revenge." Something crawls out from the bottom of the fountain. Something extra-large. XXL.

The bat leaves the scabbard.

"I'd take it out on everybody who fucked me over," LumberJane says all chill, like she just walked through a door and not from out the underground. Her blond hair looks oily and drips like Baldwin's did. Her collar's wet.

"How in the hell did you fit in there?"

Baldwin strikes a match. Danny, Sarah, and Prisha climb out of what I come to see is a small underground room, shivering, their backs wet from their drippy hair.

Danny squeezes out and shakes leaves off of his jacket. His breath comes out in ghosts.

"It's a tiny room," Danny says. "You can turn the fountain on from down there."

Danny unhooks my backpack from my arms and drops it on the ground. I stretch and crack my back. Danny massages my shoulders. Wraps his arms around me. He kisses me, and my ghosts haunt his mouth, his mine. I run my fingers through his wet hair. Have they all been taking baths in this fountain?

"We're gonna build an igloo when it snows. Be like the First People."

Oh shit. It hits me for the first time. This overnight cemetery visit isn't some teen rebel harmless bullshit. I hear my mother's voice from a couple days ago: *There's been homeless people seen in the neighborhood.* But for real, I was picturing like, old men with cardboard signs saying they were Vietnam vets.

He motions to my backpack. "Did you bring bricks to build a house?"

"Uh." I'm still trying to wrap my head around this. "Sort of. Books."

"Books," LumberJane says, swaggering to a tree and leaning on it. Poor tree. "Not blankets? Water bottles? Toothpaste?"

"No, wiseass. And if someone gets on my case for toothpaste one more time today . . ."

Prisha shows me her feet in my shoes. "They fit perfectly. Thank you!"

Danny and I are standing side by side now, his arms around my shoulders.

"No offense or nothing, but why the fuck were you barefoot to begin with? Why are you," I point to Baldwin, "wearing those ridiculous glasses? And why are you people sleeping in a graveyard on regular basis?" And why do you always look like you fell into trash cans from the fifteenth floor?

"Her parents," Sarah answers for Prisha. "They took all of them. Her shoes."

"The shoes I wore to Diwali last year even. Oh! They think, Prisha won't leave without shoes."

"But she did," Sarah chimes, crushing Prisha with a hug.

"Not that it's none of my business, but—"

"She left because she had an arranged marriage," LumberJane interrupts and lights up a cigarette. "Back home. Real Disney shit. Only not the Disney ending."

Sarah strokes Prisha's head. "First," Prisha says, "my mom caught me and Sarah together. We were supposed to be studying. My mom started yelling at me like Sarah wasn't even there, until I just broke down crying. But then nothing. No mention of the incident for a week. Until my dad casually mentions there's someone he wants me to meet online."

"Just like that?"

"They arranged a month-long trip to India last summer for our families to meet. I complained, because for one thing I was not about to leave my dog behind for that long . . ."

Prisha bursts into tears and the girls walk off together as if no one but them exists.

Baldwin leans against the tree with LumberJane and lights a smoke off her cigarette.

"So," LumberJane exhales, "Prisha's dad killed her dog. Her mom locked her in her room and Prisha could hear the dog barking. Then the barking came to a dead stop. The next day the dog was gone—buried in the backyard. Week after that, Prisha took off. The rest is herstory."

"Christ. In this day and age? What. The. Fuck? Is that why you're all here?"

"Because our dads killed our dogs?"

"No, LumberJane!" Oops. "Because you ran away from home."

Jane to Baldwin: "Did she just call me LumberJane?"

Jane to me: "What did you call me?"

I step behind Danny for protection. "Um. It's just the flannel shirt. The boots. The muscles." The shadow of a beard.

Danny laughs. "Nice to use your boyfriend as a human shield!"

Boyfriend? Boyfriend! *Xoxoxoxoxoxoxox.*

Jane scowls and puts out her cigarette on the bottom of her boot.

"I'm sorry," I say. "Still learning."

"Okay, J Lo."

"Hey, I said I was sorry."

Baldwin grabs Jane's hand and whispers I-don't-know-what. Jane nods. "It's just, we lost a friend of ours. Cops couldn't figure out who he was because they kept deadnaming him. Then the parents who threw him out finally turn up. Dressed him like a girl for his funeral."

Blood is rushing to my neck. My cheeks are hot. I don't entirely know who I am, but I know who I am not and will *never* be. "I said I was sorry, and I meant it. But me making a mistake doesn't make me those people."

"Okay. Moving on. Anyway, yes," Jane exhales, "we all ran away or got thrown out. My parents wanted a boy. They thought they got one." Jane leans against the tree with her back and one boot. "They were mistaken."

Baldwin lays their head on Jane's shoulder. "My parents wanted their son to be a computer science engineer. I could do the computer science part. Just not the son part."

I turn to Danny and he looks at me while he's talking to everyone. "My dad runs an evangelical Christian bakery. Communion for all. Cake for some. He tried to send me away to some camp to get reprogrammed. So here I am."

Programmed. Maybe Danny and I and the Underdogs are the only ones who aren't robots.

I hug Danny and we stay like that.

Sarah and Prisha come back from the dark, renewed. Their teeth are incandescent like the moon. They sit cross-legged and take turns braiding each other's hair.

Jane piles wood for a fire. Baldwin uses the matches I bought to light it, then sits their skinny self between Jane's legs. I try not to stare.

Danny motions for me to sit down. I dislodge my bat from my scabbard. We're all in a circle by the fountain of angels.

"Who's got the s'mores?" Baldwin says.

They all hold imaginary sticks in the fire.

"This is just like the Lost Boys in Peter Pan," I say.

"More like the Donner Party!" Danny says, laughing.

Baldwin and Jane are making out hard and I'm not looking. I'm not looking. I'm not looking! But I'm thinking. Specifically, about Danny with a hard-on. Does Danny want a penis? How would I feel hooking up with Danny if he had one?

Dany is behind me, wrapped around me like a blanket. I am in so much trouble. I lean my head into his neck. "How am I going to leave you in the morning?"

"You mean you're going back home?"

"I mean—yeah." He didn't think I was running away for good tonight, did he?

Danny's hand tugs out of mine hard.

I swallow. "You're mad?"

"No." But Danny nods yes. "Not exactly." He throws a pebble at Jane's shoe.

Jane and Baldwin come up for air. Danny snaps his fingers

and Jane responds by throwing a pack of smokes in his direction.

"Yeah, and I hate to bust your bubble," Jane says to me, "but *can* you go home? 'Cause it's not a choice for us."

"Of course I can go home." I hate cigarette smoke. I cough. "How can this be?" I wave the smoke fumes out my face. "At our age. How can you be homeless?"

"Welcome to our world." Danny takes a drag and aims the smoke away from my face. He pulls me closer and I can't help thinking that smell's gonna stank up my hair. "The Crooked Queendom."

"Wait. The Crooked Queendom?" I search my brain's database and get a hit. "Like *The Crooked Kingdom* by Bardugo. You guys r—I mean you find the time to—"

"To read?" Jane interjects. "Yeah. The library is where we go to get warm. Use the bathroom. The librarians don't bother us as long as we're reading."

"If you join the cooking book club on Kingsbridge, you can get food." Baldwin's cracked lens has fallen out completely. "If you go to the library on 231st, they'll bring you hot tea when it rains. I heart librarians. I asked Ms. Ramos if she could adopt me. She said yes, and I ran out screaming."

"That's—I—But, how could your family do that? Just—They must be worried about you!" The cognitive dissonance in my brain is so high, the walls of my glass house are shattering at the noise. No mother or father could be that cold. "Don't you miss them?"

"Verdad," Sarah asks, "what is your mom doing right now?"

"What she's always doing. Working. Where's your mom right now, Jane?" I will not picture her mom as Slue Foot Sue. I will not.

"She's at the airport keeping America safe. The funniest

shit, though. She's never even been on a plane."

"Me neither. But when I am it will be to Puerto Rico. My girl B—we were planning on making the trip together senior year. We were gonna get jobs to pay for the trip ourselves. It's easier to be an outsider when there's two of you."

"So Cinder-ella—you're not Puerto Rican?" Funny. Baldwin was trying to place me like I was trying to place them.

"I'm a Puerto Rican who's never been to PR. It's embarrassing. But with—my girl, we would've been embarrassed together. Somos uña y carne."

"Meaning?"

"The nail and the meat. Like two peas in a pod. She wanted to go for the beaches and los ranas and the coqui, the little frogs. I wanted to go to figure things out. Figure me out."

"I'd like to go back home too." Prisha hugs her knees. "To visit—not to live. I'm an outsider too. But oh—to walk the marketplace stacked with pomegranates. Pluck sugar apples from the trees. Eat stuffed bhati, aloo samosa. You know, Verdad, your native Puerto Rico is second best to India. I would love to go back there someday."

"Really? *You've* been to Puerto Rico? Dang. I'm so embarrassed."

"Oh, Puerto Rico is in your DNA the way India is in mine. God created India and Puerto Rico on the same day she made the sun. We're sisters."

"Sol sisters. S-O-L."

Jane says, "Shit-out-of-luck?"

"No! Sol. Sun."

"I like that." Prisha rests her head against Sarah's shoulder. "Sol sisters. Sisters of sand, salt, spice." Prisha looks at Sarah. "I miss my auntie's chana dal so bad. The food here is so bland.

And everywhere, processed meat."

"I could not live without meat," Danny says. "I'm a carnivore."

I chime in, "Same."

"Meat!" Prisha clucks her tongue in disapproval. "If you would eat flesh, what stops you from eating a man?"

A discussion follows in which Prisha attempts to prove animal sentience and Baldwin and Jane scheme to get some Taco Bell. Danny and I face each other.

"So you're going home." Danny pushes my hair out of my face. "But just in case you find there's no home to go to, I'm here."

We kiss deep, and my brain turns off the thought of me being homeless and my body pushes closer to his body, his promise that I'm not alone.

"Hey. Is this a violin? Verdad, can you play?" Sarah and Prisha interrupt our PDA, having used my distraction to go through my things. I'd have been pissed but Prisha is actually holding it right, even reverently. "You could make good money playing this." She places the instrument in my hands.

Sarah and Prisha each take one of Danny's hands. Jane leads Baldwin to the safe outskirts of the fire. The Underdogs aren't asking.

I take a minute to decide my piece before I play.

Jane is a surprisingly graceful dancer, an orca up for air. Prisha necklaces her arms around Danny. She's touching his hair, her fingers walking a trail they've obviously traveled a hundred times. I weigh my options and come to the conclusion that smashing Prisha on the head with my violin would not go over well. But the worm has poked out of the apple, and I wonder if Danny has ever hooked up with Prisha or Sarah. Or both of them.

My fingers speak the jealousy that I have too much pride to articulate. I'm a demon, summoning my music from all the unspeakable things in the shadows, from the tongues of fire.

Prisha separates from Danny and mirrors Sarah, banshee ballerinas traveling at the speed of dark, hiding and seeking, losing and finding themselves. When we're half-dead with exhaustion, I replace my bow and violin with a pen and skin. The others follow, tattooing themselves in the firelight. No one wants to be the first one to break the silence. We start in whispers that could be mistaken for the wind.

A big thermos is passed around. I gulp water, out of reverence for my heathen homies. But I have to admit I'm not down with sharing the same drink with so many mouths. Especially ones that that don't floss daily. Everybody's conversating freely now, talking about people I don't know, things I couldn't understand because I wasn't there. I have to pee.

I search for a private spot to do my business. I do not like popping a squat without toilet paper. I almost pee on my own self. I literally pray I don't have to poop and God's like, *Really? Do you know the shit I'm dealing with right now?*

I want my shower. I want my scissors. There are rituals that I have performed for months and right now it's Sunday in the church of my mind. Just stepping out of the Underdogs' circle, I realize I'm burning out like our fire. I don't belong here. I am not an Underdog. As much as I needed to talk, I doubly need the silence.

I linger in the shadows on the periphery of our camp. Prisha is laying her head on one of Danny's shoulders. Sarah the other. I can't hear what they are whispering. Why weren't the girls so cozy with Danny before? Prisha is telling Danny a secret and he is laughing. Did her lips just brush his ear?

I try to block out the image of them kissing, but the more I try the more the image plays like an annoying commercial break that won't stop till you buy what it's selling. The true test: if all this is innocent, the girls won't act differently when they see me.

I step my stalker ass out of the shadows. "Hi!" I interrupt, scaring the crickets into cardiac arrest. Sarah and Prisha startle and slide away from Danny. No!

Danny jumps to his feet. "Hey!" He sidles over and reaches for my hand. I cross my arms and shiver.

"Aw. You're cold." He starts taking off his hoodie, but I stop him mid unzip.

"No." I step back. "That's okay. You need it."

"Bae—"

"No need for a spat, young lovers." Jane stretches and a button pops off her shirt. "I got an extra flannel you can have in my bag, under the fountain. Could you actually bring the bag back though? It makes for an excellent pillow."

"So do you." Baldwin lays their head on Jane's lap. I think Baldwin is pretty when they smile.

Danny takes a step in my direction. "Thanks, hon," he says to Jane. "I'll just—"

"No," I answer passive aggressively as I step completely out of his reach. "I'll get it."

I head towards the backpacks.

Danny attempts to follow me but Sarah and Prisha have tied his sneaker laces together. The last giggles are behind me, the darkness ahead.

The Underdogs have dug a trench under the fountain. It won't be long before the caretaker discovers it and they'll have to move on to new territory. I step down into the pit, knowing

I can't possibly be alone. Nature is like everywhere. Slimy, creepy nature. Yuck. I lurch forward, snatch the closest bag and unzip it.

My phone flashlight reveals piles of McDonald's napkins and two neatly folded T-shirts— stained with what I realize is blood. Oh God. Somebody must be on their period.

In a panic I calculate the days till my own period—till my mind autocorrects itself, because it doesn't matter how long. I'll be back home TOMORROW.

Our church collects food, clothes, diapers, and toys for the homeless. But never once have I considered collecting tampons. Shit, I know nothing about the world. I knew nothing about my family and their homophobia. I knew nothing about my racist-ass, ignorant-ass self. If there was a survey, I couldn't even answer basic questions. Sexual orientation: ? Race: Human? Ethnicity: ? Emotional IQ: possibly retar—intellectually dis—differently abled?

I grab the next bag, now more scared of what I'll find in it than of what is slithering around me. I reach in and feel what turns out to be two toilet paper rolls and a used tube of toothpaste. Well, hallelujah! I can get through the night without a shower if I can finger-brush my sugar-coated teeth. Blow my runny nose on paper instead of my sleeve. The cold is giving me the sniffles.

The roll is wrapped in unmarked blue paper. Synapses fire and I'm back to my violin recital, catching Danny in the janitor's closet. Danny was stealing toilet paper. Duh.

I finger-comb my hair into a bun, blow my nose and bury the tissue. Pop the cap on the toothpaste and begin to finger brush when, spitting into the pit, I think, *What serendipity, I love Uncle Tom's lavender toothpaste!* . . . 'Specially since this is my damn toothpaste! Danny must've swiped it the first time he was at my place.

I zipper up the bags. I've been gone too long. I find Jane's spare flannel, throw it on, and head back to the fire with our pillows. I'm not ready to sleep with Danny. I mean if things keep moving this fast, we'll be married by next week, divorced the next. I decide to say good night to the Underdogs and find my own place to crash. Blanca and I will have our first slumber party in years. I need to be close to her. Maybe if I'm patient she'll give up on trying to get me to the theater and come back here, and things will be back to—the most normal they ever could be.

"What took you so long?" Danny asks.

Sarah is lying on her back. Prisha rubs her temples, her hands, her belly. To Sarah: "There aren't any more." To me: "Maybe Verdad can get you some Advil, huh Verdad?"

I nod and Danny helps me distribute everybody's backpack pillows. Prisha props up Sarah's head with the backpack of McDonald's napkins. Head cradled in her arms, Jane is snoring, Baldwin rising and falling with each of her husky breaths. But when Danny slides a backpack toward Jane, she reaches out her hand mid-dream and props her head on it without opening an eye.

"Wow," I whisper to Danny, gazing at Baldwin. They finally took off their glasses. "That is a gift."

"Survival. PS, just for *your* survival, don't even accidentally touch one of them in their sleep. With what they've been through. Let's just say they've become light sleepers."

"Jesus. Got it." I load myself up with my violin and my backpack of books. "Gonna build me a house of brick nearby." I look away from Danny's disappointed face. "Is that okay?"

"Of course it is. Yeah." He hooks his hands in his pockets. "So—"

I plant a quick peck on his lips. "So buenas noches."

"Good night." His lips are as cold as my heart.

Blanca's grave is where I'll make my bed tonight. I'm out of whatever zone I was in with Baldwin when I was the bat-following radar and proceed to trip my clutzy ass over every piece of matter in my path. Whatever the hell just crawled across my leg now has me feeling all creepy crawly up and down my body. I got to chill out.

I make my way toward Blanca's grave, expecting to see the familiar dangle of her feet. I wonder if I'll see her breath the way I do mine. I'll tell her about the stalled elevator that was my life now shooting through the ceiling like a rocket. I haven't spoken to her in minutes, hours, eons. And for the first time I have confidences to share, secrets to tell.

What would it mean to lose your virginity to a boy with the body of a girl?

Can you have love without loss?

Would you still be my friend now?

If you were still here, would Danny and I have gotten together?

Are Danny and I together?

Am I in love?

Would you, me, Fernando, and Danny all have gone out on a date?

Heavy silence, the kind old novels call pregnant. But I do not want to be answered with riddles. Or with prayers.

"Hello? Answer me, Blanca! I'm tired of chasing me. You! I can't live without me. You! Fuck!"

I'm kneeling in the dirt. I'm pulling my hair out. I'm

punching the shit out of a tombstone. I'm being lifted off my feet. Hugged, held against a heart. Cradled like a fucking baby.

"Verdad! Verdad! Baby. I got you. I got you."

I'm being rocked. I'm in a trance. The stars die behind a cloud like birthday candles blown out on a cake.

After a long time, Danny says, "Can you tell me?"

I can't talk. But I can write. I fumble with my pockets and find it. My pen. I squirm out of Danny's arms and start to write on my arm. He gently holds my wrist to stop me. He rolls up his sleeve to expose his own arm and guides my hand so that the pen rests on his skin.

I write. And write.

For the moon never beams without bringing me dreams
Of the beautiful Boricua Blanca, just fourteen;
And the stars never rise but I see the braces and wires
Of the beautiful Boricua Blanca, only fourteen;
And so, all the night-tide, I lie down by the side
Of my darling—my darling—my life and my bride,
In the sepulcher there by the city of broken dreams.
In her tomb, only fourteen.

Danny shivers. I've covered his whole arm with words. I drop my pen.

We wear each other like fall jackets. Our fingers run like little kids jumping through the leaves. We taste lavender toothpaste in each other's mouths and laugh. We hold each other's bodies down and buoy each other's hearts up, up, and far away from this fucking graveyard, this fucking planet.

16

Baldwin drives me home in the morning.

When Baldwin pulls up to my house, I hop out, grab my backpack and violin, and lean into the passenger window. "Hey, am I gonna see you at school?" If it wasn't for that banana incident in the cafeteria, I wouldn't have known they were even enrolled.

Baldwin shrugs. "I like school. Used to be good at it. But a fountain bath doesn't cut it. My shorts are crispy. I smell. It's embarrassing."

"You're not going to school because you need a shower? But why not the locker room showers?"

"Oh lawd, dealing with the school bathrooms is hard enough. You offering?"

This is nuts, but . . . "Yes. We can shower. Then head off to school. My moms will be back"—I check my phone—"in a couple of hours. That gives us plenty of time."

"Holy Mary, soap, here I come!"

I head up the porch stairs with Baldwin skipping behind me. Lay my violin down gently and fish for my keys in my backpack. My hat is crushed. My baseball bat is still in my scabbard.

I open the three locks and twist the knob, but the door doesn't open.

"Huh. I'm so tired I can't think straight." I try again slowly. I shake the door. Kick it.

"Honey. Verdad! Neighbors. They'll call the cops on us."

"Call the cops on us? On me? This is my freakin house!"

"Do you have anything on you to prove that?"

"I don't have to prove I live here!" If I do, I'm screwed. What would I do if a cop pulled up? Brown and black people do not fare well on porches outside locked doors. Fuck!!!!

"Oh shit. I know what it is. My moms used the door stick. But wait . . ."

"That means she is inside, honey. What's her car look like?"

"It's a Toyota Camry." I run my fingers through my hair and scan the street. Yup. "That's her car in front of our neighbor's house. Right across the street." It didn't occur to me to look.

"Ma!" I pound on the door. I scope the curtains to see if there's an eyeball peeking through them. "Open the damn door!"

Nothing. No rustle of the curtain. No eyeball. "Aren't you even gonna yell at me?"

All I hear is a delivery truck. A car door slam. An engine warming up. "Are you kidding me, Ma? It's like that?"

"Let's go." Baldwin grabs my violin case and drags my backpack down the steps. "C'mon!"

I grab the bat. If God don't open the door for you, a baseball bat could surely bust open a window. "So that's it, Ma? Bye Felicia?" Swing batta batta sw—

Baldwin launches themself forward and grabs the bat. "Verdad, are you fucking crazy? Jail is just, just, yucky!"

"Jail? No, no, no. I'm going to college, not jail. This is not my life!"

"Please." Baldwin begs with sugar on top. They crawl to the

top step. Lower their head and stretch their hands out toward me, eyes pleading. "Please give me the bat."

I huff, I puff, but I hand it over. Hands in my pockets, I crumple, lean against the locked door. I feel a gum wrapper, lint . . . "When do we get to be done changing? To be butterflies?"

"Don't know." Baldwin shoe gazes. Lifts their head. "Thing is, Verdad, maybe it isn't us who is changing. Maybe we're just more ourselves. Less of everybody else. And maybe the people we thought we knew are less the selves we thought they were."

"What?"

"I've eaten only a pork bun and a bag of Mickey D's I scooped out the trash in the past two days. I don't know what I'm saying."

I am so damn tired. "Fuck! What am I supposed to do?" I dig deep into my pocket. Thirty crumpled dollars is all I have left to my name. I've got no messages from Mami on my phone. Is she going to cut my service? My stomach is angry. I've never been hungry for more than thirty seconds in my life before my mother and an armada of tías swooped in, armed with pots, pans, and secret recipes to slay the beast. And I want to change my panties!

"My moms is mad. That's all. This is temporary."

"I hope so." Baldwin risks it and grabs my wrists. Tugs and tugs and tugs, leading me forward. Down the porch steps.

I climb into to the car. "Ugh!" I slam my head against the passenger seat.

"Damn. I was so excited about that shower." They put the car in gear and pull out. "So, not to interrupt the drama currently in progress, but I have a few things to do. You could come. Or I could try to find Danny."

Find Danny and do what? I mean I'm gross. Even if I know Danny is gross, I don't want him to see me gross. "Maybe I can go to school?"

Baldwin's glasses rise with his eyebrows.

I sneak a glimpse myself in the side mirror. Yup. I look that bad. I get it now. Why the Underdogs were skipping school. So where can I go? Tía Sujei's? I could easily find her office at the college. Then what? Sujei might take me in but she'd tell the entire East Coast my business. Am I willing to pay that kind of rent? My privacy in exchange for a place to stay? Is there an alternative?

Then it comes to me.

"Baldwin. Take a left."

"Why, Cinder-ella? That's the interstate."

"We're going to the suburbs. Time to pay my papi a visit."

17

I can't tell if it takes us just ten minutes to get there because of Baldwin's driving or because my father and his family really live only ten minutes away. It's not the smallest house on the block, maybe twenty-five hundred square feet, but most of the houses tower over his. The mansion my mother said my dad was living in has two stories, a porch and a yard. Fancy. Only his mansion needs a paint job. A piece of aluminum siding is rattling in the wind, threatening to fall off.

"I'd offer to walk you in, but that will probably cause more problems than it will help."

"Thank you." I look at Baldwin. Squeeze their hand. "Raincheck on that shower, okay?" They squeeze back.

Baldwin leaves and I'm left to walk up three steps that feel like three hundred. The spin of the earth is no longer undetectable, and I am dizzied. I know for the first time that the ground I've stood on has never been still.

I glance to my right and notice a pink bike leaning against a small tree. My dad left while I was learning to ride. Fun fact: My moms didn't have time to finish the lessons and I still can't ride a freakin bike.

I skip back down the steps and run to the park across the street to center myself. Climb to the top of monkey bars.

When I think about my father's presence instead of his absence, all I can remember is kindness. My mother is the one who rushed me through everything. My dad is the one who took time to explain. My mother expected me to use all my time productively. My dad once opened the window and we both climbed out to play in the yard. My mother was so pissed when she locked us out, and we shrugged our shoulders and got Chinese for dinner. Perhaps that was foreshadowing.

We've been strangers to each other for so long. Will he even recognize me? I don't recognize me.

No, that's not true. These last few days have been a wild experiment, but there's still a control. That is the part of me that will always be me and doesn't give a shit what body it's in, hetero or homo.

Damn, I hate the word *homo.* I hate the word *gay*. It's impossible not to when all I have ever heard *gay* used for is an insult.

Queer. That's better. Yes. I am queer! Queer is a magical word.

Blanca: Took you long enough.

So who am I? What is this body? Just packaging? A container? Because the only thing that matters in love is the heart, the brain, the soul.

Which gives me a bigger headache. Because isn't that what religion teaches? The body is just a shell. A vehicle. So who cares what's under the hood? Or who's sticking what in your hood. (Snort laugh.) But all of sudden when it's about queer people, the body matters?

Are these my real thoughts, or am I making excuses to do what I know is wrong?

I scan the park, the mothers and fathers pushing strollers, kissing scraped knees.

The wind blows my hair loose. Normally each asymmetrical imperfection of every strand would demand to be cut, pulled, or braided. But today my hair is a flag. Every thought a lyric to an anthem of me.

I grab my pen and make a list on my leg where there is still space left to write. Things I am: A girl. A Boricua. A fucking genius. A seer. A mystic. An insomniac. An Underdog? An astroNOT. Queer. Pan like Baldwin said?

Things I am not: a bad person. A good person can make mistakes that hurt other people sometimes.

Like I did with Nelly.

A bad person doesn't give a shit. I give a shit.

I climb down from the monkey bars and check the group message. Nelly is still on it. I message her privately, ask her if we can meet.

I cross the street to my dad's house. I reach to ring the bell. The door flings open. "Lo sabía!" my dad crows, holding his cell away from his ear.

My dad with the hair that's all salt and pepper, except for his mustache. Aside from the gray he looks just like that old family photo, the only one of the three of us who's barely aged.

My dad waves me into the foyer and motions for me to kick off my shoes. He's back on the phone talking in English, which means he's talking to my mother. Behind him, his wife holds a stack of towels. Beside her stands my replacement, the girl who gets to sit down to dinner with my father every night, a beautiful girl with pink lips, pinker cheeks, black hair, blacker eyes, a mini-me of his wife. A girl who needs my tuition for violin.

"So that's Verdad?" she says to her mom like I'm not

standing there, throwing me shade.

"Guess I don't need no introduction," I say to her. "So that's her?" I say to my dad. My dad nods, holding the phone away from his ear, my mother screaming on the other end: *Put her ass on the phone!*

"I heard that." I hold out my hand. It's going down.

"Fair warning, mija—"

"Don't mija me." I beckon with my fingertips. "Bring it."

My dad hands me the phone.

"You locked me out the house?" I say.

"She could have been murdered, raped, or worse!" says another voice.

"Wait. Sujei?" Conference call? And there's a "worse"?

"She disobeyed the rules of my house, Sujei."

"You don't put rules in front of what is right."

"Oh, Sujei, so we're gonna be all righteous now. When Ma took all my shit—"

"Hey."

"And threw it in the street, did you stop her?"

"Hello—"

"I wasn't down with that. But what did you expect me to do? I was young. And because of that you of all people should know better than to do that to your own—"

I get yelly. "HEY!"

"You get your ass back home, right now. How much is that now? Two days of school? Or more? What else don't I know?"

"You're not even giving her a chance to speak her—"

"What, so she could tell me what I already know, Sujei? She thinks she knows everything! She thinks!"

"That's right, she does think," I say, particularly freakin brave on the other side of a phone. "For my damn self. You can't tell me who to be. You think you know, but you don't."

My dad slaps his forehead and paces.

His wife Simone: "Que mejor que no ven aquí—"

"What?" my mother roars. This would be the part in the comic where she grows one hundred feet tall and her clothes rip off. "What did my daughter just say to me?"

"She said," Sujei says, chewing gum, I can tell, "you can't be telling her—"

"Cállate, Sujei! I know what she said!"

"You do? Because it's funny. You always say you want her to surpass you. But that only works if you two are in different lanes. Can you see yourself? You're chasing behind, pushing her to the finish line you never got to. She needs her own lane, stupido!"

"Oh, so you think you can call me stupid because you a big-ass *profesor*!"

"Big ass?"

"Holy shit, should I just hang up? Because I'm am obviously not in this conversation."

My dad waving frantically: "Por favor, no cuelgue en su, please!"

"You wouldn't dare," my mother warns.

I wouldn't. My mother put me in this world, and I know she could take my culo out. "No. But. But Mami. What is home? What exactly are you expecting of me?"

"What is home? Home is the place I bust my ass paying for. Like your clothes. Your food."

"I can't ever thank you enough for doing that. I love you, Mami. But that's not home. That's a place. A home is where you are loved."

"What kind of bullshit is that? Me working two jobs

doesn't show that?"

"It does. It does, but . . ." my hand drops at my side.

Sujei: "I got to go to the bathroom."

My dad takes a step closer to me. "She won't get that, Verdad."

"Is that your father? What? *He* gets it? You think he's 'home'?"

Flush. "Listen." Pants zip. "What we have here is a failure to communicate. What we need to do—"

My father grabs the phone. "What she needs, ladies, is to get a shower. Get some sleep."

Simone rescues me and motions me to follow her.

"Don't tell me what she needs," my mother shouts into my father's ear on the phone, loud enough for me to hear even though I'm halfway up the stairs.

My father holds the phone away from his ear: "Verdad! Don't go looking for bread at the hardware store. You hear me?"

Hear her? There are dudes at NASA picking her voice up on satellite. I still hear her voice while I turn on the shower. I have to set the stage. I prop up my cell and play some music. I stand in a puddle of my clothes and wait for the room to steam. Under the showerhead, I shed skins I've outgrown. Down the drain goes my pain and uncertainty. What I'm left with is the girl who had her first kiss. The girl who snuck out of her mother's house and spent the night in a cemetery.

My scar, my bullet hole, for once doesn't make me want to run away from everything but reminds me I'm still standing. I cry because of who isn't. My tears blend into the shower water and go down the drain.

I wrap my head in a towel, borrow the guest robe hanging on a hook, and leave the clouds of my tears behind me.

The room is crisp, clean, and pale blue. Pastel paintings of flowers hang on the walls. Ribboned vases are filled with silk flowers. Simone has removed the "show pillows" and replaced them with pillows I won't feel guilty drooling on. I swan dive under a layer of cool sheets and thick comforter. Dream of bakeries serving hammers. Hardware stores serving bread.

There's a knock. I sit up in a strange room in a strange bed. Somehow, I fell asleep in a department store showroom. My backpack and violin have been placed in an open closet with pink silk hangers. I check my phone. There's a text from Nelly, saying she can meet me this morning before school starts. At her new school.

Reality sinks its teeth. I keep reading and rereading the text. Does she get that I just want to talk, or did I accidentally challenge her to a fight?

My dad pokes his head into the room. "Hey, mija, want some breakfast?"

I scan the guest room, the scent diffuser and the box of Kleenex by the bed. The bathroom door is open, revealing hotel hand lotions on the sink. The same jealousy I felt about Danny's friends resurges. What guests have they had? Why is this a guest room and not my bedroom? But I swallow my bitterness because I have a vagenda today. And also because I smell pancakes and I'm freakin on the brink of starvation.

"Papi, I need your help."

"I don't have money, Verdad. No matter what your mom has been telling you."

"That's so gross, Papi. I wasn't gonna ask for money."

"I'm sorry. What do you need?"

"I have to make restitution."

"I think you better let your mom cool off for a couple of days or she's going to restitute your ass."

"No, not with her." I sit up and stretch my back. It feels like I've been sleeping in a cemetery or something. "With someone else. A girl. A girl I wronged."

I explain how I got Nelly into trouble and he agrees I have to apologize.

My dad says he'll drive me to meet her, on one condition. We both go to morning Mass—damn it. But first, family breakfast.

In the kitchen, Simone is working the sausage grill. My dad and I sit down to sausages wrapped in apple pancakes.

"Young lady." Simone turns her head in my direction. "Un tenedor?" She points to the unused fork next to my plate.

"Whhhdmopf. I mean it's like a sandwich." I think I just got syrup in my hair.

"So, Verdad," my dad says, neatly cutting his pancakes into rectangles, "how often do you eat alone?"

I roll my eyes. I'm under his roof for less than a full day and he's already opening a freakin FBI file on me. "That's insulting to Simone. Her pancakes are to blame." Simone actually smiles and flips a pancake. Wow, that was charming of me, even with three sausages in my mouth.

"That's my chair, Papi! She's sitting in my chair."

I look up. Ms. Monster High is standing there whipping around a wolf's tail pinned to her culo. I make a big show of checking my phone calendar: "No. Not Halloween. Still September. You auditioning for the circus?"

"Verdad." My dad wipes my mouth with a napkin, his eyes

darting between me and Ms. Monster High. "You know, you two have a lot in common. A flair for the dramatic. A love of costumes."

"Costumes?" Monster High stomps. "I'm not wearing a costume. Ick, she got my spot all sticky!"

Holy shit. I stand up. "I'm finished. Later."

This I hear as I head for the shower: "I can't believe you let a homeless person sit in my chair."

"Mija, hold up. Let Papi clean that up for you. She didn't know . . ."

Oops. I get lost. And accidentally take a shower in her bathroom by accident. Forget to flush. Use half a bottle of rose-scented foot lotion from an extensive collection and think, *Prisha and Sarah would love these glittery ones.* Before I step out of the princess's palace, I take note of the walls. It's like a parallel universe. Monster High has been in almost as many plays as me. I wonder how many of her shows my dad attended. I scan the photographs for evidence of treachery, and yup, I find it. There's my dad, handing her flowers. Just for that I filch her expensive-ass perfume—oh look at the tag: *Love, Papi.* Since I'll give it to Prisha and Sarah, it doesn't count as stealing. It's a donation. Also, it's a public service. Them girls stank.

I call shotgun. My dad is driving Veronica to school before he takes me on my odyssey. Monster High is sitting in the back seat smelling me, I know it. Tee-hee. I can feel her mal de ojo tryin to bore into my cranium, but I've faced off with my mother. This kid can't penetrate my head space.

I use my theater voice as Veronica slams the car door and heads toward the school: "Have a wonderful day! It's so wonderful to get to know my little sister!"

My dad raises an eyebrow at me as he drives off. "You are

just like your mom."

"Hardworking? Dedicated? Goal-oriented? Thank you." Yeah, I'm mad at my mother, but he better not talk smack about her.

"Relentless."

Time for morning Mass. Time to take all my belief in my ultimate goodness and douse it with hellfire.

We enter the foyer. I mechanically bless myself with holy water. A church no longer feels like a sacred space. I was baptized, I have taken communion, and I have been confirmed. Blanca and I always imagined a formal church wedding, her to Chadwick Boseman, me to whomever. I never imagined myself having to worry about whether I'd even be allowed to get married. I am no longer a VIP, one of God's chosen people, guaranteed a first-class ticket to paradise. I am officially on the highway to hell.

The pews are filled with the ancient ones, who are always at the very front of the church. It's funny the progression you make: in the way back as kids, way up close and personal the closer you get to the pearly gates. We recite the Our Father. Our Father Who Art in Heaven, you're just like my dad—always in my head, but never with me. Do you even want me here? Now that you know the real me? How long before my dad asks me to leave his house?

The priest is doing the homily now, something about sheep and straying from the path of righteousness. If only sheep knew their literary significance when they were being sheared for sweaters.

Time for communion. I'm kneeling and laying out my sins.

O my God I am heartily sorry for having offended you . . .

But my brain does not cooperate. I stare at the cross, at the being who is 100 percent human and 100 percent divine at the same time. The being who is at least three things at once in the Holy Trinity. So all of us sitting here accept transubstantiation, but we can't accept that a kid can be transgender?

Mass is over. My father signals me to kneel in the aisle before we go up front to get our confessions heard. We sit in the first pew outside the confessional and prepare our hearts with prayer. I squint at my dad, who's got his chin up, hands clasped, and eyes closed.

I close my eyes and think about what my mother would want me to confess. Anything to do with sex. Anything to do with Danny.

But, Jesus, why does sex have to be considered impure? I am sorry, but humanity would've been so much better off if Mother Mary just had sex. I sign the cross and shiver. I don't believe in so many things anymore, but belief in hell I can't shake.

My dad taps my shoulder. He's already been to the box and back. What did he confess? Has he confessed to betraying me and Mami? Has he been forgiven? Not by my ass, he hasn't.

I step out of the aisle, kneel, sign the cross, and head to the box. Part the curtain and step inside. "Good morning, Padre. It has been almost a year since my last confession."

"Good morning, child. What do you have to confess?"

"Honestly, I don't know. Should I be confessing my first kiss? That I like a boy? Who," I mumble, "isn't entirely a boy?"

"How old are you, my dear?"

"Fifteen."

"Ah. Well, let me ease your mind. Thinking is not a sin. To think makes you human. To be human makes you part of the divine. By the way, to be a teenager is not a sin either."

"It's not?"

"No. Jesus was a teenager. Imagine what was going through his head."

"That's pretty mind-blowing. But Jesus made all the right decisions."

"He did. But that doesn't mean he wasn't tempted. And don't forget he had Mary and Joseph. Who is helping you make your decisions?"

"Right now? My best friend is MIA. My mother and I aren't on speaking terms. My dad and I barely know each other. Right now—me, myself, and I."

"Can you think of any decisions me, myself, and I made that maybe weren't the best?"

I think of Danny. Wanting Danny was instantaneous. But being with Danny is a decision. He's one of the best decisions I ever made. Sorry, not sorry, Padre.

But what is glaring, what rises to the surface like a body formerly tied down with a rock—what I did to Nelly. Or didn't do. I went after Nelly in class because she made me uncomfortable, and then I threw her under the bus in Ms. Perez's office to save my own hide. "Yes. I was a chickenshit when I shouldn't have been. And I'm sorry."

"Then I absolve you in the name of the Father, the Son, and the Holy Spirit. Recite three Hail Mary's and one Our Father and think about how you can make better decisions in the future. But also, remember you are not alone. No. Matter. What. God loves you. And I suspect your parents love you more than you know."

"Love and acceptance are two different things." People think they know what love is. They confuse it with conformity. "Peace, Padre." I step out of the confessional.

18

"This is Our Lady of Angels!" my dad exclaims, pulling to the curb in front of Nelly's school. "God works in mysterious ways. This is where we want to send Veronica."

"Yeah? I heard it was top notch." I slouch into my seat and fold my arms. "They do violin lessons here and everything."

"Verdad," my dad says, rolling to a stop, "we need to talk about that."

"Yes." I unbuckle. "Let's talk about God's mysterious ways—and yours too—at dinner."

"Damn, the mouth on you."

I visor my eyes. "There she is!" One of three black/brown kids out of dozens and dozens of white girls, standing by the door.

My pulse picks up as I step out of the car. Nelly would be well within her rights to give me a fat lip. I assess the scene to verify if she's bringing any of her peeps with her. I hope I can talk things out with her, but I'm prepared for the worst. What I'm not prepared for is a cop pulling beside my dad.

Red and blue lights flash. The officer motions for my dad to roll down his window. "You have a student here, sir?"

"No, but—"

"Then you need to move along."

"My daughter." He motions with his head. "She has a

friend here."

I nod, turn on the video of my cell, and walk over. "Hi, officer. How do you know my dad doesn't have a kid here?"

"Quiet, Verdad," my dad commands, all patriarchal. "Officer, I can just circle the block till she's done."

"Yeah. That makes us nervous. Someone circling the block of a girl's high school."

Seriously? What's he trying to say? I scan the double-parked streets. Dodge Caravans, check. Jeep Wranglers and BMWs, check. A 2013 Subaru with bullet holes in it—not so much. There was a drive-by near my dad's work and he figured people would be less likely to try to steal his car if he just left it like that.

"Sup, Maquina."

I whip around. "Nelly!"

The officer stares at Nelly. She pulls a lanyard out of her blouse and holds up her ID. What. The. Fuck. He finally rolls up his window. He lets the car idle, talking into his radio.

I button up the oversized jacket I'm borrowing from Simone. It's cold. "Jesus," I say, nodding toward the police car.

"Yeah," Nelly says, leaning on her hip, "just imagine what it was like for my dad when he first tried to pick me up—and the second time. And the third. Sucks, doesn't it?"

I nod. My dad takes a call. The officer finally finds something better to do like IDK, his job?

"You know what else sucks?" I stuff my hands in my pockets. "I do." I look her straight in the eye. "I'm sorry."

"Sorry for what exactly?" She looks at my eyes like she's picking a lock. "'Cause you had nothing to do with why I am here."

"I don't?" What the—?

"I'm here because a security guard decided to act like a

police officer and treat a school like a jail. Treat a kid like a criminal. To be honest, I've been a thorn in the administration's side for a while. They been looking for an excuse to get rid of me. Whatever you said or didn't say in Ms. Perez's office wasn't gonna make a difference."

Wow. This from Nelly, who I really thought was gonna knock me out. Why? Because I didn't expect a black girl to be able to engage in civilized dispute. Why am I so messed up?

I look past the gates to the literal ivory tower behind it. "Well, I'm still sorry. I'm sorry I didn't act differently in class. I've replayed those moments so many times. Seems that's something I do a lot."

Nelly pulls up her hood. "How do you see it playing out?"

"I shouldn't have got up in your face, first off. And when everything was going down, I should have stood up. For you. I should've at least texted you to see if you were all right afterward. So that's why I'm sorry."

"I accept your apology." She tucks her lanyard back in her blouse. "The world still owes me one."

"No question. What now, though? The school. Brooke and Annie are still there. That's messed up."

"Annie and me don't have no bad blood anymore. She actually showed up for the rally."

I blush in embarrassment.

"Anyway, my sisters gave me some advice about how to fight the powers that be. We're suing the school district. Admin thinks they plucked me out, but I'm gonna make sure and leave a scar. And thanks to my girl Frida's protest, I got a news interview lined up. I'm getting the chance to really do somethin. I'm not gonna blow it."

"Words to power," I say.

"So." Nelly checks her cell. "We done?"

I nod. "Guess so. See you." I head back to my dad's car. Then turn around. "Nelly!"

"Yo."

"One more thing. Those words you said to me—*Dónde está tu abuela?* Why'd you say that? I looked it up—there's that song about people hiding blackness, sending their black grandmas to the kitchen when company comes, but . . ."

"You Puerto Rican. Which makes you Taino Indian like my aunty. Taino is Indian. Black. Act like it."

"Nelly, how'd you get so—so—"

"Woke? I got two sisters in college."

"Wow. They made it."

"Yep. With scholarships."

"Damn!" I notice that Nelly's hoodie is from Notre Dame. I point at the emblem. "Is that where you going?"

"I don't know. Whoever it is got to woo me." She rubs her thumb and pointer together.

We laugh.

"What about you?"

What about me? That is the question. "Maybe everything needs to stop being about me for a while."

She nods. "Well, good luck figuring it out. I do worry about you."

I'm taken like far aback. "Why?"

"You book smart. But emotionally—challenged. I'll pray for you, my child." Nelly starts walking backwards. "And you're welcome, but it's not my job to change your world. It's my job to change mine. Bye, Maquina."

"Verdad. It's Verdad."

"Ain't that the truth."

19

"You do what you needed to do?" my dad asks as I climb into the passenger seat. "Do right by that girl?"

I close the door and buckle up. "I'm working on it."

"Then I'm proud of you, mija."

I text Danny on the drive to school. He is waiting for me at the top of the steps. I bundle up, pulling on my hood, but toss the gloves Simone loaned me. My dad waves and I know he'll wait in the car until I walk inside the building.

Danny grabs for my hand and stops short. "Can I?"

"Hold my hand? Aren't we a little past that?"

"No, I mean." He nods at all the kids trotting past us. "Here."

I hold his hand, pull him to me, and take a breath. Hug him. We hold on too hard and too long. His clothes and hair waft bonfires, minerals, and leaves. He shivers because of course, he doesn't have a coat. I should've brought him the gloves, damn it. Our lips meet the way a stone and stick do when making fire.

We come up for oxygen and I realize we've just gone viral. Pics have been snapped.

"Can you walk me to the office?" I say, warming Danny's hands with mine. "I feel like I'm walking the plank."

"It's just a tardy slip, babe."

He called me babe. Can I call him babe back?

"I know, babe." He doesn't blink! "It's just—tardies, detentions, skipping school . . . That didn't used to be me."

"Yeah. Didn't used to be any of us either."

I'm slightly freakin irked. "Right." We're in the office at the computer terminal, signing in. "Beyond that, it's been rough. I'm sure Baldwin got you up to speed?"

He nods but honestly looks bored.

I try again: "Baldwin told you I got thrown out, right?"

Another nod. "Is your dad a perv? Sarah's dad is. So going home—not an option for her. Or any of us. The rest of us."

"Do you always have to frame things that way? Us and them? With me being them?"

"It's just that I'm protective of the Underdogs. They're my family."

"And I'm not?"

"Gross!"

I snort-laugh despite myself. Secretly calculate that this must mean he and Prisha did not hook up. "Seriously, Danny. What am I then?"

"Oh, you're doing the girl thing. Making me define our relationship."

"Ew." And eh?

He turns away from the computer terminal with a sigh. "Look, the night in the graveyard—was intense. You didn't just write on my skin. You wrote on my heart. But you also offended the shit out of me. You were so oblivious."

"Like you are to my feelings right now," I point out. "This is not a contest. I need to be who I am and feel what I need to feel, every bit as much as you do."

My words are like a visible smack across his face. He's

probably had to say the same thing so many times.

"You're the last person in the world I want to fight with," I tell him.

"Same." He pulls me to him. "Did we just get real?"

"Completely." I bury my face in his chest. "I want to kiss you." I look up. "And punch you in the face."

He pulls away and motions toward the secretary, who's just come out of the back offices and seems to want my attention. "I guess you can make that determination later?"

"Miss Reyna. Can you sit and wait here for a minute?"

What now?

Danny heads to class. Like ten years later: "Miss Reyna. Head on to the back. Ms. Quinones, the counselor. She's been hounding me for days to get ahold of you. Third door on the left."

I instantly plot my escape.

But Ms. Quinones, who's apparently been stalking me, heads me off at the pass. She's pretty but has a hard look in her eye. Like she's been there, done that, heard it all. "Ten minutes, Verdad. That's all I ask. I've got Malta. I've got Takis."

I roll my eyes.

But the Takis are "fuego" and the Malta is ice cold. Blanca grabs a Taki and starts touching everything on Ms. Quinones' desk. Just like that, Blanca is back in my life. The prodigal BFF has returned.

Ms.Q's office is lit dim like we're about to have a séance. Stuffed with fat, fluffy aqua pillows, bean bag arm chairs, and a cushy couch, I suddenly feel the urge for a nap.

I plop down on the couch with the Malta I've accepted. Like Goldilocks, Blanca tries every chair. She could never resist a spinny one. Once we raced them down a hallway and almost fell down a flight of stairs. Her idea, of course. "So why am I here?"

"You're here"—she stands up and grabs a file from her desk—"because I want to apologize." Planting herself beside me on the couch, I notice old scars on her arms. Holy shit. She was a cutter. "I'm sorry we are meeting today and not the first day you set foot in this school. I don't know if you're aware there's a shortage of counselors in the entire district. But there should be a counselor for every grade in every school so every kid—"

I am, of course, not listening. I'm staring at the cuts. She's ignoring me stare. Will there be a day when I'm not pulling my hair out?

"I'm sorry for what happened to you and your friends last year."

I can't see Blanca, she is spinning so fast. Just a blur. My hand instinctively grabs my hair like a skydiver grabbing the rip cord. "You know about that."

"Yes. Hard to forget a mass shooting happening so close to home."

I shake my head. It was a blip in the news, even right after it happened. The only reason it got any attention at all was because of the shooter. What brought him to make this decision. *He* had a family. Held down a job. Yeah and *he* was white. "Tomorrow is the anniversary."

She places a silky balloon in my right hand. The fingers on my right hand enjoy kneading the flour inside.

"That word is strange. Anniversary. Anniversaries should be for weddings. Not mass shootings. What is that even supposed to mean?" The fingers on my left hand comb my hair. Get stuck in tangles. Tear them out.

"Doesn't matter what it's *supposed* to mean." Ms. Q places another silky balloon in my left hand. "Just matters what it means to you."

"It means every year I have to remember." Flour. Is. Everywhere. "Whether I want to or not." The bullet that ripped a hole in my thigh and a hole in my life, through which Bambi and Fernando left and didn't return. A hole in which Blanca lingered that night after the shooting, suspended between two worlds, and has ever since. "Every time I think about it, I relive it, it's like"—the shooter, whom I will never dignify aloud with a name—"he pulls the trigger. Takes us all out again."

"He doesn't deserve to have that kind of power, Verdad. Does he?"

"Fuck no. And it's not . . ." My chest is tight. "It's not how I want to remember Blanca."

"I checked with your middle school. They don't have anything planned but—"

"Nope. They don't. There's shootings in my old hood all the time. I wish we could leave an empty desk for every kid who dies that way." I can't stop the tears, the gasps for air. The sobs. "Blanca's abuela died a few months ago. Blanca had no one else. I'm the only one who really remembers her now. The way she should be remembered."

"How should she be remembered?"

I am covered in flour and tears and my scalp burns. I rub my hands over a trash can, freeing my fingers of bloody hair. "Ten minutes is up, Ms. Q."

"It is. But your time here never really runs out. Will you come see me again?"

"I can't make any promises." Promises are dangerous. Maybe

I don't break a promise to you. But someone with a gun does it for me.

"I can," says Ms. Quinones. "I will be here whenever you need me."

****

I autopilot through class. I don't know if Nelly communicated with her girls, but they're paying me no mind. A pic of me and Danny shows up on the group message right before lunch.

@ShutUpU2: I don't know how I feel.
@frodown: Who cares about how your dumb ass feels?
@ShutUpU2: It ain't sexy.
@frodown: Why do they have to be sexy for you, perv?
@Rican_Havok: It's disgusting.
@frodown: Calm down, Carlos
@Rican_Havok: Obscenity, Obscenity, Obscenity, that I will need therapy for, for the rest of my teenage years.
@frodown: Yr canceled

I turn my phone over. Man, it's just like Sujei said. I've now added a reputation as a "disgusting dyke" to the list of shit I have to deal with.

"Jesus, Verdad." Danny sits beside me. Right beside me, so our knees touch. "Your hair."

"I'm disgusting." I poke at my tray of who-the-hell-knows-what with a side of WTF. "This is disgusting." I fling a pea across the room. "Everything is disgusting."

Danny rubs what I know is flour from my cheek. "No.

None of that. You just need—"

"You." I stand up.

"Okay." He stands up.

"I want to go back to the cemetery, but I know Blanca isn't there."

"Okay."

"The theater. I have to go to the theater." My hands are shaking. "But I can't go alone."

"Uh . . . okay." He grabs my hand and cradles it.

****

Danny and I cut school and hop the bus. "I'm a delinquent dyke."

Danny nuzzles my ear. "That's a delinquent end table." He hugs me hard. "My delinquent end table. Shit, your skin is so cold. Are you okay?"

"I am trying so hard to be okay." But I am rocking in the familiar sea of anxiety. My throat is dry and my armpits are wet. I am freezing hot and burning cold. "But I'm not."

Danny holds up my chin. "Don't try to be anything when you're with me, okay?"

I nod and lay my head on his shoulder. Memory Lane has fast-forwarded past every place Blanca and I have ever been to every place we never would be. What Blanca planned for her quince became her funeral. The church was decorated in pink balloons, gauze, and ribbons. Blanca was dressed in her pink sequined dress, so poofy it didn't fit in the coffin. She looked like a doll in a box. A gift to be opened on Christmas, not buried on a cold, shitty day in September.

Blanca's abuela had her playlist on speaker. Our playlist.

Every song we ever danced to, karaoked, laughed to, cried to. Every song from the musicals we worked on. Basically the soundtrack to both our lives. Now songs I could never listen to again.

That wasn't even the worst of it.

"This. Our stop," I mumble.

I swear I get off the bus throwing up next to the same drunk. This time, though, somebody is holding my hair. Danny ties it into a sloppy bun.

"I got you." Danny rubs my back.

The worst part was I was supposed to get up and speak to honor Blanca. But all I did was stand there frozen and silent. Melt into tears.

I full-out hurl.

The drunk hands me his AA card. "You really need to get some help."

"Thank you."

"God bless you."

I spit into the gutter. "I can't do it." I sit on the sidewalk and sob.

Danny just sits there beside me. "So let's not do it."

I sob louder.

"I mean. Let's not you do it alone. I mean let's both of us do it!"

Through a waterfall of tears, I look into Danny's extremely confused and gorgeous eyes. And I can't help it. I laugh. "You have no fucking idea what is going on."

"No. I do not." He stands up. "But whatever it is. The thing. We should do this thing!"

I hug my knees and craugh hysterically. Get over myself and point across the street. "The theater. It's where Blanca died."

He looks across the street at the theater. Which was the 'Heater. And is now the 'Eater.

Blanca: Laugh. It's funny.

Me (laughing): So you're back to take me down the black hole.

Blanca: It's not a black hole. It's a cave, stupid. Don't you know nothing about philosophy and shit?

"So we need to go to the theater. To . . .?"

"To . . . I don't know. To—to make it not just the place where she died. Where part of me died."

Danny nods. Basically carries me and his skateboard up the street. Across it. Right in front of the theater.

Fuck, I get the whole creation myth thing where rivers and lakes are created from tears. And snot. Danny dabs at my wet nose with his sleeve, I wish I were crying like somebody from the movies, but I sound ugly and weird, like a congested raccoon. At some point, some viejita hands us a pack of Kleenex. I run through the Kleenex, surrounding us with bunched-up snot wads. I soak Danny's shirt. My stomach hurts like I did sit-ups.

I finally look up. And as if I'm looking through a window of rain, I see it. The booth where the pervert handed us our tickets. The cisgender misogynist porn (Baldwin would be so proud) is weathered beyond recognition.

"Do you think the booth is unlocked?"

Danny throws me an impish look and holds out his hand.

The booth is locked, but Danny has acquired a few talents living on the street and we're inside in minutes.

"What happens now?"

I look into his eyes. "You know what's supposed to be happening now? I am supposed to be ripping out my hair. I'm supposed to be in pain. That's what the shooter wanted—to punish us. He thought all those Indian kids were Muslims, terrorists. The rest of us—he called us immigrants, dirty Mexicans."

"I'm sorry."

"You know what else the shooter wanted? Not just to kill us. To destroy our souls. To make it so whoever survived would only see hate and blood and horror. I want Blanca and Bambi and Fernando back every minute of every day. I don't think the pain will never leave me. But the ugliness—it doesn't belong to me. To us. Blanca was beautiful and good. I need the ugliness to leave me."

Danny dries my tears with his sleeve.

"And it does with you. I'm happy I'm with you. Every minute I'm happy, I stop a bullet. From killing my soul."

"You make me happy too."

My mouth is salty and hot when we kiss. We're kissing in a broke-down ticket booth, not sucked back into the vortex of time, but propelled in the now of each other's bodies.

Between kisses: "You taste mmm."

"There's more where that came from, V. Yeah, I went to a shelter and showered."

I laugh. I want to touch him, all the parts that make him the person he is. I'm not afraid of duality. I want his halves, his thirds, the whole fucking pie. But Danny stops me when I try to unbutton his shirt. "Not yet."

"Why?"

He kisses my fingers. "It's complicated." He looks away and mumbles, "Different than—what you're used to." His eyes meet mine. "If you . . ." He closes his button. "You wouldn't be touching *me*."

I lift his hand and kiss it. "Then show me how to touch you. PS, you're the only person I've ever touched. So . . ."

I like seeing Danny shy. He guides my hands and my lips and I learn him bit by bit. We take turns. I moan as Danny's cold hands slide under my shirt, goosebumping my skin, and it's like it's summer and I just dove into the pool for the first time. He makes my body feel tight and loose, warm and wet in all the right places. I let him shimmy off my jeans. Kiss my scar. When his hands slip inside my panties I feel a buildup, for the first time in months, of ecstasy, not pain.

After, we dress each other like dolls. I sit between his legs, and we're laughing. He's smoking a Newport and I'm smoking a pretend cigarette, because it was that good.

"This place"—I exhale fake smoke—"I want to do more."

"Really?" Danny unzips his pants.

"No! I mean yes! But no!"

Danny is cracking up. I smack him.

"Like, I mean—this theater is a tomb. I want to do something about it."

I look away as Danny googles the shooting.

"It's just been abandoned," he says, scrolling. "The previous owners went bankrupt. The city keeps it boarded up, but me and the crew have broken in before to escape the snow."

"What does it look like inside?"

"Cleaned out. Except for the chandelier. Too high up for anybody to get their hands on that."

In my mind I see an idea like a diamond from that chandelier. "Even before the shooting the theater wasn't a safe place. What if we made it one? What if it were a community center or something?" I tip my head back and kiss his chin. "Or a shelter just for teens. Both?"

"That's ambitious. I'm just happy I showered."

I turn and lie on top of him. "Me too."

20

I'm coming down from a major life high and the reality—that I'm still semihomeless, that my missing assignments are piling up, and that I can hear Monster High and my dad screaming on the front porch—makes me feel like I'm landing flat on my ass. For once, I just want to stick the damn landing.

Monster High is standing her ground in front of the flat screen. "Why doesn't she have to go?"

I open the door and enter the living room, stage right. "*She* is home. And go where?"

My dad is center stage sitting on an enormous armchair. Simone is knitting on the couch.

"To a church retreat." Monster High rolls her heavily made-up eyes. I mean, she looks good, but how can she blink? I start blinking for her, it annoys me so much.

Monster High throws her hands up in the air. "Instead of my drama club's party."

I plant myself on the freshly vacuumed carpet. "That does sound harsh, Papi."

"Verdad!" I get a *you're not helping* look. "We've been planning this for weeks. And we need this family time to reconnect—"

"Weeks, huh? My invitation must have gotten lost in the mail."

Simone throws my dad a *what did I tell you* look. I never knew knitting could be—loud.

Monster High: "You want to go?"

"Yeah *no.* Just sayin."

Simone, who I wish was meaner so I could hate her, says, "You are always welcome." She turns to my dad sitting across from her in that armchair like it's a throne.

"Veronica," my dad proclaims from his armchair, "Veronica, you will be going on retreat. Or you will not be going anywhere else, including drama club, for the rest of the year. Get your priorities straight—"

"Priorities, straight," I mutter. "That is interesting." I pause, surprised at their attention. "Why are priorities always straight?"

Simone smiles with her mouth, but her eyes throw me a look like, *Maybe I should lock up the silverware so she can't sell it for crack.* "Anyway. In this house, God first."

Monster High: "It's not fair that whenever I disagree, you make it about God!"

Me: "Good point!"

El Rey is displeased.

Simone: "This is an opportunity for us to work through some stuff, honey." And OMFG she starts rubbing her belly the way women do when . . . "The retreat might be a good place—to talk."

Monster High folds her arms. "Talk about what?"

"Whatever is going down is going down here." I fold my arms, joining in the protest.

Simone: "I'm pregnant."

Monster High: "Ew!"

I laugh. To my dad: "You're telling Ma." To Monster High: "Sucks, doesn't it?"

"Verdad!" My dad pounds the arm of his throne. The ice in his seltzer water jiggles. "It does not suck!"

El Rey is angry.

Me: "So when are you all leaving?"

My dad: "Tomorrow. The neighbors will be looking in on you. I expect a call from the school office indicating you are AT school, Verdad, before and after school. Then straight home." El Rey downs the seltzer water like a shot of brandy.

"There's that word *straight* again."

Simone asks me, "Have you been drinking?"

Ha! "Keep that sort of thing coming, Simone." Because I can't like her. My mother would kill my ass. "And no. Just drunk on life, I guess." My head is swimming, though. I want Danny to dive in my pool. There is no way I'm gonna be able to sleep tonight. Blanca got herself off all the time. I think I'm gonna have my first time with . . . myself—I snort-laugh—or implode.

I head to the guest room while the arguing continues over where the future kid will sleep. No way is it gonna be Monster High's room and so, obviously, it's gonna be this room. A few months from now the only space I'll have in the house is gonna transform into a pullout couch.

I fantasize about sneaking Danny into my room—and realize with a shiver that other than a pop-in from an eighty-year-old neighbor, I'll have the house to myself tomorrow night.

After school, Danny and I meet up by my locker. "I have something to show you." He slips his arms around my waist. "I don't want you to feel ambushed."

"What do you mean?" With just one comment, I feel like the whole day is going to avalanche. It was actually going fine—I've been catching up on assignments, nobody was giving me shit. But there's always a catch.

"I'm not making sense." He runs his fingers through his silky blond half-a-hair. I run my fingers over the shaved part of his head, my heart leaping that I have permission to touch him like this. "Can you just come with me to homeroom?"

"Homeroom? Now?" All I want to do is take Danny home to my room.

But I head upstairs. I don't like how quiet Danny is being or how his palm is sweaty. My senses go on high alert. Through the glass window of the door, I can see my whole homeroom sitting in there. Frida, Rudy, and Penelope are talking with Ms. Moore at the board.

Everything gets quiet, and being that my homeroom has not been thrilled with me of late, I am wondering if I should run.

Frida opens the door. Straightens the flower in her hair. "Verdad, please, please come in."

She's calling me by my name. "What is going on?"

Danny nudges me over the threshold, steps behind me, and closes the door. He lays his head on my shoulder and hugs me from behind.

I scan the room past Frida. The first thing I see is the desk. Blanca's desk. "Ay Dios Mio." Her whole desk is painted with sky blue. Intertwined around the back, the arms, and the legs of the chair are paper flowers.

"They didn't know," Penelope says. "The other day Rudy was saying he thought maybe you'd lost somebody, and that's when I realized nobody here knew. Blanca and I weren't close, but I knew her. I was at her funeral. My hair was black then.

I couldn't imagine losing my best friend like that. I'm so sorry."

I cannot move. I stare out at the class—people who are enemies at worst, strangers at best.

"I talked to Danny to make sure I wasn't gonna make things worse for you. Then to Ms. Moore," says Penelope, "who talked to the counselor, who made sure we got the extra desk back in here."

I think of a heartbeat. The clench, a closing in and off, a retreat against pain and hate. But the exhale, a full bloom, a proud opening up to love and everything that comes with it.

"I painted the desk," Boricua 1 says all proud, linking her arm through her friend's. "My girl Jessie did the paper flowers."

Jessie—Boricua 3, the one with all the shirts for Latinx metal bands like Tierra Santa. It's about time I learn people's real names.

Even with a gun, the shooter couldn't stop Blanca's heart. The love that she gave me is in the room right now.

"I had no idea that's why you were acting so cray," Rudy says, almost talking to himself. "I mean, I'm sorry."

Danny hugs me. Frida hugs me.

"Oh damn, I'mma cry!" Rudy tackles us, and we practically tip over. Everything's all warm and fuzzy until Rudy realizes he's hugging Danny.

"Sorry, dude. I don't hug on dudes."

Danny rolls his eyes before turning away. At least Rudy acknowledged that Danny's a guy—that's progress, I guess.

"Verdad, tomorrow evening, in honor of the anniversary of Blanca's death," Frida says, wiping tears on a handkerchief, "we would like to hold a vigil. I know we're late, but can we consider it POC Standard Time?" Every POC laughs. Nobody else does and nobody else should.

I nod. I have no words.

"We're thinking four o'clock in front of the theater," Frida goes on.

"Christina already got Perla's to donate a whole bunch of teddy bears," Boricua 1 says, all proud, beaming at Boricua 4 with the dope cat eyes.

Thank you, I mouth at them—Gloria and Christina, I'm pretty sure.

"And," Boricua 1 aka Gloria continues, "my Tío William is going to donate all these flowers from his shop. We know what you're going through. I lost my cousin to guns."

Everybody starts talking about all the godforsaken miserable shit they and their families have been through, and I start to feel like I belong less than ever.

"Are you okay?" Danny asks, brushing away a tear from my cheek.

"All these people and all their baggage," I whisper back. "The weight. And I'm all wrapped up in myself."

"I'm here to remind you of what you said to me. You need to feel what you need to feel.

"All of us get wrapped up in ourselves. You have to. You have to heal. The baggage never goes away. But that doesn't mean other people can't help carry it. Or that you can't help carry other people's. You've helped me carry mine."

I lean on Danny's chest. Pause a beat and then take a deep breath. "Listen. Everybody." Nobody listens. "Hey! Don't make Maquina get to eighty percent."

The class simmers down and laughs. Faces me.

"Thank you. But I don't deserve this."

Rudy, folding his arms and leaning back: "You don't, but—ouch!" Frida pinches Rudy's arm.

"Oh my God, Rudy!" Frida scolds Rudy, then turns to me: "Verdad, Blanca didn't deserve what happened to her. But she deserves to be remembered. Maybe one day you can tell us about her, and then we'll remember her too."

Immortality.

"That's what I want for her," I find myself saying. "And for Fernando and Bambi, and the others too. For them to be remembered. And for the people who loved them to carry on. Like the theater. I was thinking, what if we could do something with it? It's sitting there empty right now. If we could raise the money, get the right people to sign off on it, maybe we could turn it into someplace where kids can go to be safe. To just be themselves."

"Hold up," Frida says, fingers flying on her phone, "we got to get Nelly in on this."

Nelly waves to everyone as Frida holds up the phone. "Well, I guess they couldn't kick me out completely, now could they?"

There is major applause. Ms. Moore finds something else to do at her desk. Frida catches Nelly up on the vigil and on my idea for the movie theater.

"So, here's what I'm thinking," Nelly says after a minute. "I'm supposed to have an interview with the local news tomorrow. Film crew and everything. I'll ask for them to meet in front of the theater, right as the vigil's starting. That could be a chance to plug this idea to the public. We could ask for community support to renovate the theater, organize a cleanup."

"Man, cleanup? That place was cleaned *out*. My cousin"—Rudy pauses—"I mean I heard some dude even made off with that big-ass popcorn maker on foot."

"Some dude, huh?" Frida gives him side-eye and a neck roll. "Anyway, Verdad, text me privately. My mom is on the board of advisors for Revitalize, Not Gentrify. I could talk to her about this."

Ms. Moore clears her throat, her tappy shoes bringing us back to reality. "If everyone is going to catch their bus, I'm afraid it's time to go." To me: "Verdad, I'll be there tomorrow too."

Danny comes over after school, but we are both greeted by my dad's neighbor, who looks like Grandma Moses and is actually waiting for us with milk and freakin cookies. She even sits with us at the table like we're eight. I down my milk like a shot of vodka and bitterly eat the chewy goodness.

Danny holds up a cookie like a judge from *Sugar Rush.* "These are good, ma'am. I mean really. The texture is spot on. I can taste the brown sugar and toffee, but you managed not to make them oversweet."

"You sound like a baker yourself."

"Sort of." Danny reaches for another cookie. "My dad. He owns his own shop. Every morning we had fresh homemade bread on the table."

She nods. She's picked up on the tone in *had.*

"Our pies had fresh berries we picked from our own property."

Property? Was he a rich boy? Ay Dios, my default is to stereotype. I need, like, a mind cleanse. A freakin exorcist.

"I head the church baking committee," Neighbor Lady says. "We make pies and cakes for charity. Maybe you can stop by sometime and give us the benefit of your expertise."

I send a volt of psychic vibes to Danny: *Don't. Do. It!* First it's pie. Then it's communion. Then barbecue. Of your soul.

"Thank you. Maybe. I got a whole crew who would love to be tasters."

"Oh, that would be delightful!"

What would be delightful is the look on her face when Jane and Baldwin are hand-feeding each other pie. Less delightful? The look on my dad's face.

How will he react when he sees Danny? I don't think I can take another rejection right now. Estrangement is like a little death. I already feel like I lost my dad, not so much after the divorce, but after Monster High was born. And now another sibling is coming. Maybe by coming out I'm just going to give my dad yet another excuse to stay away.

"Thank you for the cookies," I say to Neighbor Lady. "I'm about to bust out some prayers, then do my homework, so—"

"Oh! Well. I guess—"

"We better head out," Danny says. "I'll walk you out, ma'am."

What? No! His ass better be coming back.

I stuff another cookie into my face. I'm in a mood.

Two cookies later, I hear a scratch at the back door.

"Took you long enough. Did she convert you?"

Danny closes the door behind him. "If my dad couldn't do it with his threats, she's not gonna do it with baked goods. Even her baked goods." He licks his thumb. "They're extraordinary."

I wrap my arms around Danny. He wipes cookie crumbs off my mouth. Kisses them off. "I'm sorry about your dad."

"He can't threaten me now. I don't believe in God anymore. He has nothing left he can take from me."

"Don't let him take God from you." I surprise myself with that comment. Shut up, Ma.

"Huh?"

I wince. "I'm just saying—God loves you. God loves us. Don't know who the hell everybody thinks they're praying to."

Blanca: You're going to give him a headache. Just kiss him.

I do. Danny's tasting my brown sugar and toffee tongue. He walks me toward the kitchen table and sits me on it. If Neighbor Lady is on surveillance, she's getting the R-rated version of me and my purple push-up bra.

"I do have a bed, you know. And considering I don't know how much longer I'll have one—"

"We might as well take advantage."

We take advantage.

"I need a smoke so bad." Danny sits up. "What do you think your dad is gonna do? Since you said you weren't sure how much longer he'll let you stay."

I shrug. "I don't know. My dad opened the door. But he didn't realize what he was letting in."

"No kidding. But"—he lays some major puppy dog eyes on me—"now that you've got the door open, might I make a suggestion?"

I raise an eyebrow.

"Baldwin mentioned an offer you made. The shower . . ."

"Oh, yeah. I forgot about that." I remember what I said to Nelly, what I felt in homeroom when I heard bits and pieces of other people's heartbreak. *Maybe everything needs to stop being about me for a while.* "You know what. Let's have the whole crew over. We'll cook a big dinner. You can bake cookies. It'll be dope."

"Really! Oh God, after I shower and steal some more of your toothpaste, I'm going to kiss you so hard!"

"I can't wait."

21

I make sure to lock Veronica's room so it's off limits. Text my dad that I'll be having a few girlfriends over. Unlock the door. "Sup, Underdogs." They are all barefoot. This time on purpose. Prisha, crouched on the porch straightening a row of sorry-looking shoes, stands up and smiles. A carnation is pinned to her billowy teal blouse.

Prisha hands me flowers. "For you. As a thank you."

I hold the slightly crispy brown-edged petunias. "They are—*For Henry? May he always be rem*—"

Baldwin snatches the plastic card holder out of the bouquet.

Jane points at my T-shirt and jeans. "That outfit looks better every time you wear it, honey." She and her enormous feet stomp into the house like a T-Rex.

"Yours too. No one could work overalls better than you!" I rewashed the clothes I last wore the night my mother threw me out. I don't expect Simone to buy me new clothes, my dad hasn't had time to offer yet, and I sure as hell couldn't borrow anything from Veronica.

"Oh." Jane winces, scoping out the area. "It's so Better Homes and Gardens in here."

Baldwin, who appears to be wearing an octogenarian's glasses, consoles Jane and rubs her back. "Breathe, honey." To me: "Jane is a bear. We love the bear. But she will break all your shit. The harder she tries to be careful, the more she breaks."

"I'm in that genre too. It's all good. Come on into the kitchen. I've laid out some ingredients on the island. I thought I'd play head chef and you all could be sous chefs. And Danny will be Rachael Ray."

Jane claps and faces Baldwin. "There is an island in her kitchen. Hold my hand."

Danny holds my hand. Each of my fingers feels like a note being perfectly played. I am a charmed snake and want to wrap around Danny's whole body. I smile like an idiot.

We move slowly like we are kids crossing a street. Danny walking forward, me backwards, our fingers intertwined.

"Oh God. It's a refrigerator." Baldwin releases Jane and flings open the fridge door. "And look! There are eggs in an egg compartment. Fruits and veggies in the fruit and veggie drawers. Holy. Jesus. There are Rice Krispie Treats in here. Homemade! Please tell me there is Kool-Aid . . . Yes!"

"Don't be rude," Prisha scolds, tugging on Baldwin's ear. "You didn't even offer her the food we brought. Where is it?"

Baldwin stands up like a guilty dog and closes the fridge. Pulls a banana out of their pocket. "Here?"

Sarah smacks her forehead in disgust. "Really?!" Prisha folds her arms and frowns.

"I'm sorry. I did get the buns. But . . ."

I fill in the blanks. Baldwin ate the buns.

"You know what?" I reach out for the banana. It's warm, bruised, squishy. "This is . . . We could . . ." I bust out laughing. "No. We can't. It's dis-gross-ting." I grab it and toss it at Jane, who screams as she catches it. And tosses it to Baldwin. We are in circle formation playing hot potato with a warm banana.

"What are we going to do now?" Baldwin says, tossing. "We can't stop! Ha ha. Ha ha ha. We'll be jinxed."

"We have to eat it! Everybody stop!" Jane catches the banana and unpeels it. Takes a bite. Passes it to Sarah, then Prisha on her right. Baldwin. After Danny it will be me. I am not homophobic (anymore), but I am germophobic. I try not to imagine all the microscopic cells in their unbrushed, unflossed mouths that haven't seen a dentist in who knows how long. I now hold the banana.

"All right," I say with a mouthful of immune-building or death-inducing warm mush. "Let's get cooking! On tonight's menu: arroz con pollo con tostones." I toss the slimy banana peel to Jane, who screams and drops it on the floor. Nobody picks it up. We walk around it like it's sleeping.

I make stations at the island. Prisha volunteers to cut onions. "Firstly," she says, "put the onions in the freezer for about ten minutes." She holds up a potato masher. "I'll work on mashing these stewed tomatoes while they chill."

"In the freezer?" This is new. My moms taught me to chop the onions underwater, but I could never do it right.

"Yes. To prevent the acid from being released. I'll also need your sharpest knife."

"What do I do?" Sarah asks, looking around the kitchen like a puppy just freed from the kennel. "I'm so excited. Cooking in my house was using a can opener."

"Come and I'll show you how to mince the herbs," Prisha sings. "Oh, I miss the smell of fresh cilantro!"

Jane is sniffing the bottles of oregano, garlic salt, the cumin for the rice like they're cocaine. Until she gets too much up her nose and starts sneezing like a cartoon. She knocks over an entire collection of ceramic angels, Paschal

Baylon and his holy ladle separated.

"Contain!" I holler at Baldwin. "Contain!"

Baldwin—all ninety pounds of them—tackles Jane. Which causes Jane to sneeze and laugh hysterically.

Jane: "I almost feel like I've had an orgasm. Another one."

Danny aims the sink hose at them both: "TMI!"

I survey the kitchen. Prisha is all Julia Child showing Sarah the difference between mincing and dicing. Any minute now, Jane will slip—yep, is slipping—in the puddle Danny made, and I'm wondering where Simone keeps her Crazy Glue with a calmness and reserve that only comes from knowing you're probably screwed.

"Okay, okay, enough!" Baldwin leaps up, further splashing water every-freakin-where. "We've got to get organized!" They clap. "Jane, you are DJ. Sit down right here." Baldwin places Jane on not one, but two of the still-upright chairs. "Don't move. I'm on cleanup. Danny, rummage for paper plates, plastic forks—for the safety of everyone." They look at Jane playing on my phone. "And whatever baking items you can find. Verdad: Cook. I'm hungry, damn it."

Order is as restored as it's gonna get. I join Prisha and Sarah in chopping red and green bell peppers for the chicken. I make a mixture of garlic powder, earthy cumin, black pepper, YUM, and fiery cayenne pepper in a Ziploc. After stabbing the chicken, I toss it in the bag to absorb the deliciousfreakiness.

Danny has made room beneath the cupboards for what looks like will be some kind of fancy custard.

I absorb the sifting, the chopping, the talking, the fragrances that make a kitchen a sacred place. This is what I imagine college will be like when I move out. Except for Blanca, who should be sitting up on the counter and testing the ripeness of the peppers, everything is perfect. We have a pot of rice going in no time. While it boils under the lid with the stewed tomatoes, waiting for the peppers and onion, I mash the plantain for the tostones. While Danny is doing whatever witchcraftery that conjures up the prettiest pink custard, I fry up the chicken just right.

Danny: "Taste."

Me: "Heaven."

Danny: "This I learned how to make from my aunts. They were the experts on desserts."

Me: "You have an armada of tías too?"

"Yeah. Zias! I couch-surfed with them for a while. But they've got their own kids. Their own problems. As cool as they were, their husbands, not so much."

I turn off the stove. "How long has it been? If you don't mind me asking."

"No, it's okay. It's been almost a year. For all of us."

"A year and counting without family. That's hard."

"Sometimes you have to make your own family."

Everybody nods and gets quiet. Jane hands me my phone. I buy the song she wants and toss it back to her, and she fumbles. Sarah catches it before it hits the floor. "Do you ever think about going back?"

Jane runs to the sink, holds up the island sink hose and belts out, "If I could turn back time!"

Baldwin turns the water on.

Jane looks like she's dog paddling against the deluge from the hose. "Sweet baby Jesus! I'm drowning."

Sarah throws a dish towel at Baldwin like a fastball. "Okay!" Baldwin turns off the water, *ha ha*'s, and tenderly dries off a pouty-faced Jane.

"In all seriousness, you guys," Jane says, dabbing at her beard, "I'm curious. I want to go back . . . and see that everybody is sad and they, like, kept my room exactly as it was. But what if it's completely the opposite?"

"Yeah." Baldwin hugs Jane. "What if I go back and my parents changed all the locks?"

"That is true." Prisha lays down her knife by perfect mounds of spring-green chopped cilantro. "But if that were the case, we would haunt them."

"Yes!" Sarah says, fist bumping Prisha. "Rearrange the furniture. Leave a message. Steal all the shoes!"

I join Danny by the stove and fry up the tostones while he turns the chicken. "I would go back with you to get your shoes." I nod to the girls. "And"—I nod to Baldwin—"your glasses."

Baldwin pinballs a look that hits every target around the room. "Cinder-ella, are we hatching a plan?"

"This is so exciting!" Jane almost accidentally steps on the banana peel. But manages to catch herself.

Everybody sighs with relief.

"The banana," Sarah declares, "is magical."

We wash hands in the sink—and manage to soak half the kitchen floor. Between that and the sink hose, Baldwin just decides to mop up. Prisha finds candles, lights them on the table, then takes one look at Jane and blows them out. Baldwin sits on Jane's lap. After Sarah wipes down her counter, she joins Prisha, sharing the same chair. Danny sets a plate at the table but leaves the chair empty. "What would be Blanca's favorite?" That is it. I love him.

I point and Danny serves Blanca tostones. We sit beside each other and hold hands. I try not to cry into my rice.

We all argue over whether we should pray, whom we should

be praying to. Settle on holding hands and saying what we want in our own heads.

Baldwin shrieks, “I’m going to stick my face in the rice bowl, y’all!”

I lift the lid of the rice and sprinkle in fresh cilantro. “Vamos a comer!”

The two kinds of food that are best in the world, food made for you by someone you love and food you make with friends. No grain of rice is left, no morsel of juicy tender chicken is not scraped from the bone. Of course, Prisha sticks to the rice and plantains and lectures all of us on the intelligence of chickens. Jane’s strangely tiny burp signals the end of the meal and erupts us all into laughter.

“We got friends, food”—Jane slaps the table, sending a fork flying—“now music.”

Jane’s music is K Pop that sounds like K Hip Hop, which makes me feel conflicted because anyone can appropriate pop, but rap is a no-no.

Baldwin: “Oh! Verdad is making a frowny face.”

Sarah: “Verdad is gonna kick your ass.”

Jane switches it to Bollywood. At which point Prisha busts some major moves. Which makes *me* bust some moves. I’m that girl in the horror movie who can’t walk without falling down, but I can bring the salsa.

Jane stands up and almost knocks over the table. Danny pulls the table against the wall and sits on it, watching. I like being watched. Baldwin waltzes Sarah around the room. Jane twerks, which is surprisingly sexy but also comforting because it keeps her in one spot.

At some point this leads to us all doing a Gloria Estefan conga up the stairs to my bedroom.

Jane sits on my bed. When Baldwin joins her, I worry it might crash through the floor. Prisha and Sarah perch on the windowsill. Danny sits at their feet. They braid his hair. This annoys the living shit out of me.

"So I have a surprise for everyone," I announce. "Wait here." I run to the linen closet, load up, and return. "For you," I say, laying a thick, fluffy towel on Sarah's lap maybe a little hard. And on everyone else's.

"Sarah and Prisha first?" Nobody questions that they will shower together. "Toss your clothes out the door and I'll throw them in the wash." The door closes and the shower water runs. The two girls laughing and undressing sound like birds uncaged. Clothes fly out of the bathroom like discarded feathers.

"This is going to sound weird," I announce, "but can the rest of you just undress and wear towels? I should probably throw all your clothes in a quick wash together."

Jane gestures like a queen. "You just want to see me naked."

Are you there, God? It's me, Verdad. I really don't want to see Jane naked. Amen.

"Yeah no. I'll wait outside. Just toss the clothes out the door." No offense, but I run downstairs and grab a pair of tongs. I mean, think about it.

The washer is set on thirty minutes. I return to Prisha and Sarah singing. To Jane wearing a towel like I do wrapped around her chest, sitting on the bed all lady-like. Baldwin on the edge of the bed hiding under my blanket. Danny in a T-shirt (thank you, Monster High) with the towel wrapped around his waist. Makes sense.

Prisha and Sarah emerge and so does the smell of every single bath and body product Simone keeps in the guest room.

Sarah says, "I feel like I've been baptized."

Prisha spins her around the room.

Baldwin smiles at Jane: "Our turns!"

"Oh! Hey, Verdad. Your phone's vibrating." Jane holds up my cell.

Now it's my turn to be horrified. "No offense, but where was my phone just now?"

"You wish you were so lucky, honey. It was just lying on the pillow."

Jane hands me the phone as the songbirds and the scents of their shampooed hair whirl around the room. And Danny watches them. If I see just one of his nostrils inhale, I swear the girls will wake up bald.

My phone vibrates again. The text says, "Hope all is well. Miss M says she had a great time meeting you and your friend. Our neighbor Ms. J will be stopping by any minute. She might want to stop in your room to measure for curtains she's making us. Do you need her to bring dinner?"

"Oh. No." I say aloud. I check my text about having friends over. Somehow, I never actually pressed *send*. Shit.

Also: The curtain bullshit is clearly just an excuse for neighbor lady to spy on me.

"Oh my God, my dad's neighbor is coming over here and everyone is naked!!!!!"

Danny flies to his feet. "He's what? What?"

I run to the washer, peel the wet clothes out, and toss them in the drier on quick dry. Bang into Danny when I turn on my heel to haul ass to my bedroom.

"So let's take a breath here," he says. "I replied to your dad's message. I asked him if your neighbor could bring dinner. That will buy us some time."

I nod and exhale.

"He said Ms. J is packing up some Tupperware for me—I mean you."

"I'm laughing on the inside, Danny. How long do I have?"

"Your dad said maybe twenty minutes? Baldwin and Jane are showering now."

"Together?!"

"They promised they'd only engage in oral sex. No worries."

Okay. I'm laughing on the outside. "But for real, what am I going to do with another dinner? How will I explain the kitchen downstairs?"

"Prisha and Sarah are on it. They're Hefty-Bagging the evidence. Listen, you did tell him you were having us over though, right?"

"Yeah. I mean, I meant to." Did I? Was not sending the text a Freudian slip? "Regardless, you all need to be dressed and get going."

Despite the ticking time bomb that is my life right now, I grab Danny by the waist. "It's not fair. You are the only one who isn't getting to shower."

"True. But I stole your toothpaste and deodorant."

"Really!" I pull him closer.

I get hit in the culo with one of a pile of wet towels flying at my head. Make-out session, interrupted. Everybody sits in front of the dryer as I dole out clothes that are still burning hot.

Shit shit! Fuckity fuck! is the general interjection as hot buttons and zippers cause second degree burns.

"All right, Underdogs!" Baldwin claps. "Ándale!"

A moment later they're all fresh and frisky and waiting in the car—except Baldwin, who's dashed back for one last trip to the bathroom. Danny and I are standing on the porch. I love standing in the dark with him, looping my fingers through his belt loops.

"Thank you for coming here tonight. I needed to be in the present. Before tomorrow."

"Tomorrow is gonna be heavy."

I grab Danny's hoodie and bury my face in his chest. I hear Baldwin run past us, down the steps to the car. "I don't think I can make it through school." I look up. "Mental health day?"

"Definitely. Maybe we can go get Baldwin's glasses."

****

My dad's neighbor, of course, wants to sit down and talk. I know she smells the food, but she doesn't ask about it. She asks to use the bathroom, but I'm pretty sure she's just seeing if there's any evidence of a party. She tries to talk, but I pull the I've Got Cramps card and get her out of the house so I can decompress.

That night, I pray.

I'm not a hypocrite. I pray because everything I've ever understood about math—science—the universe—proves God exists. I don't need faith.

I pray that I can walk up to the movie theater again and take it back from the man who stole it. Who stole our stories, ripped out pages, and forced Fernando and Bambi and Blanca to the end. Forced me to rewrite my story, myself, without my sidekick, my sage, my best friend.

And who was that man? That thief of our paragraphs, chapters, lives?

An illiterate piece of garbage who thought his existence, his thoughts, feelings, and ideas entitled him to delete everyone else exponentially. The selfish, soulless asshole who held a gun and shot Fernando, Blanca, and Bambi before they could duck. Shot me in the leg as I turned to run.

I played possum. Waited for the sound of sirens. Dragged myself to Bambi and the hole in his head making a tunnel straight to his afterlife. To Fernando and the bullet that stopped him from ever telling his mom and little sister *I love you* again. To Blanca, the red circle on her chest spreading into a pool, thinking like an idiot *You spilled your slushie! You spilled your slushie!* because I knew it couldn't be blood. Blood spilling from her chest emptying the most beautiful wild heart I had ever known.

I pray the rest in tears.

I don't sign the cross when I'm finished because *that* would make me a hypocrite.

22

At school, I meet up with Danny and the others in the parking lot. I'm carrying an emptied-out backpack stuffed with bags for everyone. Baldwin is wearing suspenders over their Afro Punk T-shirt. Prisha and Sarah have braided each other's hair and Danny is wearing a tie over his standard skater outfit. What they don't have are jackets.

Baldwin raises their hand. "Cinder-ella, shouldn't we be doing this in the dark?"

"That depends," I say, handing a duffel bag to Jane. "Do your parents work? If they do, then we hit the houses now when they're gone."

Baldwin adjusts their big-ass octogenarian glasses. "My mom and dad run a salon. Sometimes they even sleep in the back. I used to work there after school. I hated it." Baldwin rubs Jane's beard. "I wanted to tell all those hairy girls, keep those mustaches!"

"Seriously," I say. "We say we have souls but we define ourselves by skin. Do souls have vaginas?"

Prisha buries her face in Sarah's chest and cracks up. "Verdad, you're terrible!"

"What's terrible is not that I say vagina but that your parents think they own yours. What do your parents do?"

Prisha answers, "They're in IT. I'm going into IT too. I'm going to design computer games. Ones for lesbian Indians who like to skateboard and be gangsters."

"And," Sarah says, "I'm going to go to school for business. To get our company off the ground."

"Wow. Are you going to go back to high school? I mean eventually?"

"We are." Sarah pulls on her hood. "For now we use the library to study up. Prisha wants to be emancipated."

I must admit I'm impressed. Still venomous and poised to strike if she touches my man. But impressed.

"What about you?"

"I was emancipated at ten when my parents started—"

"Well, now we will emancipate our parents from their earthly belongings for all their misdeeds," says Prisha. Sarah laughs but is clenching and unclenching her fists.

"My dad is in the military and my mom is a wedding planner," Jane volunteers. "They won't be home. But there will be an alarm. I think I know the codes, and maybe their guard is down because it's been a while so they haven't changed them."

"Danny. What about you? Your dad will be at the bakery, right?"

He looks away, jaw clenched. "I'm not going back." He wipes his eyes real fast, and I know he hopes I don't notice. "There's nothing I want. There's nothing I need. I got everything I want and need right here."

•••••••

Forty minutes later, we're parked beside cars plastered with MAGA bumper stickers. Jane's neighborhood is divided into lots, each with two trash cans waiting for pick up, a mailbox, a front lawn, and a rancher with an American flag. These are the kind of houses little kids draw with a lemon-yellow sun shining over them. In the back are small fenced yards, each containing a doghouse and a barbecue grill. We instantly consider suicide.

"Oh my God. I'm having a desperate desire to go to a mall!" Baldwin acts like they're flying backwards, pulled by an invisible vortex. "I need to buy clothes. Help me!"

Sarah grabs them by their suspenders and brings them back to safety.

"Tell me about it. I had to live there. It's that one." Jane points to a rancher on the west end, with a sign that reads "God and Country" on the porch.

"So help us God." I sign the cross. "Let's give this a shot. What's your goal?"

"Besides my favorite flannels? Like personal stuff? I want a picture of my brother. He went into the army. I'm so proud of him. I miss him so much. If I'd want to see anybody again, it would be him. He's stationed in Virginia last I heard."

The door to Jane's house opens and out walks an old man collecting firewood. I pray so freakin hard this is another relative Jane didn't mention. But Jane's facial expression tells us all that he's a stranger.

"Hey! Hey!" Jane barrels at full speed to this man's porch, and we follow on her heels praying we won't all be shot dead.

The old man jumps up fast and backs up to his door and hopefully not the rifle he's got behind it.

"Who are you?" Jane says.

"Who am I? None of your damn business, and I believe you are the strangers on my property."

"Where are the Redfields?"

Something in her tone makes the man's eyes seem to soften. His voice is quieter when he says, "Why don't you all come up here and we can talk without shouting."

A neighbor steps out onto his porch. "You all right, Bert?"

"I'm all right."

We advance on the leafless lawn onto the perfectly swept porch. Bert's neighbor, apparently the neighborhood watch, gives us a once-over and plants himself on his porch.

"So," Bert says sitting in a rocking chair, "the Redfields moved. They got stationed in Germany."

Jane doesn't say a word. We all wait to see what will happen. Then she erupts.

Wailing, Jane runs off the porch and down the street with Baldwin in tow.

"Hey, sir," I say. "Did they leave any forwarding information? That's the Redfields' kid."

"Yeah? He looks like his dad. Or did." Crackly laugh.

"Sir?" I ask, steering him back from the road to dickdom.

"I collected their mail for a while, so I can give you their forwarding address."

We all meet up at the car. Baldwin warms it up. Jane's crying in the passenger seat.

Sarah and Prisha rub her shoulders. Jane closes her eyes and leans back. "I knew it. In the back of my head. I feel like an abortion or something. I never really felt homeless until now."

More to God than any of us, Baldwin says, "At least I know my parents didn't go back to Korea. Fuck!"

Jane blows her nose on what looks like an old sock and tosses it on the floor. "Oh my God, Baldwin, what if we go back to your house and it's the opposite? What if they want you back?"

"Nah." Baldwin takes off their glasses and their eyes are

squinty and raw. "They told me, this is what we come to this country for? For you to become an outcast? A freak?"

I am clinging to Danny. My moms may be pissed, but leaving-the-country-without-me-pissed? No—I don't think. "I am so sorry, Jane."

"Thanks, Verdad, but I needed to know the truth and I'm glad I didn't find out alone."

Everyone gets buckled, which amuses me because driving a Lego car would be safer, and Baldwin turns the ignition key.

****

Baldwin lives in an apartment building where everybody and their mama knows your business. When the place gets gentrified, these will be the last people standing.

"I feel like I need to say something before this round," Jane says as we stand at the bottom of the steps. "We go in together. We leave together. No matter what." I pity anyone who tries to take Baldwin away from her.

Baldwin walks up to the third floor in a trance.

Almost every door has a neat mat flanked with a Buddha or a highly breakable vase with stark dried plants inside. I want to have a god statue by our door at home. Shit, what happened to all our gods?

Baldwin stops in front of a door and presses their head against it, hugging it like it's a raft after a shipwreck. "Oh that kimchee. I can't take it!"

Of course the door opens and Baldwin falls into some viejita's entryway.

"Can I help you?"

I can't identify what the teeny tiny lady with the giant

wooden spoon is cooking, but I'm feelin Baldwin. It smells so good I want to eat my face.

"Uh, no!" Baldwin backs up into the rest of us. "Sorry!"

"Wait. What's your name?"

"Baldwin?" Baldwin tries to deflect her paralyzing gaze.

"Your given name." I think she's doing a retinal scan of Baldwin's brain. She and my mother share that superpower.

"Ji su Pak."

She nods. "I thought so. I've lived in this complex for twenty years. I know you." The woman's black eyes focus on Baldwin, but somehow see us all. "And who's with you?"

"Just some friends. Um, everybody, this is Mrs. Joung, my neighbor."

"You look hungry." The wooden spoon is now a scepter. "Why don't you come in—why don't you all come in? Have a bite to eat." She smooths her blue dress and bows slightly. Baldwin nods and bows lower. Oh God. There will be bowing. Do I bow?

"Thank you, Nanimaa!" Prisha does a sort of head dunk and signals everyone to toss their shoes in a pile.

Sarah follows Prisha—always—and whispers to me, "That's a term of respect in Hindi." Baldwin gives Jane a helpless look and follows the smooth-skinned, iron-haired woman into a long sunlit hall full of black-and-white photographs. I want to look and see how beautiful she has always been. I love old people. I wish we all started old and grew young.

"Help." Jane lowers herself to the ground as gracefully as a bulldozer and attempts to yank off her size-too-small shoes.

I come to her rescue.

Yes! I get Jane's right shoe off. But she knocks over the Buddha at Mrs. Joung's door. I try to catch it. She tries to bear-hug it.

"You two!" Mrs. Joung scolds at us from above. "You two are not in the right bodies. You come in and sit still!" We scurry inside. Danny helps her right the jolly fat immortal.

She inspects Sarah and Prisha. "You two, help me in the kitchen."

Jane and I breathe a sigh of relief because we are seated at a plastic-covered table but freak out when Prisha and Sarah come out carrying trays with loads of tiny ceramic bowls.

Me to Danny: "Why is the rice in a silver bowl? That's got to be hot. Why is there only one bowl of soup? Why is there one spoon? Do we just like take a whole bowl for ourselves? Do we just stick our hands into it?"

Danny to me: "Should I slap you? You are totally losing your sh—itaki."

"For tasting," Mrs. Joung says to us all. To Baldwin, "Tell everybody what they are eating."

"This is banchan, appetizers. Here you have Tteok Kochi, rice cake skewers. Here, radish pancakes. There, Swiss chard fritters. I'll pour the soup into the rice. You all choose something and spoon it onto your side plates." Baldwin pats Jane's hand. "We don't pick up the bowls. No handles for a reason."

Mrs. Joung and Prisha talk shop about the types of chili paste in Indian food and gochujang—fermented chili paste in Korean food. Once we've all chilled out and started filled our plates, Mrs. Joung says, "So Baldwin," surprising me by using their new name. "You've come home. I told your parents you would."

Baldwin eyes the door.

Mrs. Joung lays her hand on their arm. "Stay. Tell me your story."

While we empty bowl after bowl on the table and Mrs. Joung signals the girls to refill them, they talk in Korean. I'm instantly a hater. I want to speak my native language, erect it around the gringos like a wall. But it's so hard. If a white person learns how to speak Spanish, it doesn't matter if they mess up. They're expected to. But if I do? How am I supposed to get my feet wet when everybody is always expecting I'm an Olympic swimmer in the pool?

I'm finally full, but Baldwin and Mrs. Joung are in no rush and the rest of the Underdogs are still stuffing their underfed faces. Mrs. Joung is just like Blanca's abuela, getting full from what other people eat. Her first taste is a tiny sip of soup after everybody is onto the thirds. She lowers the spoon. "I suggested we have a funeral."

That was plain English. (Which, I realize as I think it, is a racist term.) All you could hear is munching and slurping before, but now silence.

"What Mrs. Joung means is a funeral for Ji su," Baldwin explains. "Not *me*."

"Your parents need to mourn. They need closure. They need to bury old ideals and expectations. I have spoken with your father many times. What is a disgrace is fighting to keep your family together only to tear them apart."

Baldwin covers their face. Tears spill through their fingers. Jane grips their hand. Possibly breaks their pinky.

"Ow."

"We already have buried so much. Our thoughts, our hopes, our dreams. I reminded your parents what we came here for. That is wasn't for themselves, it was for you to be you."

Mrs. Joung lifts up Baldwin's chin. "Such a dashing young person, you make." She picks up a napkin and dries their tears. "But not in those glasses."

Baldwin looks up at Mrs. Joung and laughs, giving us all permission to breathe.

"We actually came to get his glasses," I say with a mouth full of spicy, sticky chicken, "and a few of Baldwin's things."

"I can get what you need. I have everybody's keys in case of emergency. But on one condition."

Jane is hovering protectively over Baldwin. I know she is ready to attack if Mrs. Joung threatens to take away her boo.

She looks directly at Jane. "On the condition you bring Baldwin back here to meet with Mr. and Mrs. Pak, I'll arrange it."

Mrs. Joung leaves to collect a few of Baldwin's things, and we get ready to head out.

"So all's well that ends weird, huh?" I say to Danny, who is helping me with my coat.

"We are the WE in weird." He stretches his long, lean, muscley back that I want to. . . "I don't think I can handle two more houses today."

"We have to. We promised."

Mrs. Joung does the most complicated exit of all time. She catches Baldwin mid-bow and hugs every fiber of them. She and the girls exchange bows and hand clasps. The woman kisses me on the cheek. "All the quiet was killing you. Good job."

I smile. I get an A for *not* being an asshat!

"Mrs. Joung, how come you had all that food? I mean that was unreal."

She smiles and folds her arms. "Well, you never know who's going to show up."

•••••••

We're standing in front of Prisha's sprawling house, the perimeter surrounded by beautiful dangerous rose bushes Prisha says her mother planted. In the giant backyard there's a greenhouse and a soon-to-be harvest of peppers and tomatoes. She points out a butterfly garden and talks about her parents' beekeeping hobby.

I'm trippin. "Like with the suits and everything?"

"My mother's been stung over twenty times! But it's all for the good."

"Too bad she didn't show you the same love she showed bugs," Sarah whispers and gets a nod from Jane.

Prisha fishes a key out of a rosemary plant at the top of the steps. I'm trying to process Prisha's story, but my brain is rejecting pieces that don't fit. "I'm sorry, gang," I interrupt as Prisha talks about her dad running away screaming as her mom rescued a freakin snake, "but none of this makes any sense. Prisha. Your parents—are vegan, right?"

She turns the handle of the door. "Yes."

"And they basically have the circle-of-life conservationist thing going on here."

Now the whole crew is staring me down in annoyance.

"Hello! Do these sound like people who would kill a dog?"

Sarah looks like she's about to throw down. "What the fuck do you know? The things people are capable of—just because we want to exist?"

My brain revs up and I slam on the gas. "Fuck you, Sarah. You ever take a bullet aimed at you simply because you exist? Every person of color knows that the minute they step into your world. And that ain't even counting being queer."

Baldwin: "Tone it down, you two. The whole turn-against-each-other thing is played out."

Jane puts her hand on Sarah's shoulder and eyes me warily. "What's your point, Nancy Drew?"

"My point is, did *you*," I say, looking at a very teary-eyed Prisha, "ever see the body of the dog?"

Prisha's all choked up. "I saw the—burial mound . . ."

She bursts into tears. It's possible everybody, including Danny hates my guts right now.

But no—Danny rolls up his sleeves. "Where's it buried, Prisha?"

She points toward the greenhouse before she's enveloped in Sarah's arms.

Danny says, "Verdad, you're digging."

Jane and Sarah sandwich Prisha on the porch steps while Danny grabs a couple of shovels leaning against the greenhouse.

We tromp down a grassy slope behind the sunlit greenhouse. He's speed-walking ahead of me.

"This is taking things to a whole other level," he mutters. "Have you thought about the fact that we could get arrested?"

I stop short. "Is that what I need to do to prove I'm on your side?"

"No! But—I do need to know that you're not treating this like a game. It's serious for us. And we don't like people flaking out on us when things get tough. We do the leaving these days, not the other way around."

"Look, I know I'm not really one of you. But even if I do have a home, I'm not gonna leave you behind."

"That is a huge." Danny looks into my eyes and I look straight back.

"It's the first promise I've made in over a year. Now let's start digging," I say, pointing to a mound of raised dirt.

No more than ten minutes later, we're carrying a dirty collar up the hill.

I hand it off to Danny and let him go talk to Prisha. From the distance, I watch as Prisha jumps into Sarah's arms and they all hug. The grave, as I suspected, was empty. Her parents lied to her.

"Verdad," Danny calls from the porch, "get your hot ass over here!"

I take my time strutting my hot ass over because I'm feeling like a left-out kindergartner, and I still don't like seeing Danny all hugging up on Prisha.

"So Velma," Jane says, apparently still bitter about me calling her LumberJane, "what's the plan?"

"Well, jinkies, Jane," I say, "I guess now we can case the place. For money, jewelry, and info on wherever that dog might have ended up."

****

Baldwin drives us to the Maheshwari residence. According to Prisha's mom's emails, this is the family who got Prisha's dog.

Base is blasting through the walls of the townhouse, and I'm feeling nostalgic for home. There are two cars in the driveway, and through the windows we can see toys in the living room. A dude on the phone, a woman typing away at her computer.

"Oh my God! Tavi! That's Tavi on the balcony!"

Prisha almost slams the car door on Jane's fingers in her eagerness to get out of the car. We follow in her hyper footsteps, and I'm crossing my fingers that the base is loud enough that the lady inside doesn't register our motley asses assembling under her balcony.

"Tavi, it's Prisha! I miss you so much!"

Over our heads, the dog is wiggin out, whining and pacing and whipping its tail so hard it knocks over a potted plant.

"I need to get up there!"

"Prisha, babe," Danny pleads, "there's no way!"

He called her babe. This negates all the times he's called me babe.

Oblivious to my brewing wrath, Danny lays his arm around Prisha. "Tavi is happy. Safe. It might have to be enough."

"No fucking way," Prisha screams. "Jane, let me get up on your shoulders." Before we can determine who's gonna catch Prisha when Jane inevitably drops her on her ass, music blasts even louder through the front door.

"What in the hell are you kids doing? I will call the cops!"

I freeze. Danny's words echo in my brain: You know we can get arrested? I've been flippant about it. But now I'm thinking back to the police questioning me after the shooting. Asking me why I'd been out so late at night. Was I pulling my hair out because I was on something? Those memories deal me the next card: the Underdogs hearing the siren and trying to run.

I face the man—Mr. M, I assume—who's glaring at us from the front step. "Please. Please don't. We're here because our friend thought her parents murdered her dog because she is a lesbian. But they gave it to you. And she's homeless now and how the hell could she possibly take care of a dog—"

Danny wraps his arms around me. "Okay! So we'll be getting the hell out of here."

"Wait!" Prisha says. "Can I please, please just see Tavi for a minute? Just to give him a hug! I know I couldn't take care of him now even if you would let me have him back, but could I at least say a proper goodbye?"

Mr. M. frowns at us. "All right, young lady," he says, talking only to Prisha (rude!). "You can come in for a minute."

Sarah tries to follow Prisha inside but Prisha says, "I'll be fine, you can all wait for me out here."

This was not the plan we all agreed on. Jane runs her hand through her hair and paces. Baldwin follows in Jane's footsteps, trying to chill her out.

Sarah takes too long to let go of Prisha's hand. Eventually Danny pulls her back. "She's okay."

We lean against the Maheshwaris' truck parked in front of the windows and play it off like we don't even care. As Prisha talks, Mr. and Mrs. M get closer together until they're holding hands. Until Mrs. M holds out her other hand to Prisha. Mr. M leaves the room and heads upstairs. A minute later, Tavi hurtles down the stairs. They both lose their minds, Prisha talking in a high-pitched voice we can hear all the way outside, the dog leaping into her arms. Eventually Mr. M snaps his fingers at Tavi and she traipses over to an armchair, grabs a chew toy, and lies down contentedly chomping on its neck. Prisha and Mrs. M sit on the couch, talking. Mrs. M steals glances at us outside pretending we're not spying.

Mr. M opens up the centerpiece of the living room, a large, narrow carved wooden cabinet. Above the cabinet is a jeweled mosaic of what I think must be a god. He/she/they has a body of a human and the head of an elephant.

"That's Ganesha," Sarah explains, because I guess she's been educated by Prisha for a minute. "Ganesha is the god of new beginnings. The ultimate obstacle remover."

Sarah straight-up bites a nail off until it bleeds. Goes for another one before Jane intervenes and holds her hand. Rubs her back. "You are the new beginning, honey."

Danny hops off the truck and looks off into the distance.

I wonder if it's out of respect or because prayer of any kind is a painful reminder to him.

"They're going to do puja," Sarah says, interpreting again. "Indian prayer."

I want her to shut the hell up, but I guess I get it. I think she's going through what Jane went through at Mrs. Joung's house when she thought Mrs. Joung was gonna kidnap Baldwin.

"So is that an oil lamp?" I ask.

"It's called the diya," Sarah answers. "First they light the diya. Then they begin the puja with an offering."

We see Mrs. M duck out of the living room and come back with all these dumplings and bars that make my mouth water for my mother's absolutely everything she has ever cooked for me. Yeah, I want my damn mami.

Sarah mumbles, "modak" and "ladoo" pathetically, and I get to wondering about her life before Prisha.

"Makes me think of us leaving my abuelo's fave foods on the table for him on his birthday every year," I offer.

Sarah rolls her eyes and starts pulling a thread out of her already threadbare booty shorts. I try again.

"So, I'm missing my ma's flan right now. Sarah, your mom ever make you anything especial?"

She shakes her head. "Please."

Mrs. M has laid the offerings on the altar and disappeared into an adjacent hall. She comes back with head scarves.

Sarah continues, "Lucky we heated up the Chef Boyardee."

I shudder. Oh the horror.

"Prisha took me to temple once to pray—and get warm. She believes in a bunch of gods. I wish I believed in just one."

Prisha and Ms. M's covered heads are bowed and they are—pujaying?

"Yeah. I'm having that kind of crisis right now."

"Prisha gets sad for what she's lost. I get wrecked because the more I'm with her, I realize everything I never had."

I nod. There are exactly zero words of consolation I can give.

23

Of course, Prisha can't take Tavi with her. But Ms. M gives Prisha her number so they can stay in touch and sends her off with a backpack full of tampons, baby wipes, and clean underwear.

Now for Sarah's house. Turns out her dad molested her, and her mom didn't do jack. We all but set the place on fire. There's nothing to steal except a bag of pills hidden under the dresser. Sarah promises Prisha she'll sell it, but I see her poppin a bunch before we even leave the house.

We think that's it, until Danny says, "Do we have time for one more stop?"

"Yeah?" Baldwin asks, their hand on his shoulder.

His jaw tight, he nods.

I grab Danny's limp hand. "We're your ride or die."

His dad lives in the gentrified side of town where Nelly goes to school but can't afford to live. His house has well-tended rose bushes, bird feeders, and a bird bath. Storybook fruit tree and berry bushes. I can't help but picture the man who trims those roses, fills those feeders, prunes those trees, and turns his child out into the cold.

Baldwin expertly parallel parks the car and Jane jokes about the time Baldwin got so tired of seeing some lady struggle to park that they got out of the car and did it for her. Jane is feeling a little better.

We all nod as we head toward Danny's backyard. Danny jiggles the fence and lets us in. It's just as beautiful out back as it is in the front with neatly manicured evergreens and even a squirrel feeder.

Danny pulls a key out from a ceramic toad's mouth and lets us in. Jane agrees to be lookout and sits on the steps.

Inside the mudroom, I ask, "Ground rules?"

"Take whatever you need for yourselves. Don't destroy anything. Just—alter things ever so slightly."

We walk into a sitting room—as opposed to a living room, Danny tells a very confused me. He makes a Bed Bath and Beyond portrait of a jazz band crooked.

Baldwin cracks their knuckles as they look at all the family portraits on the mantel, which are all of Danny when he looked like a girl.

I look away because that isn't him.

"So," Baldwin says, "we're gaslighting Dear Old Dad?"

Danny nods, looking miserable. He sits on the couch and props his Vans on the coffee table. "Notice there are no pictures of me beyond elementary school."

I adjust the grandfather clock on the mantel to an hour earlier. Go sit beside him and clasp his hand. "I'm sorry."

"You know the last conversation I had with him?" He outlines it for me.

His dad: You go to the conversion camp. Or you don't come home.

Danny: To be converted into what?

His dad: Back to what you used to be. Back to what you are supposed to be.

Danny: Used to be? Dad, I never was.

His dad: Your mother. She didn't take care of herself when she had you.

Danny: Trans is not a birth defect. How can you throw me out? Do you know what happens to kids like me on the street? They end up prostitutes, raped, selling drugs . . .

His dad: That's what being gay leads to. That's what you're fighting so hard to be. Just like your mother.

Danny: What the fuck, Dad? There's nothing wrong with Mom. She's a lesbian. That is all. I'm sorry she broke your heart. But she is who she is, and I am who I am.

His dad: silent stare.

"I ran out the door and didn't look back."

I climb on Danny's lap, wrap my legs around him, and hug him so hard. Feel his breath on my neck. I admit to feeling distracted from the original purpose of this embrace . . .

Sarah and Prisha are bounding down the stairs with beautiful scarves in their hands.

Danny stops kissing me. He looks pale. I slide off him.

Danny stands up. "Those were my mom's."

"I know." Prisha hands them to Danny. "I remember when you told me about them. Your mom wearing them and how she would let you play with them and pretend you could fly. They belong to you."

Prisha and Danny hug. They've had these conversations already and I'm late to the party. I'm a jerk and I hate all the whispering going on between them. Danny stows the scarves in his bag.

"Everybody ready?"

I motion to Prisha. "Where is his mom?"

"He doesn't know. His dad got full custody because he said

she was unstable. Made her sound crazy. But it really it was him making her crazy because she was gay, and he couldn't stand it."

My stomach churns. "That held up in court?"

Prisha nods. "I had the same question. I have a cousin who's studying law in Cali. She says we make the assumption that our courts deliver justice. But how can they when the people in power don't represent the people they're supposed to serve?"

Prisha is dope. Damn it. "I guess I get why she had to leave," I say. "But I don't get why she had to disappear."

Prisha shrugs. "I know he's tried searching for her online and hasn't had any luck. He's not sure what name she uses now . . ."

"Well, damn, we tracked down your dog. Shouldn't we be able to track down his mom?"

Danny's dad has stronger passwords for his laptop and his email account than Prisha's parents had, but we still manage to get in pretty fast. Middle-aged white men aren't that imaginative.

We end up with a ten-year-old email address for his mom, plus confirmation of her maiden name. I write both down on a scrap of paper and give it to Danny. He folds it up and puts it in his pocket without a word. Stands stone still. Then grabs a pen and my wrist. Writes *THANK YOU.* I grab it back and write *when you're ready* on his.

We're all dead silent as we pile into the car.

This wasn't supposed to be about me, but I can't help it: Danny's dad's words dance with my mother's words in my head.

Like Padre said, it all comes down to decisions. My mother decided to not trust my judgment. Decided who I should be and who I should love. My mother decided I'm not good. Funny how homophobic people think being gay or transgender leads to misery but never consider that they're the ones who cause it. Never consider that they are the ones who separate God from their kids.

Hell is now. Saying it happens later is a power play.

24

We all separate an hourish before the vigil because we need a breather. Simone's cooking wafts out of the house as I climb my dad's front steps, juicy pork ruined by the odor of mashed potatoes. I can't stand potatoes. (And French fries ain't potatoes.) My dad is cutting up tomatoes from Simone's garden for a salad and Veronica is setting the table. I hear something about a banana. And tongs. Fuck. Shit. Crap. Damn. Their voices drop as I try to beam my guilty ass up the staircase.

"Hey. Verdad. Ven aquí."

"Hey!" I give my dad and Simone kisses hello. "I'm gonna try to get some homework done. Then I'm gonna head out for a bit."

Simone side-eyes my dad and fake-smiles at me. My dad says, "Okay. But this weekend, we need to have a conversation about ground rules."

I salute him. "Yes sir."

Veronica throws me serious shade. I let her have it. The whispering that they think I can't hear starts as I climb up the stairs.

I plop on my bed and pray to God, even though Simone thinks I'm probably toking a joint up here. I have to believe what I told Danny earlier today. To hate is human. To love is divine. God loves whoever I figure out that I am. But I'm not praying about me.

Prisha talked about a cousin in California. I'm praying she finds her.

Sarah left her house after raiding the medicine cabinet. I'm praying she doesn't OD.

I'm praying that Danny will be able to track down his mom.

I check the time. It's 3:24.

My hands are shaking when I rummage a pair of nail clippers out of the bathroom drawer and start snipping my split ends. I know the vigil isn't about me. But going to it forces me to make public the feelings I've locked in a vault for so long. I won't just be wearing my heart on my sleeve. I'll be like my screensaver Jesus, my heart ablaze for everybody to see.

Dear God-Force/aka Multiverse: Make today bigger than me. Make it about Blanca and her abuela, Bambi, Fernando, and every other kid who deserves to dance on their fifteenth birthdays.

I decide that I have ninety-nine problems and being bald shouldn't be one of em. I need freakin help.

I can't call my mother. I know she loved Blanca, but she also disapproved of her. Like I told Padre, love ain't acceptance. Love on its own isn't enough. I don't want her there with all her judgment, remembering Blanca through a tainted lens.

I don't want to ask my dad to come either. We're not at that level yet. And I'm already in debt to him.

I call Tía Sujei.

"Took you long enough. I'm insulted."

"I'm sorry, Titi. My head is just—"

"Up your ass?"

"Can you come get me?"

"I'll be there in twenty minutes."

Never mind the drive from where she is should take like fifty. Not only does she arrive in nineteen minutes, but she packed Tupperwares of food, which she hands over to an excusably annoyed Simone.

Sujei sniffs the air and wrinkles her nose. "This is what she likes." She taps the lid covering the pasteles. "Take some for the family. Just boil what you want for about an hour. Freeze the rest."

"How's Ma?" I ask her when we're in the car.

"Honestly, I can't tell if she's more pissed off that you're on a collision course with hellfire or that you're staying with your dad. He actually called me right before you did."

"About what?"

"After your stepmother discovered an elephant must have bathed in your bathtub, amongst much other strange shit, she and your dad had a discussion. Being that they have their hands full with Veronica losing her shit over you and the new baby, and your mom and dad are at war over stupit shit, they called me. Once I call the school and straighten shit out, you're moving in to my place."

"My dad's throwing me out?" Even though I knew it was coming, the sucker punch still hurts.

"No." She grabs my hand. "I am not letting him or you get to that point. You and he are good right now. I want to preserve that. The problem with tug-of-war is that nobody really gets all of you. You just get torn to pieces. And that ain't happening to my favorite niece. Your dad and your mom love you. But they need to work on their shit without shitting on you."

I'm trying to take this in. Trying not to think about my split ends.

She side-eyes me. "You okay with this? Because you look scared shitless."

I twirl my hair till it hurts. "I mean, of course I appreciate it, but at the same time—with them I know what to expect. And what *they* expect."

"What I expect is for you to live your best life. But I also expect you to make mistakes. Life isn't a multiple choice. Your parents got no answer key. They want you to do better than they did, but mija," she glances at me in the mirror, "you already are."

Okay. I can make that work. Living with Sujei. Living my truth. "Thanks, Titi."

She cradles her ringing phone with her ear as she parks the car.

"Listen, I got to take this. You do what you need to do."

I head to the theater and there is Ms. Q holding a box of electric candles. Ms. Moore is carrying a princess crown in honor of Blanca. Gloria and, I'm guessing, her Tio William are each pushing a laundry cart of white and pink roses, sprays of baby's breath. Beside her there's Christine, with clear giant bags of stuffed animals on her back. I'm sure all will be stolen by the morning. But even that thought is kind of fly. A little piece of Blanca, a little love will be played with in parks, slept with in bedrooms, given to lovers before a kiss in the dark.

A camera guy is setting up in front of the ticket booth. A journalist is talking to Nelly. "Let's talk about the school-prison pipeline . . ."

Rudy is taking a panorama with his cell. Frida struts in my direction with her hands on her hips.

"Verdad, why weren't you at school today? Ms. Q"—she nods at her—"was pissed." Ms. Q finger wags me but smiles.

"Sorry," Danny says, curling his arm around my waist and planting a kiss on me. "She needed a mental health day."

Rudy makes porn music and gets nasty with his hips.

Frida stomps her foot. "Boy, I'mma—"

Frida chases Rudy until he trips on his parachute pants. His camera goes off on the way down. Frida grabs it.

"Yaas." She holds up a shot of Rudy with his eyes closed, his hands and legs sprawling before his ass-busting finale. "Send!"

I receive. "This." I hold up the picture. "This makes today suck so much less."

The cameras are still rolling on Nelly, and I overhear her saying something about a city council meeting. The journalist talking to her eyeballs me.

"Penelope and I talked to the reporter before they started filming, told her about your ideas for the theater. Nelly's gonna work a quick mention of it into her interview too. A little press and maybe something can happen." Frida lays her hand on my shoulder.

My neck and ears feel hot. I didn't think I'd be the one in front of the camera. I didn't think this through at all, really. I shake my head. "Frida, I'm not talking to nobody."

"Well, that's your call. If Nelly's little shout-out airs, that'll be a start at least. But it shouldn't only be up to Nelly." Frida gives a peace symbol and starts helping Gloria and her Tio arrange flowers all around the perimeter of the theater.

Eventually, Nelly goes off to help Ms. Moore pass out electric candles. The journalist keeps talking to the camera. "Now what we're seeing is a student-run vigil for the victims tragically taken by a mass shooter a year ago today, the youngest among them being Blanca Lopez, Bambi Melendez, and Fernando Zarrin. Nelly Hamilton, whom we just spoke to, hopes to collaborate with Blanca's best friend, Verdad de la Reyna, to turn this site into a community center in honor of them and all youths taken by gun violence."

Now their names are out there and somebody on the other side of the camera, maybe a few somebodies, will sign the cross, whisper a prayer, light a candle for them. If even half the people in this city who have lost somebody stand up and say hell yeah to our idea, maybe that chandelier will shine over kids running after basketballs, not running from bullets.

I stand as if I'm watching a movie. I don't feel closure. I feel a responsibility that I am not ready to fill, as if Blanca raised her hand in a fist bump, and I left her hanging in eternal limbo.

I'm making her sit in a school desk when God's got someplace so much better for her in the sky. I believe in an afterlife. Matter is not created or destroyed. What matters can never be created or destroyed. Good gravitates toward good and Blanca is now everything good about her condensed. She's in that galaxy—if I let her be. The show must go on. I need to let that star be born.

"Verdad?" Danny hugs me and sort of rocks me, and we're swaying, slow dancing.

I open my eyes, and there are my Underdogs on skateboards: Jane cleanly shaved and trimmed rockin a new pair of red cowgirl boots, the someday-to-be-emancipated Prisha, her hands adorned with henna, Sarah, her booty cheeks actually covered, and Baldwin, wearing slacks and a hoodie. The hoodie has a quote from Baldwin's namesake on it: *Love takes off masks that we fear we cannot live without and know we cannot live within.*

And there is Titi Sujei, with her hands on her hips.

"Ah, so this is the boyfriend." She sticks out her hand. "We haven't been introduced."

Danny blushes and shakes her hand, and she won't let go of his.

"Jesus, you need some Nivea. And a manicure. You know men get them these days. I'll send you to Nina." She assesses the Underdogs from head to toe. "Hey, cowgirl. Where did you get those boots?"

It's Jane's turn to blush. "TJ Maxx."

"Oh, I love that store. You should come with me tomorrow. They're having a sale on all plus-sizes. Verdad can give me your number, I'll pick you up."

Turning her attention back to me, Sujei says, "Hey, I heard a little of that interview with the other girl. I want to talk with you about this theater project at some point. I have a lot of students at the university that can help you make it happen. Be standing by the booth after this is over. No nightlife tonight. The news is here. Don't make me slap you."

Titi Sujei moves away right before a microphone gets all up in my face. Danny takes a step back.

"Excuse me, Verdad. My name is Liz Nelson. I'd like to talk to you for a minute."

I can't do this. Blanca could do this . . .

Blanca: Por favor.

"I'm sure there is no one here who can memorialize Blanca or tell her story better than you," the reporter is saying.

"Her story?" My jaw is clenched because I don't want to break down. "Nobody asked about her story a year ago. The media only cared about the killer's story. The white supremacist's story. You all showed pictures of the man with his family. Smiling, clean cut, respectable. You gave him the benefit of the doubt that people like us, the people who were shot down, the brown and the black, never get. You gave him humanity. You bought him empathy."

"I can understand—"

"You can't. Blanca's story will forever remain unwritten." I think back to the movie. How many times my mind has written the ending of the movie and the ending of that night. "But if we can reopen the theater—if we can make it a place for the community. For people like me and my friends, LGBTQ kids who are being robbed of childhoods, because of rejection, because of homelessness—then Blanca doesn't have an unwritten story anymore. Blanca's storyline becomes the storyline of every kid who could come in here and find comfort, solace, love."

The reporter nods. "Thank you."

Blanca: Thank you, Verdad. BTW, you just came out on TV.

Oh shit.

I exit my trance and realize everybody is dead quiet and looking at me. "I'm done talking to y'all."

Rudy: "Maquina is low on charge, y'all. Nothing else to see here."

Everybody laughs. Danny holds my hand. Jane, Prisha, and Sarah swoop in and hug me.

Sujei steps into the ring that has formed around me and lays her hands on my shoulder. "Then talk to her. To Blanca."

I flash back to her funeral when I failed. Couldn't find the words to eulogize my friend, my sister, my heart.

Baldwin reaches through the group and hands me my violin case. "Verdad, don't leave her hanging. You can do this."

My violin? "So that's why you ran back into the house."

"Yes. And to steal toilet paper from your powder room. And—"

I open my case.

I don't know if the violin is the instrument or I am. If I'm playing or being played. I didn't ask for silence, but I get it. The candles are lit and the barrio is our church. We are not just the actors, the players, we are the directors of the new script, the new story. We will decide how it ends. I will.

25

I'm gonna say more than I've prayed.
I rest my chin on the violin, Blanca's shoulder,
knowing she's gonna get younger and I'm gonna get older.
I can reach my arms out but never hold her.
We were supposed to be kids not soldiers.
But Fate says, I could have told ya.
Cast my bow into the River Styx.
My notes try to swim but sink.
I'd follow you to the brink.
Cosmic strings my veins circulating the pain again and again.
How could God say Blanca wasn't meant to be?
What does that mean for me?

Blanca, I'm married to our memory
Our ring that chandelier.
But what is crystal clear
is that our stories don't end here.

26

This is how it ends . . .

. . . with a plane taking off. I sit in the window seat that Tía Sujei reminds me she usually takes. Sujei is chatting it up with the attendant and I know this will mean bebidas gratis and under-the-table snack packs. Wherever she goes, she seems to become a VIP.

While the plane cruises, I think of all the weight my heart carries, but how light it feels, like a whale in water.

"Nobody celebrates Navidad like the Borinquen." Sujei unbuckles her seatbelt and kicks off the chanclas she wore in thirty-degree weather in anticipation of the trip. She tells me about the unforgettable parrandas, when a small group of friends link up to asaltar or surprise another friend. It's the Puerto Rican version of Christmas caroling. Most parranderos play an instrument, like the guitarras, tamboriles, güiro maracas, or palitos.

I'm going to play the violin. So will Blanca, who is with me whenever my bow and strings touch. The parranderos all sing too. Or in my case, rap.

"Too bad your mom couldn't be here. Every year when we were kids, we would break out the straw hats, the pavas, pretend to be the jibaros from los campos. My mom and all of us would do the parrandas. You show up outside your neighbors' door after they are asleep. Then at a signal, everybody sings and plays their instruments. Afterwards, your neighbors invite you in for pasteles, lechón asado, arroz con dulce, tembleque—coquito for the adults—and dancing."

"Wow. Didn't people get mad you showed up at their house in the middle of the night?"

"No! We would give them a heads up. Drop hints. You'd stay an hour or two, then move on to the next house. Or in our case, apartment. The parties went on till dawn! Your mom was the only one who ever managed to stay up the whole time! It's too bad she can't come."

Can't is the word my moms used. She can't get off for Christmas, she said. That's the busiest time of the year for hospitals. She can't stop worrying that Fate will take away everything she's worked for. She's afraid of "assailants," the devil, poverty, life. Can't deal with me.

My moms and I haven't exactly made up. I have *can't*s of my own. The main one: I can't be anyone but myself.

I'm roasting in my coat. Titi Sujei was right to dress for the destination, not the departure. I wrestle out of my sleeves. My furry hood doubles as a shield against her mal de ojo, as I'm disturbing her whole setup. I squeeze past her to the aisle, knock over her book so she loses the page.

"Ay!" I've now managed to bang my head on the light switch and in an epic move, drop a whole bunch of some dude's luggage all over the floor.

"Necesito ayuda?" The beautiful brown person looking at me has that same half-a-hair thing as Danny, only it's thicker and longer on one side like in a Pantene commercial. In Danny's defense, he was dealing with a shortage of Pantene at the time.

Danny, my Danny, whom I messaged just this morning. He's in San Francisco, with his mom, living his best life. Sucks hard that it couldn't be with me.

Prisha and Sarah are sort of next door to him. They moved to California to live with Prisha's activist feminist cousin. I miss Danny so hard—no matter what drama went down. He didn't hook up with Prisha because she wasn't into him that way. But he did hook up with some chick in San Fran. That heartbreak was the first scar I wanted to keep.

Baldwin, Jane, and I have become besties though, and that makes it easier. Baldwin and Jane are still together. Baldwin is back at home. Mrs. Joung is helping the family plan the renaming ceremony. And I linked Jane up with Ms. Quinones, who helped get Jane set up with social services. Apparently there's this program where kids her age can go to school, work, and have their own crib, albeit a teeny-tiny crib.

The biggest news: there was a miracle. Turns out Prisha was right about the chandelier. It was worth so much, the city decided to buy it and donate the proceeds to turn the theater and the adjacent building into a shelter and community center. Renovations are still in the works, and I've been to about a million city council meetings in the past year, pitching ideas for how to use the space. In a few weeks Frida, Nelly, Baldwin, and I will be speaking at a fundraiser that Baldwin's beloved librarian helped us organize. We're asking for money to put a stage in the soon-to-be community center. I'm thinking *West Side Story* would be a great first production. Sujei hooked us up with donors to get special theater chairs dedicated to Blanca, Nando, and Bambi. I don't need to set aside one for her anymore.

Blanca comes and goes as she pleases now. I don't hear from her often. She's always been a free spirit. But when she shows up in my mind, in my heart, we just pick up where we left off. Exactly as besties do. The same way we'll do when I'm finally, one day, with her on the other side.

People always talk about first loves being crushes, lovers. But my first love, my first true love, is my first true friend, Blanca.

I get a text from Danny. He wants me to come see him in San Fran. Because of course ain't no other chingona as dope as me. I forward that text to Frida for consultation. But no matter what happens with Danny or any other lover, myself is nonnegotiable.

"I'm sorry," Guapx says, looking at the spilled suitcase contents in the aisle between us. "Need help?"

Titi Sujei huffs, "Pendejos!"

Our hands touch as we pick up a pair of SpongeBob SquarePants drawers and crack up, which is the universal language for *We are having a moment. Let's have more.*

But the moments will have to be later, because Sujei smacks me in the culo with her book. "Sentarse ya!"

Guapx waves and sits across from us in the aisle seat. How much would I be risking if I asked Sujei to switch with me? Life and limb. I settle for exchanging looks. Is Guapx looking? Yes. Yes, Guapx is.

I situate myself with books. Poetry, essay collections by Puerto Rican writers. Yes, I am treating myself like a research project. That's how I roll.

Who is myself? Myself is queer. Myself has mental illness and needs to take pills so I don't rip out my hair. Myself can be a scientist and a poet. And the truth is, myself ain't entirely myself yet. Why do I have to have myself figured out already? The answer is I damn well don't. And once I get myself figured my out, I'ma try something new and start all over again. Myself is also sort of talking to myself.

Myself is distractible. Because Guapx with the Pantene hair is smiling at me. Yes they is.

I've been learning to love the self I am now. The self who is first chair in violin and kicked ass at the state competition last spring. The self who got into AP math. The self who used her Genius Hour project in Ms. Mercardo's class to start a literary journal: *Dichotomy*. The self who my moms still can't accept.

But I do love my moms and I know she loves me—even if, for now, only in fragments. Hopefully at some point we'll like each other. I love my dad even though he's less of a dad and more of an uncle. I love my sisters, Veronica and the new baby, Vanessa. I especially love interjecting confounding ideas about life and love into Veronica's head and then hearing her irritate the hell out of my dad with her questions.

The truth is, loving myself is not a given. It's hard work sometimes. And loving other people is hard work too—if you're giving them the love they deserve. But love is something we all have to do for ourselves, and for each other. It's the only thing worth fighting for.

VERDAD'S READING PLAYLIST: A PRIMER

Latinx Rising edited by Frederick Luis Aldama

Feather Serpent Dark Heart of Sky by David Bowles

Like Water for Chocolate by Laura Esquivel

Magic for Beginners by Kelly Link

Yaqui Delgado Wants to Kick Your Ass by Meg Medina

Shadowshaper by Daniel Jose Older

Anger is a Gift by Mark Oshiro

The Revolution of Evelyn Serrano by Sonia Manzano

Puerto Rican Poetry, An Anthology from Aboriginal to Contemporary Times edited by Roberto Marquez

Remedios by Aurora Levins Morales

Marti's Song for Freedom by Emma Otheguy

Out of Darkness by Ashley Hope Pérez

When I was Puerto Rican by Esmerelda Santiago

Boricuas, Influential Puerto Rican Writings edited by Roberto Santiago

ACKNOWLEDGMENTS

First and foremost, all my love to Miguel for being my eternal support in every writing endeavor I undertake. 2020 will be OUR year, baby.

Mad props to my editor Amy Fitzgerald, who helped me honor the intersectionality of my characters with dignity and respect.

Thank you to Gabrielle Bohnett, the grand maestra of the Little Mozart Academy, for finding time to educate me on some violin basics. Thank you to the brilliant Lily Gold for helping me to understand the draw of K Pop, and I apologize that my Verdad did not end up a fan! Thank you to my dear friend Jerry Park, for educating me on some aspects of the Korean culture so that I could write Mrs. Joung and bring Baldwin to life, fully-fleshed. Puja Parikh, I could not have done justice to my dear Prisha without your friendship and counsel.

Much love to the Tía Sujeis of my life, those who have saved me when I was stranded or just straight-up kept me from being homeless: xox Susan, Richie, Carmen, Seth, and Clarissa. Susan and Richie, you have rescued me a thousand times (Remember that book cult in Iowa?), filled a thousand summers with golden memories. Carmen, the year my mother passed to the next dimension, you gave me a room of my own (sorry about the candlewax and glass) and made me a brown bag dinner (with a side dish and snack lol) EVERY day for me to take to my second job at Barnes and Noble. Clarissa, you saved me from being stranded in New Jersey, and sent me a first-class ticket back to WVU—with Seth waiting to take care of me on the other side. Seth, yeah, that time I ended up in WVU, homeless and in debt to said cult, you opened up your home.

To all of you, I am eternally grateful.

TOPICS FOR DISCUSSION

1. How has Blanca's death affected Verdad? Why do you think Verdad still imagines having conversations with Blanca?

2. Why is Verdad so embarrassed that she doesn't speak fluent Spanish? How does her Puerto Rican heritage shape her in other ways?

3. What do you think Verdad could have done differently during or after the confrontation with Nelly in history class? Why is Nelly expelled while the white girls involved in the fight are only suspended?

4. What initially draws Verdad to Danny?

5. What misconceptions does Verdad have about trans people? How does her understanding of sexual identity and sexual orientation grow over the course of the novel?

6. What terms does Verdad find liberating and helpful in her quest to understand her own and others' identities? What terms does she find limiting, hurtful, or ridiculous?

7. Verdad frequently catches herself stereotyping others, even as she resents the ways she is stereotyped. How does

she work to overcome her ingrained assumptions? What is one instance when she still falls short?

8. Verdad's mother reacts negatively to her relationship with a trans person and to her emerging queer identity. Later, Danny describes his dad's reaction to Danny being trans. Compare and contrast the two parents' attitudes and actions.

9. Sarah is upset when Prisha goes into the Maheshwaris' house on her own. In what ways is she an outsider in this context? In what ways is Verdad an outsider among the Underdogs?

10. Verdad says, "God is a hundred billion things but humans are expected to be one." How does this reflect her feelings about the role of religion in her life?

11. For much of the novel, Verdad refers to her classmates by their messaging handles or by labels gender-and-ethnicity-based labels like "Boricua 1" and "White Girl 3." How does this limit her perception of their identities? How do her classmates defy her expectations?

12. What ways does Verdad find to honor Blanca's memory?

13. Verdad has many intersecting identities. How is she navigating them at the end of the novel? What do you think her future holds?

MORE FROM NONIEQA RAMOS:

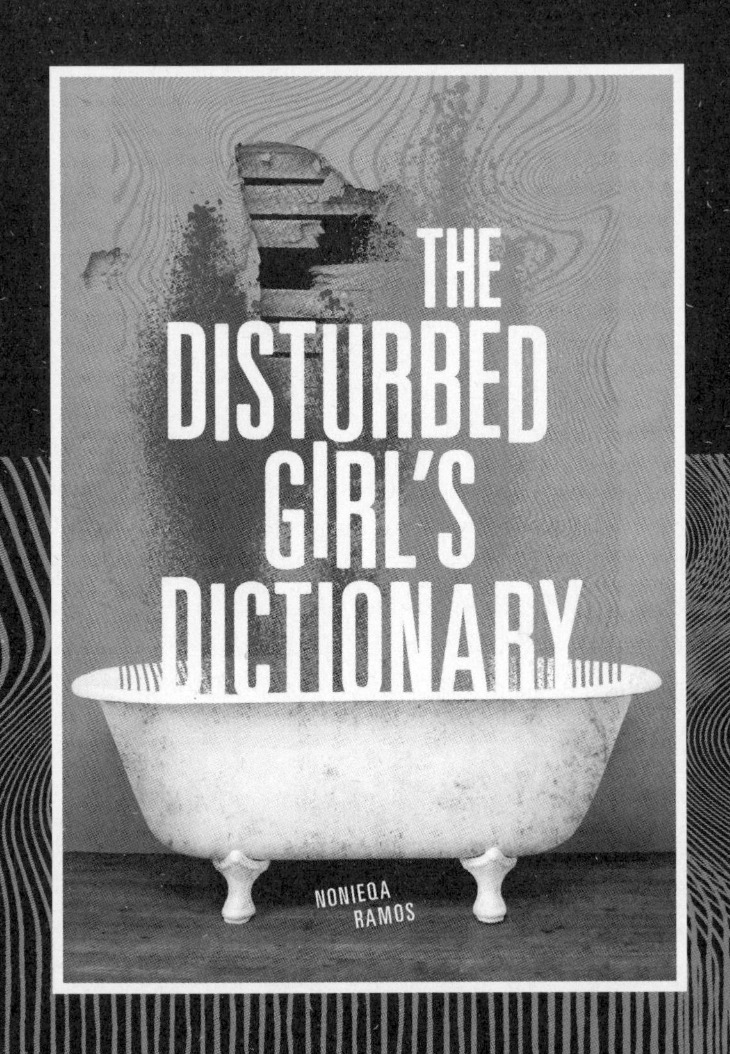

ALWAYS/NEVER

Interjection. Sometimes hated. Always feared.
Never disrespected.

"Still getting radio silence." I scroll down my list of followers. "But she didn't unfollow . . . or unfriend me."

The word *unfriend* makes George tighten the strap on his helmet. (See H for Helmet. George is what you call special. But not to his face if you want to avoid me jackhammering yours.) "Look, look. Alma posted another one of her kids." Alma's got so many siblings and half-siblings and cousins living at her house I lose count.

I hold up my iPad and George leans over, almost tipping his desk. "Yo, see that in the background? The little dude there on top of the fridge!" He scrolls and laughs, slamming into the seat so hard it crashes into the desk behind it. If you sit near George, it's highly recommended you wears a helmet too.

Teacher Man glares at us. He is annoyed because our ignorant asses broke the school firewall again to check social media posts, but we can't even pass a daily quiz. Right now we're supposed to be doing a historical analysis between suffrage and civil rights, but I got to know if my friendship with Alma is history first. We haven't talked in two weeks and I'm in serious bestie withdrawal.

History is the only class the three of us have together anymore. The only reason Alma is in a regular class—and rest assured there's nothing regular about the cray-crays in this class—is because all her other classes are AP and she needs a breather. Alma's not here today though. She's on another field trip in this program called Tomorrow's Leaders Today. (See G for Gifted and Talented.) George and I are not in this program because nobody appreciates our gifts or talents today—or any other day. Currently George is displaying his talent for appreciating my jokes. Every time he laughs he bashes into desks like bumper cars. Any minute he'll start wheezing and get sent to the nurse. George has the asthma.

Me: "Alma always never posts pics of herself. Even her profile pic is of one of her kids. Check it out. This girl is Alma's mini-me. She always never—"

"Macy! George!" Teacher Man is staring us down. "Let's talk about why we cannot use the words *always* and *never* in the same sentence."

"What do you mean by *we*?" I lean way back in my seat. People are always talking like that to me. Saying *our* and *we*.

Our plan for Macy is . . . I think we can all agree that . . . We don't want THAT to happen, do we?

Teacher pops a cap off a black marker and writes the sentence I said on the whiteboard in Caps Lock.

ALMA ALWAYS NEVER DOES THAT.

He's trying to turn this into what he calls a teachable

moment. Like that time he made us proofread all the graffiti in the bafroom.

With a red marker, he crosses out the word *always* and rereads it. He says, "See, *always* is what we call superfluous. It's clutter."

Clutter? Like he knows my life.

"You're pissing me off," I say. I stay seated. I don't get in his face. Yet. I stay in my circle—draw a imaginary one around my desk. (See C for Circle.)

Teacher turns his back. "I hear you, Macy," he says. "I'm sorry you're angry."

"I didn't say I was angry," I shout. My circle is bursting with flames. "I said I was pissed."

The teacher turns on the projector. He's got a PowerPoint with GIFs. He's got Vines. He's got everything but a top hat and a cane. He is ignoring my behavior. This is a time-honored teacher strategy that also royally pisses me off.

I reach into my desk. Take out *History of the American People Volume 1* and clean house. Cross out all the pages about shit that's got nothing to do with me. What's left? Not much. The teacher keeps clicking through his slideshow until he hears the silence of the other kids. Until he hears the slashing of my pen.

"*Macy!*" he whips around, blinking in the light of the projector. "What are you doing?"

I guess he is no longer ignoring my behavior. "Are you angry?" I crack my knuckles. "Or are you pissed?"

If he were a cartoon, smoke would be pouring out his ears. A kid coughs as if he can smell it. "Put the Sharpie down, Macy. Vandalism will not be tolerated. You—"

"Vandalism? I'm not vandalizing any more than you. I'm just deciding which words count and which ones don't. Which words mean something and which don't. That's exactly what you do."

"Macy! You can't argue two plus two is three, and you can't argue that *always* and *never* should be used in the same sentence. You're not in middle school anymore." He slams his marker on the lip of the board. It rolls onto the floor. "I expect—"

Me: "You dropped something."

His nostrils twitch.

Yeah. He's pissed.

"What you're not picking up on is how much is at stake here, Macy. Nobody's gonna give you a lollipop anymore just because you throw a tantrum."

"What did you say, motherfoe?" I throw my desk.

The other kids hide under their desks like it's a tornado drill. Teacher Man pushes the office button. I'm going. Don't even need to give me a lollipop. It's a violation of my civil rights, though. Depriving my ass of a education. I walk out and slam the door.

I sit outside the principal's office and take out the dictionary you're reading right now. (By-the-fucking-way, you're reading this because I'm missing or dead or in a nuthouse, or CPS stole it, and maybe you don't know I'm standing right behind you, motherfoe.)

Back to *Always/Never*. Miss Black, my English teacher, says that to prove your point you have to give many examples. Here's mine: Mothers always never leave.

I remember the first time my mother left. She thought I was asleep, but I saw her packing her bags. I don't know why she left the house that night or what made her come back, but she did. I mean I guess she's got enough reasons to leave, but what I always never get is what brings her back. Is a bad mother the one who leaves or the one who stays even though she should go?

I checked what was inside those bags. In one bag was a ratty old stuffed dog missing a ear. Her honey-bear bong and a dime bag. (And let me share my disappointment that a dime bag don't actually got no dimes in it, believe me.) Pictures of herself at the beach. Queen Helena hair gel. A lock of my brother Zane's hair. (See B for Burner and G for Gas.)

She always leaves a note. It says: *I know you'll never forgive me. But you'll always love me. I know it. I still love my mother. The bitch.* (*The bitch* is crossed out, but I can still read it through the scribble.) *All my love, Yasmin.*

But she always never leaves. Always acts like those bags aren't still in the back of her closet, waiting. In the morning, I always look for the piece of tape hanging on the front door where the note was. Always find all the empty kitchen cabinets open like she wants us to know there's nothing left for us here. The stuffed dog is back in that bashed-up box of hers. She got it from the group home when she left at thirteen. The bong and the dime bag are back in her panty drawer. The gel is on the kitchen sink where she does her hair when somebody's stunk up the bafroom. The pictures of me on the dresser have never left.

ABOUT THE AUTHOR

Raised in the Boogie Down Bronx, NoNieqa Ramos is an educator and literary activist. She wrote the young adult novel *The Disturbed Girl's Dictionary.* She believes Halloween is a lifestyle, not a holiday. If you're in Virginia, you might catch NoNieqa getting motorcycle lessons from her soulmate, Michael, or going indie bookstore hopping with her preciosos, Jandi and Langston. Connect with her works on www.nonieqaramos.com or on the Latinx collective www.lasmusasbooks.com.